# ONCE UPON A TIME IN AMERICA ...

*HOW CONSERVATIVES' IDEOLOGIES CHANGED AMERICA . . .*

## THOMPSON K. GEORGE

## ISBN

978-1-958690-44-4 (Paperback)
978-1-958690-45-1 (eBook)

# TABLE OF CONTENTS

## PART-II: WAR ON IMMIGRANTS



## PART-III: AMERICA.....THE SOCIO-ECONOMIC POLITICS WITHIN

# **PREFACE**

AT THE TURN OF THE 20^TH century, a president by the name of George W. Bush got elected as the 43rd president of the United States. A highly contested election in American history, which led to the nation's Supreme Court deciding him as the final winner of the election between him and former vice president Al Gore.....a first time scenario ever in the history of America.

However, little did America knew that the man whom the nation's Supreme Court had declared as the winner of the 2000 presidential election had a deeply rooted imperial agenda to lead America into a path contrary to that set forth by the founding fathers. The result:.....all hell broke loose within America and across the globe as the administration defiantly embarked, in the following years, on series of chaotic and dysfunctional policies that had served no other purposes than soil the good image of America across the globe. The nation, since then continues to grapple with the rude awakening and the ensuing consequence of the mess spelt everywhere by the administration.....a huge liability resumed by the succeeding administration. Not even to mention the crushing economic consequences to the nation due to the administration's reckless war spending and its protectionism of corporate sectors' culture of unregulated and deceptive business practices that almost brought the nation to her knees.

Most troubling has been the forefront role the administration championed through its eight years in office, approving policies that has been aggressively and ruthlessly enforced by the nation's various security agencies on foreign nationals within and outside America. Such horrendous policies led to similar measures being adopted by other like-minded administrations against foreign nationals in various other countries.....an extremely dangerous moral precedent set by the administration.

America, as the whole world knows, has remained a nation of immigrants since its founding. In fact, the nation's socioeconomic might and standing in the world is indisputably attributed in large part to the invaluable sacrifices made by generations of immigrants who came to America voluntarily or otherwise from different parts of the world. Sadly enough, Mr. Bush made it one of his administration's top priorities to toil with one of the most fundamental strength of America.....turning a nation of immigrants into a nation that resent them.

Not only ending the trend, but ending it on a very sad note on the part of American economy and for millions of foreign nationals who came to America with legitimate intentions. For the most part of Mr. Bush's eight years in office, the immigration laws he approved to be amended and signed into laws led to swift apprehension, detainment and repatriation of millions of both documented and the so-called undocumented foreign nationals and the like. The hunt for foreign nationals in America got so intense and ruthless to the extent that even a handful of local municipalities, and even some states like Arizona, were also emboldened by Mr. Bush's hostile immigration policies by enacting their own version of draconian local immigration ordinances to assist the administration in making life a living hell for immigrants who resides within those states and locales. First time ever in America history....allowing U.S. municipal and even state governments to mettle with immigration enforcement.... an obligation that has always been under the control of the federal government in almost every country across the globe.

Immigration enforcement during Mr. Bush's administration got so out of hand to the extent that the operation escalated to the level of harassment of immigrants and citizens alike by the nation's Immigration agency that conducts the raids across the nation. Such reckless raids of foreign nationals across America led to tens of thousands of aliens languishing indefinitely in prisons across the country awaiting removal. Even Geneva Convention refugees and asylees, who may have committed relatively minor infractions, were forcefully removed by the administration back to their countries of feared persecution.....na violation of the Geneva International refugees treaty which United States is a signatory state.

The Bush-Cheney's administration used the travails of the 9/11 incident to unleash various hostile foreign policies that has left the Middle-east Islamic nations in a more dire state than ever. From the invasion of Afghanistan to that of Iraq in particular, to the abuse of the captured Prisoners of War (P.O.W.) by the U.S. troops, to the secret rendition program and the torture policy inflicted on foreign nationals held in secret detention facilities in various countries across the globe by the C.I.A. operatives....including the internationally renounced U.S. detention in Guantanamo Bay, Cuba, and the one in Bagram, Afghanistan....all approved by the Bush-Cheney's Republican team.

How shameful that the United States security agencies, during Mr. Bush's watch, adopted the same Stalinist tactics they decried so intensely during the cold war. This explains why the America's reputation all through the free world had become so tarnished.

The administration lapses were numerous, so also had been the devastating effects of the reckless foreign policies it had championed. The flawed intelligence leading to the invasion of Iraq caused so much havocs, financial liabilities and huge loss of human lives on both ends and unprecedented ripple effects across the globe....the list goes on.

Arbitrary rule of both domestic and international laws became so prevalent during the Bush-Cheney's administration to the extent that his administration was reported by the media for the detention of hundreds of juvenile foreign nationals from Iraq, Afghanistan and other foreign states reported to be as young as thirteen (13) years of ages, as terror suspect detained in their own countries and in other states' facilities. Such disheartening practices carried out by the Bush-Cheney's administration makes the whole world wonder how much influence should United States try to exercise......if any at all over another country's behavior? And should that country be receptive, given the abuse, indefinite detentions and closed tribunals that has been part of the United States record in recent years?

Freedom of "Speech" and that of the "Press" which is protected by the nation's Constitution was on major assault as the administration secretly eavesdrops on telephonic and Internet communications of citizens and particularly that of foreign nationals without the consent of those being violated, or first seeking court's approval. The same administration sought immunity for the telephone companies that were partners in invading these violated citizens and non-citizens' rights to privacy and freedom of speech.

Mr. Bush's administration tried to ostensibly justify its hostile immigration raid and the mass-repatriation of the so-called undocumented immigrants as a drain on the nation's social services and also blaming them as the ones taking the jobs intended for the American citizens. That said, one would think that after several years of the administration's mass-expulsion of these group of aliens there would be so much jobs for the citizens and the state of the American economy will recoup and even become stronger. Rather, the exact opposite was happening. It seems like the more immigrants are forcefully expelled from America, the more job losses accrue and the worse the state of the nation's economy seemed to get.

The real fact of the matter behind the administration and the Republican's draconian immigration offensive against foreign nationals in America has been left untold to the general public.

A testament of the administration's failed economic policy became so evident during the final years of its presidency and thereon after.

However, Mr. Bush, haven been the captain of the boat for eight long years, was not a lone architect to this divisive and dysfunctional style of governance. His right-wing conservative constituents within his cabinet and the vast-right old guard colleagues outside the cabinet, playing behind-the-scene influence peddling role within the lobbying industry in Washington, have been co-architects of the woes brought about by eight years of his presidency as well.

Eight years later, the American public finally decided they had enough of Mr. Bush or another Mr. Bush's style of divisive politics that led America astray. Barack Obama, an Illinois U.S. Senator, a half black and half Caucasian U.S.- born citizen, was overwhelmingly voted into office on November 4, 2008 as the 44th U.S. president. His vision reflects that of an individual with fair and sound bi-partisan leadership style, unlike the

Bush-Cheney's. He was embraced by both the American public and the international community as the leader of the moment to undo a wide range of damages which the Bush-Cheney and their Republican teamsters in Washington has done to America image across the globe. He was definitely the messiah God sent to save the nation.

Mr. Obama, among other things, undid lots of the nation's conservative dominance of the courts and their partisan politics that was the root of so much division in recent time in America. He made quite an impressive effort to change the old order of things while in office. He made himself clear with passion about breaking out of the partisan mold of bickering and catering to special pleaders, and to end the Bush-Cheney's type of abuses of power and subverting the Constitution and disown the big-money power brokers who have corrupted Washington politics. The very same Bush-Cheney's vast-right Republican teamsters in Washington who were co-architects to all the political and financial mess created by the administration to the nation stood in the way of some of the necessary restorations he intended to accomplish during his tenure.

With all the red inks contained in Donald Trump's report card, surprisingly to all....including himself, folks who were impressed with his record still went out and casted their votes for him.....enough to win the 2016 presidential election. All hell has broken loose once again with the treatment of immigrants....particularly those from some Spanish speaking and Islamic countries. Trump's assault on immigrants since he took office has been worse than the era of Bush-Cheney. He not only apprehend the Spanish folks at the border. He detains parents and their kids/babies and then have their kids forcefully separated/taken away from them to undisclosed locations...all carried out under the guise of stopping Mexicans from entering the country through the back door. This is nothing short of 'child kidnapping' being carried out by U.S. government officials with impunity....wow!

Trump has pretty much rescinded almost all the meaningful reforms put in place by Obama to protect the American public like the consumer protection laws on various sectors, banking regulations and so forth. He is pushing hard now to fill the nation's federal judiciary seats with folks who will prioritize their decision making based on party affiliation rather than what the law says.....scary!

# PART-I

# ALIENS ODYSSEY IN THE U.S.

# 01 — AMERICA IN THE 21ST. CENTURY

GONE ARE THOSE GOOD OLD DAYS when America used to be that dreamland where people crave to visit or longed to live.....in at least once in their lifetime. The outside world's impression of America being the utopia and most sought-after society was then the real deal. Whatever the sacrifice made then to reach America was seem to worth it. When it's all said and done, the very first touch-down experience in United States' soil was everyone's surreal moment.

During those bygone days, the respect for the rule of laws was paramount as well as the fundamental norms put in place by the founding fathers. General kindness and hospitality to humankind back then was also very prevalent and well felt. And most importantly, the "In God We Trust" American motto in those days was so practical and sincere. Those unique and practical values made America stood out among other nations in the world. America, after the slavery era was abolished, was perceived by the rest of the world as the beacon of liberty and a pioneer in the respect for human dignity and rights. The whole world was craving to be in America at least once in their lifetime to experience these spectacular lifestyle there .....which in most cases was only a dream in their homelands.

Even so, during those days, life in America wasn't without a struggle. Things wasn't just readily available for grabs without the normal struggle to earn them. In other words, America, being commonly referred to as "The Land Of Milk And Honey" did not necessarily imply that the milk and honey was all over the place for grabs without working hard to earn them.....but then, the people and the general vibe in America was very unique and genuine compared to the new vibe within the country since the last decade of the 20th century.

From that point on, those unique values that once made America so sought-after around the world has been gradually diminishing. Things has got terribly wrong. It appears like America has been falling from grace and loosing its grip on its glorious days and gradually deteriorating on its once high standard for liberty and strong regard for humanity as each year unfolds. Nonetheless, the 2009 Obama administration has been trying its best to mend some of the damages.

All hell finally broke loose at the turn of the 20th century during the nation's highly contested presidential election that ended up being decided by the nation's Supreme Court for the first time in American history.....the year 2000 presidential election. A Republican presidential candidate by the name of George W. Bush was finally declared the winner by the court in a U.S. presidential ticket contested between him and Bill Clinton's former vice president, Al Gore. The Supreme Court declared Mr. Bush as the next and the 43rd president of United States.

Any society is reflective of the policies or ideologies of its leaders. Such was the case with Mr. Bush's leadership. His policies, ideologies and leadership styles was all the way contrary to those of the founding fathers whose values have in the past brought America to its attained height of social and economic trajectory.

America has long been known from history as a nation of immigrants. Other than the Native Indians, everyone else born in America has some ancestral bloodline traced back to immigrant parents at some point in time. As a nation which its economic might came about through enormous contributions of hard work by various voluntary and involuntary immigrants over several centuries, it is extremely terrible and equally troubling for the rightist conservative faction in American government to now deviate from such defining source of strength that the nation was founded upon. A unique source of strength which America needs now more than ever to be able to move forward in this globalized generation.

Mr. Bush's leadership policies as the president of the United States for eight years.....along with his vast-right conservative team.....strongly reflected their deeply-rooted resentment towards foreign nationals within America. Not only did they resent foreign nationals within America, Mr. Bush also helped spread that same sentiment they all stomach into the minds of the rest of the American public. These resentment targeted at foreign nationals has, over the Bush years as president and even thereon after he left office, led to ripple effects across the board and has been heavily put to use against foreign nationals within the country at various work places, social services and even used in the worse way against immigrants in the application of immigration laws by the nation's immigration agency.

The U.S. Republican policymakers has been rolling the dice since 1994 up till 2006 as the majority in both Houses of Congress.....and the immigration laws they have pushed, among other laws, over these years has been very critical of foreign nationals in all respects, to say the least. The coming of Mr. Bush seemed to have further emboldened these extreme-right conservative policymakers to toughen the already harsh immigration laws to clamp down even harder than ever on foreign nationals residing within the country.

The implicit hostility applied towards foreign nationals during the Bush administration has no doubt been the worst treatment that immigrants ever experienced in America other than the treatment of indentured servitudes during the slavery era by the so-called slave masters who were also migrants themselves just like some of the slaves they bought and forcefully brought into Continental America.

While it is normal for any sovereign state to tighten up on things after such horrific incident of 9/11 on its soil, it is equally a bad governance for the same policymakers using the occasion as a political tool and window of opportunity to descend hard on innocent immigrants by using them as punching bags to settle their multifaceted ambiguous motives towards foreign nationals.....a mindset which has been preexisting among the rightist faction in America ever before the 9/11 incident itself.

Speaking of extremely hostile immigration policy and its enforcement by the U.S. Immigration agency against foreign nationals in recent time at least since Mr. Bush had a chance to be the U.S. president.....imagine yourself getting detained right at the port of entry by the U.S. Immigration agency for such minor civil violation as invalid travel document. Not just being detained briefly at the airport to be put back on the next available plane back home reasonably fairly. Instead, the agency is conferred with punitive authorities by the very same vast-right Washington policymakers, to first detain such aliens in U.S. prisons among the nation's criminal convicts for a period not less that 3 to 6 months, as permitted by one of the numerous amended immigration laws by the Bush regime, before such aliens are finally sent back to their countries.

It is very cruel and unusual treatment to subject any foreign national, who have never commit any criminal offense within a foreign land, to any form of prison confinement just for having invalid travel documents..... or for having reside in such country without valid residency papers. Such a civil violation do not in any way rise to the level that any government entity infringing on any foreign nationals' liberty interest till they are either returned back home if they can not be admitted without the required residency papers. There are in fact various better alternatives like temporarily holding them in a refugee-type of facility with reasonable level of liberty till they are either returned home, or be afforded the chance to seek lawful residency papers.....and not be confined with prisoners in jail like convicts. The very same extreme-right conservative policymakers in Washington who were behind the wicked Bush administration immigration policies and their manner of enforcement, have been trying to make laws that will make it a crime itself, punishable by jail time, just to be in country without valid residency papers.

The troubling part is that some of these aliens subjected to such cruel measures of confinement are in fact good citizens in their countries of birth and have never bee in prison back in their homelands till they arrive in America. For those who were detained right at the port of entry, their first anticipated taste of the proclaimed land of liberty filled with milk and honey, landed them behind bars of the U.S. prison walls. At that point, reality finally sets in....asking themselves if their relentless sacrifice made to leave their homelands to come to the so-called land of milk and honey was really worth it? Or has things changed in America that much that fast that the good old values of the founding fathers have become a thing of the past? The leadership of Mr. Bush and his vast-right Republican teamsters validated this to be true in all aspect.

Without a doubt, United States of the good old days, and to a limited extent today, offers better opportunities for better life in general, compared with lots of other countries across the globe, but it is far from the best country of the so-called acclaimed 'milk and honey' status to live in these days. Sadly, those unique values put in place by the founding fathers that has made such lifestyle and living standard possible, are fastly diminishing... due to the ideologies of the nation's far-right policymakers in Washington and in part by the influence of their corporate imperialist peers from the bloodline of the imperial era at the American private sectors.

The torments faced by foreign nationals since the turn of the 20th century carried out by the U.S. government law enforcement agencies can only be best described as being motivated by hate. A lot of foreign nationals would rather prefer to face such harsh treatment in the hands of their governments back home rather than being subjected to worse treatment in a foreign state like United States for that matter.....over mere violations like travel or residency validity to enter or remain in the country.

Those who came to America in recent years after the new millennium, have surely got a clear picture of the changes and the reality of life in America as opposed to their high expectations of the good life and the glitters they are used to seeing in American tabloids and TV networks back home, or heard from those who went there when the good old values was still intact......or at least, have come to grip with the reality that those glitters and the proclamation of America of being that 'land of milk and honey' was more of an hyperbole of how the select few lives in America, rather than the pluralistic impression created in the minds of the outside world. Life has gotten so frighteningly different in America today.

The sad news is that a lot of foreign nationals have in fact sacrificed the best life they ever had back home for a supposedly better life in America.... finding themselves entangled with socioeconomic politics of corporate dominance....a new-age system of servitude with little or absolutely nothing to show for all the open-ended sacrifices.

Those who made it to the country with valid residency documents have to undergo the process of assimilation and integration into the complex American society. Some fared well, while majority gets overwhelmed with unmet and accrued obligations. In the process, most aliens totally lose track of their very goals and mission they initially had before leaving their homelands....if at all they can still recall them. Most aliens get consumed in a new world that now appears to them more like a mirage rather than the real deal. The complexity of the society has forced many to compromise with mediocrity by going with the flow often dictated by the nation's heavyweight capitalist power-brokers.

The 9 to 5 minimum wage job plus overtime got most immigrants so preoccupied that they barely have spare time to reflect on the progress they 're making.......if any......since they have been in America. The earnings on these tedious jobs are barely enough to sustain them and their families till their next paycheck. A lot of immigrants have lived in America for quite some time, some for decades, with absolutely nothing to show for such lengthy time of residency. The conservative vultures in the American corporate sectors along with their conservative peers in the helm of policy-making in Washington have put laws in place that will hinder most of the aliens, and even the citizens alike, to get pass a certain bracket of socioeconomic mobility status....no matter how hard they may try. Some of these aliens' socioeconomic stagnation are self-inflicted as well. That evidently is not how they had expected their lives to have turned out in the land of milk and honey...where everything are presumably supposed to flourish.

It is a sad fact, to say the least, that a lot of immigrants has been so sidetracked in America that they can't even afford to buy a flight ticket, in the case of those with valid U.S. residency papers who can leave and be allowed to return on their own accord, to visit their original homelands after so many years of hard work away from home. Talk less of even having enough money to splurge during such reunification trip back home. Some aliens remain on extremely tight budget all year every year.

Realistically speaking, most immigrants still residing in America have long outlived the very essence of their migration to America for better life. Many in this category are merely existing in the country as figures, basically floating and continuously conforming to year by year stagnant routine of mediocrity lifestyle. All there is for some aliens who have been in America for quite some time is the mere impression to people back home that they live in America, but are barely living the so-called American life which most had craved so much for so long to be a part of.....such as the glitters and glamour which they used to see back home on American tabloids and media networks. Not even to mention the "American Dream" that, to some, is these days viewed more like a mirage than the real deal that it should be.

Has United States always been a showcase nation? Do America still remain the real deal for all? Or has time, things and people changed so fast since the last decade of the 20th century to the present time that those unique rules of engagements have become suddenly obsolete? Evidently, with the look of things today in America, it is clear to see that the hearts of people in the country that was once synonymous with hospitality and gentility to humankind few decades back are increasingly so cold like the sub-zero degree winter nights. Folks hearts are so cold in America these days, especially that of those within the like-minded rightist faction... both in the private and the public sectors, to the extent that the regard for human liberty and democratic values established by the founding fathers are perceived and implied by these set of people as values of the past. "In God We Trust" motto that has long been endowed in the spirits of most Americans since the days of the founding fathers is almost completely eroded from the beings of typical Americans today.

A much familiar mission statement among typical Americans these days is: "In Dollars We Trust." Every cause of action, both in government and in private sectors, are directly or indirectly linked with insatiable motive to get paid by any means necessary. Even though it means destroying the next man's soul to get it.

The ideology and policy of the extreme-right governmental policymakers in Washington as well as that of the corporate America today is: 'Business As Usual', even though the next man's house is on fire. They might render a helping hand only if there is potential financial incentive for them at the end of the day.

Speaking of corporate greed, this nature is more prevalent in American corporate circle than anywhere else in the whole world. This insatiable thirst to continue amassing personal gains at whoever's expense has tarnished the integrity of well-read American corporate leaders. This culture of greed led to the implosion of a number of huge American corporations since the turn of the 20th century.....particularly when Mr. Bush was the captain of the boat. Those who keep up with what goes on in the American marketplace will easily identify with these facts. Barnard Maydoff, a single entity who was operating in the American highly unregulated Hedge Fund industry, bilked his corporate and private clients a whopping $50 billion, more than the entire budget of some countries. However though, the American media are always the first to spotlight the government of other nations as being corrupt.

The very same culture of personal and corporate greed to continue amassing ill-gotten gains at whoever's expense led to the 2008 implosion of various huge American financial institutions which later rippled through various other countries. A financial meltdown that almost brought the entire nation's economy down to its knees right before Mr. Bush left office.

# 02

## *HISTORY REPEATING ITSELF*

THOSE FAMILIAR WITH THE AMERICAN HISTORY will fully understand how Continental America and particularly United States as a country and a society came about. Back in the colonial era, Europeans and Africans were forced by the European frontiers to emigrate to Continental America. Most troubling of all was how the early European frontier migrants treated the Native (Indian) Americans upon their arrival.

Having arrived in a strange land with a very harsh wintry weather with little or no resources to survive on, and knowing nothing about how or what to survive on in their Newfoundland, the Europeans had no other choice but to turn to the Native American Indians to teach them surviving skills to save them from perishing, as many of them eventually ended up due to hunger and inclement weather.

The Native Americans were hospitable by nature and taught them the much needed surviving skills. After they had mastered the surviving skills, the European colonialists plotted to extinct the indigenous Native Indians who had essentially saved their lives. Their deviously selfish motive was nothing else but to eradicate these native landowners and then take over their lands. They basically bit the hands that had fed them by strong-arming the Native Indians of their land.

## (a)   The Japanese Internment in America

--- ***THE JAPANESE INTERNMENT IN AMERICA:*** Following the attack of Pearl Harbor on December 7, 1941, President Franklin D. Roosevelt issued Executive Order 9066, which permitted the military to circumvent the constitutional safeguards of American citizens in the name of national defense.....soon after the beginning of World War II.

The Order set into motion the exclusion from certain areas, the evacuation and mass incarceration of 120,000 persons of Japanese ancestry living on the U.S. West Coast, most of whom were U.S. citizens or legal permanent resident aliens.

These Japanese Americans, half of whom were children, were incarcerated for up to 4 years by the actions of the government of that era......without due process of law or any factual basis, in bleak, remote camps surrounded by barbed wires and armed guards.

They were forced to evacuate their homes and leave their jobs, in some cases, family members were separated and put into different camps. President Roosevelt himself called the 10 facilities 'concentration camps."

Some Japanese Americans died in the camps due to inadequate medical care and the emotional stresses they encountered. Several were killed by military guards posted for allegedly resisting orders.

At the time, Executive Order 9066 was justified as a "military necessity" to protect against domestic espionage and sabotage. However, it was later documented that "our government have in its possession proof that not one Japanese American, citizen or not, had engaged in espionage, not one had committed any act of sabotage." *(Michi Weglyn, 1976)*.

Rather, the causes for this unprecedented action in American history, according to the Commission on Wartime Relocation and Internment of Civilians, were motivated largely by racial prejudice, wartime hysteria, and a failure of political leadership." Quite sadly, a closely similar scenario has unfortunately been repeating itself and relentlessly embarked upon during the 8 long years of the Bush- Cheney's leadership and the administration's vast-right Republican constituents in Washington and the rest of their faction across the nation. A war still being relentlessly waged against foreign nationals and their U.S.-born kids.

Almost fifty years later, through the efforts of the leaders and advocates of the Japanese American community, the U.S. Congress passed the 'Civil

Liberties Act of 1988.' Popularly known as the Japanese American Redress Bill, this act acknowledged that "a grave injustice was done" and mandated Congress to pay each surviving victims of the internment $20,000 in reparations.

In Canada, similar evacuation Orders were established. Nearly 23,000 Nikkei, or Canadians of Japanese descent were sent to camps in British Columbia. It was the greatest mass movement in the history of Canada. This same year, formal apologies were also issued by the government of Canada to the Japanese Canadian survivors, who were each repaid the sum of $21,000 Canadian dollars.

To quantify or even attempt to redress the grave injustices and the countless irreparable damages that has been carried out against foreign nationals by the Bush-Cheney's administration within the U.S. and across the globe, would undoubtedly leave the U.S. government completely bankrupt for the rest of this 21st century.

The reparation was sent with a signed apology from the president of United States on behalf of the American people. The period of reparation ended in August of 1998.

The following is the signed apology by President Bill Clinton in 1993:

### *THE WHITE HOUSE*
### *WASHINGTON*
### *October 1, 1993*

*Over fifty years ago, the United States government unjustly interned, evacuated, or relocated you and many other Japanese Americans, I offer a sincere apology to you for the actions that unfairly denied Japanese Americans and their families fundamental liberties during World War II.*

*In passing the Civil Liberties Act of 1988, we acknowledge the wrongs of the past and offered redress to those who endured such grave injustice. In retrospect, we understand that the nation's actions were rooted deeply in racial prejudice, wartime hysteria, and the lack of political leadership. We must learn from the past and dedicate ourselves as a nation to renewing the spirit of equality and our love of freedom. Together we can guarantee a future with liberty and justice for all. You and your families have my best wishes.*

Despite the redress, the mental and physical health impacts of the trauma of the internment experience continue to affect tens of thousands of Japanese Americans. Health studies have shown two times greater incidence of heart disease and premature death among former internees, compared to non-interned Japanese Americans. Thanks to president Franklin D. Roosevelt's leadership and his Congressional representatives' anti-Japanese sentiment.

A closely similar trend is in play today and aggressively adopted by the Congressional right-wing Republican policymakers in Washington along with their fellow right-wing constituents across the country against the current generation of immigrants in America. They have been on that path yet again since the Bush- Cheney administration laid the ground work of hatred for them to build upon during the administration's eight chaotic years of leadership. Since then, America has not been the same again. The general state of things in America continues to decline as each year unfolds.

Today in America, any foreign nationals living within its soil has a 95 percent chance, under Mr. Bush's administration and his right-wing Republican-led foreign policies, of being framed as an enemy of state, or a terrorist suspect, in most cases, without a substantial proof....and at any time, without prior notice, can be arrested and detained in prison without charge. Other foreign nationals are similarly being scooped up by the nation's Immigration agency and detained indefinitely till such aliens are forcefully removed back to their individual countries. In most cases, without substantial legal justification for the government to do so. Geneva Convention refugees and asylees who had fled their homelands to escape persecution and was granted international refuge protection are treated this way as well. Such governmental harassment and infringement of people's liberty interest could be as a result of violations as minor as over-stayed students, visitors, or tourists, or having minor trouble with the law, among others.

Without any prior notice by the government of such violation and its intended cause of action, foreign nationals are hunted down like criminal fugitives at large by the U.S Immigration agency, now called 'ICE Police' (I.C.E. stands for: Immigration and Customs Enforcement), and then taken to jail to await their repatriation.

It has been an extremely cruel way of handling foreign nationals with relatively minor civil immigration violations by the administration of Mr. Bush and his extreme-right conservative policymakers in Washington....

particularly by the government of a nation like United States of all countries....a nation with acclaimed history of immigrants and a proclaimed slogan for liberty and respect for humanity.

This is a true story chronicling the extreme hostile behavior towards foreign nationals by the administration of Mr. Bush and his like-minded Republican extremists.

Millions of foreign nationals who have once been in America in recent decades or still recently residing there, have, at some point, been victims of this right-wing government instigated xenophobia.....and can identify with this type of cruelty. Millions of American-born children by immigrant parents suffer similar torments as well.

Since 1994 up till 2006, the right-wing Republicans had the majority of both Houses of Congress and have used that majority leverage to wield enormous power, devising and legislating very harsh and cruel immigration policies against the interest of relatively law-abiding immigrants dwelling in America with legitimate intentions. The effect of these draconian policies have torn and still tearing apart tens of thousands of immigrants' families across America. Their American-born children and spouses left behind morally, mentally and financially crushed as well.

In most of the repatriation cases, public's interest should far outweigh the very threshold issue of the government's justification for removal. Mr. Bush's Republican administration and his established immigration policies and the manner of their enforcement has caused the most irreparable damages in the lives of almost all foreign nationals residing in America to date.

The outside world may not actually know how terrible this particular situation is, or the exact gravity and the impact of the Bush administration along with his extreme-right Republican teamsters' immigration policies has been like the immigrants affected by it.....immigrants who were physically residing in America during Mr. Bush's leadership. The Bush administration leadership woes has, no doubt, been an international history in the making. For the current and the future world generation, an accurate account of events as they unfolded all through Mr. Bush's eight chaotic years of leadership in America and how the policies he championed through this period and thereon after has affected America and the rest of the world community at large, has been chronicled on this text to be shared with the international community.....to educate, inform and to help make the world a better place when next we need to either appoint or elect leaders to represent or serve our society.

Very sadly, most of these viciously crafted foreign policies and particularly the immigration amendments approved by the Bush administration directly focused on immigrants, are still ongoing and aggressively enforced against foreign nationals even after Mr. Bush left office.

There is nothing cool about depriving relatively law abiding foreign nationals their due liberty interest in a foreign state by its government just for a boost of their political prerogative and ego, or to satisfy personal resentments they harbor towards these groups of people whose lineage and bloodline brought forth today's America.

It is extremely shameful how American society has become through the makings of arbitrary policies by some of the nation's vast-right conservative policymakers since the last few decades to the present time of the 21$^{st}$ century.

The nation's Justice Department during Mr. Bush's administration was operated more or less like an enterprise. The nation's laws, both criminal and civil, were and in large part, are still more protective of the select few heavyweights in both governmental and private sectors than the average Americans. They originally pushed for these laws enactment in the first place to serve their own personal interests. Rather they make the American public to believe that these laws are made to serve everyone's interest, but in practice, the laws are more beneficial to the limited few within their right-wing conservative circle who were the sponsors and brains behind the legislation of the laws in the first place.

Socioeconomically, so much has gone wrong in America and across the globe since the leadership of Mr. Bush. His administration was no different from a typical dictatorship regime under the guise of a democratic setting. His stubborn and arrogant nature and unilateral ideologies changed everything in America for the worse. The administration amassed so many ethical lapses that are yet to be accounted for......like the prisoners abuse scandal in Abu Grhaibe prison in Iraq, the illegitimate justification of his invasion of Iraq that has resulted to the lose of tens of thousands of innocent Iraqi lives and that of thousands of U.S. troops as well as that of the Iraqi security forces, and the so-called enemy combatants, and also the complete wasteful spending of the American taxpayers' hard- earned money to invade other people's sovereign domain under unsubstantiated claims of 'War on Terror', and the rendition and torture policy.

Mr. Bush along with his like-minded cabinet war hawks committed crimes against humanity and should be held accountable by the international tribunal to account for all the innocent lives that have perished in Iraq for ordering an unjustifiable war.

Other former leaders like Slobodan Milosevic of the former Yugoslavia nation of the Baltic region, Saddam Hussein of Iraq, The top commander during the Khmer Rouge's Pol Pot era in Cambodia, Charles Taylor of Liberia, among others, have all been apprehended and held to account for their roles in crimes they perpetrated against humanity and to their own people while in power. The same international law should apply to Mr. Bush, his vice, Dick Cheney, Donald Rumsfeld, John Ashcroft and a handful of other top Republican policymakers within his regime that were partners in plotting and biasly executing the so-called terror act against the world.

# 03 APPREHENSION AND DETAINMENT OF FOREIGN NATIONALS IN THE U.S.

SINCE THE 9/11 INCIDENT, THE BUSH Administration remarkably increased the number of already existing detention facilities to hold arrested foreign nationals across the country. One of such numerous facilities is located in York, a small rural town located in central Pennsylvania. It is considered one of the busiest detention facilities in the east coast of the country for the nation's Immigration agency. It has, for quite some time now, been serving as a major transit hub heavily used by the agency during the Bush administration to detain and process foreign nationals for repatriation.

The U.S. Department of Homeland Security (D.H.S.), born after the 9/11 incident, in conjunction with the U.S. Immigration and Customs enforcement agency (ICE), formerly called 'U.S. Immigration and Naturalization Service (I.N.S.) before the 9/11, have established very huge and active presence at this particular County prison facility as well as numerous other detention facilities across the country, to detain and deport hundreds of thousands of both criminal and non-criminal foreign nationals.

The methods and tactics adopted by these federal law enforcement operatives called 'ICE Police', right from the point of apprehension to the final phase of repatriation of aliens, are extremely cruel and capricious, to say the least. It is more like scenes from the movies that are not suppose to be real, but sadly, these ones are as real as it could get.

Maybe aliens charged and convicted of particularly serious crime(s), the ones that would be truly considered as danger to public safety may somewhat deserve to be subjected to such cruel process of apprehension just to be deported from the country.

Majority of these aliens picked up from the streets by this agency are either arrested at their residences, at their job sites, while commuting and even at school premises, and also at churches, mosques and other religious service vicinities. They are instantly apprehended and taken to jail pending their removal back to their individual countries. A process that takes no sooner than 3 to 6 months. Pending their removal, they remain detained in the agency's custody.

Hundreds of thousands of aliens arrested in this manner are absolutely non-criminals who merely overstayed their study or visitation visas, or were not lawfully admitted into the country. These aliens are heavily shackled upon their arrest to be taken to prison. En route to jail, they are firmly entwined with heavy-duty chains and cuffs on their legs, wrists and waist like they are very dangerous violent criminals being arrested for murder or any other heinous crimes. To further make matters worse, the agency have fleets of customized shuttle vans they use in apprehending and transporting arrested aliens to the agency's holding facilities. These shuttle vans are redesigned with no factory-installed seats. Instead, the regular factory-installed cushion seats are removed and replaced with bare metal seats with no cushion, crudely mounted on both sides of the vans. Arrested aliens are packed inside these customized vans, heavily shackled for a long ride bound to detention facilities.

The sad part is that majority of these apprehended foreign nationals have never experienced being in jail, or committed any crime in their entire lives to deserve being subjected to such treatment.....even back in their own countries. Most of these aliens have always been modest citizens all their lives. Their very first taste of prison took place in the proclaimed 'land of liberty' supposedly filled with milk and honey. What an odyssey in the proclaimed land of liberty for all.

How cruel can it get for a father of three young kids be taken in early dawn right in front of his innocent little kids when they were barely awoke as the U.S. Immigration agency arrived at his residence. All because he was charged some eight years prior and was convicted in the state of New York for having received stolen property.....a relatively minor criminal infraction that he was already punished for.

At the time, Andre, who is originally from Ukraine, was punished accordingly for his mistake and trouble with the law. He was sentenced to two years probation and to pay restitution to the victim. That would seem like a fairly adequate punishment for a permanent resident alien, considering the offense gravity. Such offense category, though harshly codified in the U.S. Immigration laws as deportable crime if a sentence of up to a year may be imposed, do not in any way rise to the level of such offense to warrant the agency hunting such aliens down, arresting them under any circumstance on the spot and detaining them in prison indefinitely without a chance of posting bond while they go through the agency's often lengthy process of removal proceedings. Not even serving such aliens any prior 'Notice To Show Cause' before their final arrest and detainment in jail.

The immigration proceeding against Andre could have been commenced and concluded on the streets without having to arrest and detain him to answer to the deportation charges as the agency prefer to adopt in pretty much every immigration matters these days in America.....a policy that was authorized and started by the Bush administration.

In the case of Andre and a whole lot of other cases involving immigrants, Andre was his family's breadwinner. It will be very troubling for anyone with soul and compassion to listen to him giving a sad account of how he got arrested right at his residence in Queens, New York......snatched away right in front of his two little kids while their mother was at work. Such a heartless application of the law towards foreign nationals by the United States Immigration agency, under the conservative leadership of Mr. Bush and his rightist Republican constituents in Washington, have left tens of thousands of immigrants' families in America torn apart like that of Andre.

Andre further went ahead to share his lamentation whenever he talks on the prison phone with his wife on how the kids have been extremely troubled for not knowing their father's where about....narrating how the kids cries to sleep at night and having nightmares, because their Daddy whom they have been so used to is suddenly not with them any more. Why? Because the ultraconservative administration of Mr. Bush along with his extreme-right policymakers in the U.S. government wants him and millions of other foreign nationals kicked out of the country by any means necessary. Their primary motive has remained the best-kept secret to the American public.

Andre's ordeal with the U.S. Immigration agency was just one out of tens of thousands of this nature faced by foreign nationals and their American families that have fell victims of the assault on their liberty and harassment at their homes by this agency.

The terrible part is being scooped up by this agency without any prior 'notice to show cause', when these aliens least expected it. It is necessary to note or somewhat imagine what goes on in the minds of these set of Washington policymakers who are behind these extremely harsh immigration laws that exist today in America.

Their intentions are unmistakably clear that they possess a deep-rooted level of resentment towards foreign nationals, and they are willing to stop at nothing in devising policies to make immigrants lives a living hell in America. Such mindsets are reflected in the enactment and the enforcement of these harsh and cut-dry new amended immigration laws to hurt the immigrants. It is not a sentiment that had just emerged after the 9/11 incident neither. The 9/11 incident merely served as a catalyst to unleash their long concealed xenophobic agenda against foreign nationals.

American history started with immigrants and still remains a strong force and asset to the nation's growth and socioeconomic standing in the world today. Even though the so-called rightist conservatives in America feels like they are now more of Americans than even the new generation of Americans and the naturalized newcomers, they still remain generations and descendants of immigrant parents from back in time.....who migrated to America, voluntarily or otherwise, from some other parts of the world.

It is very sad a development, and troubling as well, seeing the ugly things that took place during the early days of the first generation of the European migrants to America repeat itself.

The first European migrants to America who did not die from the extremely harsh wintry climate in America at the time, survived through the hospitality of the Native American Indians who thought them the necessary surviving skills. After mastering these skills, they decided to brutally annihilate the goodhearted Native Indians from their land and took it over. A closely similar scenario is repeating itself again with the new wave of immigrants residing in America these days, but this time the plot is being executed with a slightly different twist.

These immigrants are being kicked out of the country without being afforded any opportunity to retrieve any of their equities on the streets of America, or even be allowed to make an alternative arrangement with their American families, relatives or friends, on that respect, before being kicked out....or even with their Consular office abroad.

Amid the continuous proclamation of hatred of foreign nationals championed by the Bush administration after the 9/11 incident in America, some goodhearted Americans, nonetheless, continue to stand by immigrants....helping them to proclaim the injustices inflicted on these aliens by the nation's Republican rightwing leadership who has made it their utmost political priority to forcefully remove permanent U.S. resident aliens and the aliens admitted into the country as Geneva Convention refugees or asylees from America. These aliens who have lawful residency papers to stay in the country are kicked out once they have the very least encounter with the law, regardless of how minor such encounter might have been, what equities they own in the country, fear of persecution back in their homelands, and even those with strong family ties in the country.

The Bush's administration position to pluralize the retaliatory punishment for the 9/11 incident on all foreign nationals residing in America is very inimical.

Less than 10 percent of the foreign nationals arrested and detained to be repatriated barely prevail at the immigration custody after a lengthy period of legal battles to secure their release back to the street to reunite with their families in America. Such low percentage reflects the extent of damages being done to the lives of the affected aliens and their families left behind in America. Not that those conservative hardliners behind the legislation of such draconian immigration policies these days in America cares the least bit about these aliens nor their families left behind in the U.S.

If the conservative Republican policymakers in America is so bent in removing all the immigrants from America as a result of their hate sentiment for no justifiable reason they had helped created....ostensibly stemming from the aftermath of the 9/11, even though it is unmistakably clear that none of these arrested group of aliens had anything to do with the 9/11 incident, or for whatever undisclosed reasons.....it would have been judicially fair for the government to promptly notify these aliens of its intent and afford them some grace periods to enable them secure their American families and equities. After such grace period, then such swift and aggressive move to apprehend and repatriate criminal or noncriminal aliens will at least be somewhat reasonably justifiable in the public's eye. But these U.S. right-wing conservative policymakers' motive behind the mass-expulsion of foreigners are neither well- founded nor legitimate in fact and law. That is why they adopt the 'thief-in-the-broad-daylight' strategy of a swift sweep of the aliens on the spot and dump them in their custody till they are ready to send them home.

Unfortunately, some of these arrested aliens are in America all by themselves with no close or reliable relatives to help them secure their equities out there. In tens of thousands of instances of such, the affected aliens end up loosing everything they worked so hard for in America.... enriching someone else who has no idea how those personal equities came about.

It is an extremely heart-wrenching odyssey for tens of thousands of foreign nationals who are subjected to this cruel nature of treatment by the policies championed by some far-right conservative American policymakers.

Some immigrants love America so much and have lawfully resettled there, working very hard and diligently for over 20 years.......paying taxes to the government for all those number of years.......then all of a sudden, they get scooped up out of the blue at their workplaces, at their home, or even while commuting on either public or personal transportation out there by the nation's Immigration authority. They get struck by the rude awakening of the nation's conservative extremists' intent to deport them for relatively minor civil or criminal infractions like overstayed visa, lack of residency papers, or even a simple civil infractions like 'Driving Under the Influence' (D.U.I.).

A lot of legal resident aliens have been stripped off their permanent residency status and subsequently kicked out of the country back to their homelands over relatively minor offenses like D.U.I. until one of the affected aliens painstakingly challenged the government's legality of his removal charge all the way to the nation's Supreme Court.

After years of litigating the case, the United States Supreme Court reviewed the case and made a ruling in 2003-04 that became a precedent.

The Court essentially established that a D.U.I. offense is not a deportable offense for immigration purpose. Thanks to such courageous alien who made himself a sacrificial lamb to pursue justice for himself and for other aliens who were currently, or may have already been, or may suddenly find themselves in similar scenario with the agency in the future. The nation's Supreme Court's ruling on this matter should at best be considered a very rare lucky shot these days in a nation that fair and square justice for all has become so far-fetch, especially justice for foreign nationals.

After this ruling, the U.S. Immigration agency was mandated to bring back and readmit all the aliens the agency had already erroneously repatriated under this statutory case law.

For aliens with pretty long work history who have been saving up with the government for those long years on retirement/social security savings, which are mandatory deductible from workers paychecks, and then suddenly happens to get picked up by the nation's Immigration agency on very minor criminal infractions of this nature, have all ended up being removed from United States without the government making any provision to reimburse them for those saved up social security funds that was intended for their retirement years.

Such funds owed to these group of foreign nationals who were active workforces during their stay in America by the American government on social security, continues to be unlawfully forfeited and unaccounted for by the government when these aliens under such category gets deported.

Justice has not been served if the U.S. government decides to deport any foreign national for whatever immigration violation, but fails to promptly make provision to reimburse him or her on social security funds it owed them before their removal. A lot of aliens removed from United States were victims to this governmental scam. They all got surprised and did not expect such injustice and petty strong-arm dealings to be practiced by the United States government that always proclaim itself as a pioneer state in practicing as well as spreading democracy, fair and equal justice for all.

If the government of the U.S. right-wing conservatives wants to deport these set of aliens with relatively long work history that bad based on the offenses they committed at some point in time in their past, then it should also be equally fair for the same group of conservative government faction to make prompt and timely provision in paying up all the social security money it has received from these aliens for those period of years they have legally worked in the country paying their taxes before they get sent back to their individual countries. Only then will such removal be somewhat justified in the part of the government.

Foreign Consulates have a very crucial role to play in accomplishing this goal on behalf of their deportee citizens before issuing travel papers to effect their removal.

# THE U.S. DEFIANCE OF THE GENEVA CONVENTION'S REFUGEE TREATY

ALL CONTRACTING STATES ARE REQUIRED AND expected to acknowledge and uphold the United Nations' Convention Protocols, including the one relating to the status of refugees ("Refugee Convention"), 189 U.N.T.S. 150.....as binding.

A treaty put in place on July 28, 1951 after the world war II to provide protection against persecution and special safeguards for civilians by member states when people flee their homelands at war time, or persecution on racial, religious, national or political grounds. United States acceded this Refugee Convention in 1968. The U.S. Congress enacted the Refugee Act in 1980 in order to bring United States in conformity with this United Nations Refugee Convention. The United States' Supreme Court found from legislative history of the 1980 Refugee Act that one of Congress' primary goal was to bring United States refugee law into conformance with the Protocol to which United States became a signatory state in 1968.

In light of the threshold Refugee Convention obligation which United States acceded as binding, brings about the odyssey of an asylee in United States who was subject to forceful expulsion back to his country of feared persecution by the draconian judicial frameworks put in place and heavily enforced by the Republican administration of Mr. Bush and his extreme-right conservative policymakers in Washington.

Thompson, a Nigerian citizen who was admitted into United States as an asylee after fleeing the political turmoil caused by his government against his oil-rich Niger-Delta region was arrested and detained by the United States Immigration agency. The Bush administration along with his extreme-right policymakers in Washington sought to remove him for a conviction of unauthorized marketing of Hollywood's 'Visual Arts' intellectual property.

Even though the offense, in the actual face of it, is not close to the level of being categorized as a particularly serious crime to warrant the government initiating such an aggressive and ruthless removal action against him.

The government record shows that he was granted "Indefinite Asylum" status, which, by the way still remained valid and active at the time the government agency commenced the removal proceedings against him. Such ruthlessly aggressive removal action by the U.S. Immigration agency that had been emboldened by the far-right Republican teamsters in the Bush's administration simply meant stripping a Geneva Convention asylee off his refugee status and protection an forcefully returning him back to harm's way in his homeland of feared persecution.....an outright violation of the Convention's Protocol.

Both the U.S and the International law clearly specifies that refugees may not be forcefully returned to their feared country of persecution as long as they remain refugees within the context enumerated in the Geneva Convention Protocol for refugees.

Refugee status and its protection rarely get disturbed unless such individual is no longer considered a refugee within the definition of the Convention's protocol; or such refugee has engaged in a particularly serious crime, or engage in a capital offense against others. Only in such circumstances can a refugee be stripped off his or her refugee status and be returned to his or her country of feared persecution.

Thompson was scheduled to appear before an Immigration Judge to answer as well as to contest the removal charge against him. After his charge was read to him by the presiding judge, Thompson's counsel addressed the court by rejecting the charge.....making it clear on record that his client was admitted into the country as an asylee and still remain an asylee and may not be forcefully returned to his country of feared persecution pursuant to the statutory language of the United States immigration law: Immigration and Nationality Act (INA), Section 208..... which itself implement the Geneva Convention Protocol relating to the status of refugee under Article 1 of the Convention. Then the Immigration

Judge asserted that: " Thompson is no longer an asylee once he became a U.S. permanent resident".....a so-called permanent residency card 'Green Card' that Thompson was never issued by the agency, but yet the agency uses its law to unlawfully seek his removal from the country.

The Immigration Judge however failed to support her finding, either by statutory construction of the U.S immigration law nor by prior precedential decisions of similar case law by other superior courts. Knowing that her assertion of this particular section of the law was unfounded and erroneous, Thompson's counsel requested that the judge support her assertion and ruling by codified statute or precedent, then she suddenly got very upset and declined to answer nor entertain any further questioning on the issue by Thompson's counsel. To proceed with the matter, she offered one of those vague advice to Thompson, through his counsel, to fill in another asylum application as Thompson's only form of relief from removal. Thompson suddenly have to fill in yet another asylum application while his first asylum grant has never been legally terminated by the agency. Such unnecessary runaround and mental torture was pretty much the order of the day under the authority of Mr. Bush's vast-right Republican leadership.

The tactics applied by the agency is to make the aliens under this special International protection succumb to their practice of unlawful expulsion. The tactics, even though unlawful, has proven quite effective all through Mr. Bush's administration who had primarily conferred this excessive power on the agency to maltreat foreign nationals this way.

Sadly, a lot of refugees have been unlawfully removed back to their embattled homelands with the agency's strategy of detaining them in jail while litigating the legality of their removal till they subsequently become completely exhausted and finally gives in to the overbearing pressure and end up being forcefully sent home against their wills to face the very same demise which they had fled from in their various homelands.

Through its arbitrary style of policy-making and their ruthless enforcement thereof, the Bush administration basically and frankly sent a message to these refugees as well as the international law governing their protection from persecution, that, it could care less about the law protecting them or whatever happens to them upon their return home.

The Bush administration's deportation policies against Geneva Convention refugees like Thompson and thousands of others who have already been forcefully kicked out of the country over some relatively minor criminal offenses, showed that its removal goal of such refugees back to harm's way is very important and serves the public's interest than rather waving the removal charges as the law recommends to protect their lives and safety from persecution in their homelands.

What else could possibly be the logical motive behind a judicial agency, serving the government to uphold fair and balanced justice, requiring an alien to fill in another application for relief that he or she had already been accorded and the same status still remains valid and never was terminated, other than a swindle motive to strip such individual(s) off what he or she already got. In this type of governmental arm-twisting, two results are likely: either being completely denied the relief the second time around, which is basically the same as being stripped off the very same status that the government was unable to directly terminate by law; or at their most reluctant best, being given a replacement status of much lesser value and protection than the first one.

In Thompson's further effort to challenge the legality of the agency's removal action against him, his counsel filed a motion with the court on his behalf, requesting the court to terminate the removal proceedings against his client, pursuant to statutory regulation codified in the U.S. Immigration laws which supported the fact that Thompson may not be forcefully removed back to his country of feared persecution.

Nonetheless, this motion was briefly addressed by the court during one of Thompson's subsequent removal hearings. The judge yet again reasserted her erroneous finding that "Thompson is no longer an asylee after he applied and was approved of a Lawful Permanent Resident (L.P.R.) status." Still without any statutory or precedential citation of any case law to corroborate her vague presumably legal assertion of a non-existing law.....even though Thompson was never actually issued the so-called Green Card itself to verify the actual accordance of the so-called L.P.R. status as required by the agency in the first place.

In her conclusive statement, she made a statement off the record saying that: "The Geneva Convention rules governing the treatment of refugees do not apply in my courtroom. This is United States court, not international court," she asserted.

From such erroneous re-assertion, it became quite obvious that she was arbitrarily inclined to fulfill the far-right judicial wishes of the Bush administration and not necessarily to serve justice for public's interest.

Serving justice, in most cases, was never the primary motive of the agency, as implicitly delegated by the Bush administration along with his right-wing Republican teamsters who have been heavily funding the mass-deportation operation. According to Mr. Bush, the administration's goal is to "drain the swamps." Who are these swamps? Of course the foreign nationals living within the U.S.

Democracy and justice is at stake when a governmental agency charged to enforce and execute the nation's laws accordingly for public's interest is itself circumventing the clear language of the law along with the judicial adjudicators to fit the empirical agendas of the vast-right conservative inner-circle power brokers who always wants to control and dictate every policy-making to others.

With the new and continuing trend of hostility towards foreign nationals, such application of the nation's federal immigration laws are enforced at the expense of relatively innocent and law abiding immigrants in America. In Mr. Bush's tenor as the nation's Chief Executive Officer (CEO), everything became very wrong with the so-called justice served to foreign nationals.....especially when it comes to the justice served in immigration laws presided over by immigration judges with conservatively radical views of interpreting and applying the law.

Majority of the Bush administration Immigration Judges plays the role of both the government prosecutor and that of the judge at the same time in the courtroom. In such a setting, the administration of the moment or the central government's judicial motive and goal becomes highly questionable.

When these aliens are pressured with pretrial confinement strategy, either they are guilty as charged or not, most gets heavily constrained as a result psychologically forced to bow to the court's dictates without affording them the necessary Due Process of the law to properly determine the appropriate justice deemed adequately fit for the matter by the court. Any government's ultimate goal should not be winning judicial matters at all cost, but rather make it its utmost priority that justice is properly served in every judicial matter accordingly and at all cost. That would have been a proper statement to make if only the Bush administration was operating under the rule of law.

After being forced to fill in another asylum application as his only relief, Thompson finally appeared before the same judge to determine the merit to the second asylum request he was essentially forced to fill in as his only form of relief from removal......despite the fact that the first one was never legally terminated, as there was no such legal ground for the government to do so.

As anticipated, Thompson was shot down and denied all the three forms of the Geneva Convention protection against persecution of refugees. At that point, Thompson was not so surprise because he was already given heads-up of such denial forth-coming during the preliminary stage of his removal proceedings.

The government counsel along with the presiding judge avoided and failed to explain their legal reasoning in finding Thompson removable as charged. The only explanation offered by the judge was that asylees who were approved of permanent residence status automatically strips them of their refugee protection. This noncodified and vague legal assertion by the immigration judge and the agency is completely unfounded and contrary to any old or new statutes enumerated under the U.S. Immigration and Nationality Act (INA) which the agency and the judge must follow to practice and enforce the nation's immigration laws.

In United States, the Immigration and Customs Enforcement (ICE) agency is in charge of every immigration law enforcement. A name born after the 9/11 incident to replace the defunct Immigration and Naturalization Service (INS). The agency is under the regulatory umbrella of the United States Attorney General's office, under the U.S. 'Department of Justice.' The immigration arm of the nation's Justice Department is expected and portrayed to be operated civilly, but in practice, it is far from it......especially after Mr. Bush came on board and flipped the entire rules of the agency's engagement.

The Bush administration loaded the agency with pretty much open-ended authorities to enforce the nation's immigration laws against foreign nationals in the most raw and ruthless manner ever seen in America in recent generation....maybe the worst immigration enforcement in the U.S. history.

The nature of treatment imposed on foreign nationals under the agency's custody at any given time and place is far worse than the treatment received by high-profile criminal offenders who are considered to be threat to public safety. Hundreds of thousands of non-criminal aliens who have been forcefully repatriated back to their homelands can identify with the various versions of cruel and inhumane treatment suffered from the hands of the United States Immigration agency under the leadership of Mr. Bush and his ultraright Republican teamsters in Washington thereon after.

Undoubtedly, coming to America has turned out to be these immigrants worse nightmare…worse than what most of them ever experienced growing up in their home lands. The image of American government inflicting cruel punishment on foreign nationals, particularly during the reign of Mr. Bush's Republican regime, is far from the image of liberty for all and respect for human right which America likes to portray itself as a nation to the rest of the world.

Every foreign nationals forcefully repatriated from America is not just removed for whatever violation they were charged for, but also carry with them a terrible and inhumane impression of America where justice to foreign nationals is applied with high level of bias. Even the nation's hostility towards foreigners is increasingly affecting free flow of commerce and foreign investments and other forms of socioeconomic dealings with America.

Following the new Arizona law intended to empower the state police officers to stop any individual in the state that looks like an immigrant and request for their legal residence papers, and if they are unable to produce them on the spot, they will be arrested and taken to jail till they get processed for deportation, Mexican government has not been in very good terms with Arizona state in particular, and even other neighboring states with Arizona and a number of cities across America has vented their anger towards the law by boycotting doing business with the state. Even so, other states like Nevada and Virginia with similar anti-immigrants typical Republican governors and policymakers, have also joined the state of Arizona anti-immigrants band wagon to enact yet other sets of laws within their states to punish the so-called undocumented immigrants by arresting them and have them deported back to their countries.

The hate syndrome against foreign nationals in America in recent time by the nation's right-wing Republican extremists, both by governmental officials and private citizens alike, is increasingly being played out more like how the Bush administration went about combating terrorism......a highly dysfunctional and chaotic cause of action that plunged the country in a deep political and financial mess which the Obama administration tries to restore. Immigrants now in America are seen by the right-wing Republicans as enemies that must be vanquished or flushed out of the country by any means necessary.

The Obama administration challenged the Arizona anti-immigrants laws in court. The court struck down some of the key parts of the laws, agreeing with the administration that immigration laws and its enforcement is solely rested on the federal government and not state or local authorities.

Arizona state, which is one of the states in America that is so cash-strapped... deeply sunk in financial woes stemming from the Bush administration's failed economic policies....with one of the nation's most messed-up state budget, still have the state's taxpayers' money to waste on litigation expenses to appeal the federal court judge's preliminary injunction placed on it not to enforce the key parts of the laws the state had expected will go into effect by mid July 2010. Such money could have been put to better use to provide meals or shelter for the homeless citizens within the state.

This and other shocking new developments across the nation shows how far the right-wing Republicans in America today are determined to go just to demonstrate their hatred towards immigrants living within the country. With this level of hatred on foreign nationals by the nation's Republican faction, if the ugly trend is not contained quite soon, it won't be a surprise to see this current trend escalates into a full-blown war against foreigners in America by the nation's right-wing Republicans just like the ongoing battles against insurgents in Iraq and Afghanistan.

The Obama's administration challenge of the Arizona state anti-immigrants laws is expected to be battled by the state all the way to the nation's Supreme Court. This is how deep the Republicans mission to root out the new wave of immigrants from the country has gotten these days in America.....the nation of immigrants for that matter.

Article 94 of the United Nations Charter requires member states' law enforcement agencies to inform any foreign national arrested of any offense within its soil, of its right to seek assistance from their diplomats abroad during the time of their arrest. Such notification to foreign nation nationals facing criminal charges is required by the Vienna Convention.

The Article which governs the enforceability of world court decisions, provides that "each member of the United Nations undertakes to comply with the decision" of world court in any case to which it is a party. Such Vienna notification is constantly violated by United States.....particularly during the Bush's administration. He withdrew the United States from the world court's jurisdiction over future Vienna Convention disputes.

# 05 THE IMMIGRATION COURTROOM SETTING IN THE U.S.

IN A DEMOCRATIC SOCIETY, ANY COURTROOM of law, either for criminal or civil proceedings, should, by law, be accessible to the general public who are interested to follow up with such legal proceedings. It is however not so at most immigration courts venues across the U.S. It gets even worse when such courts are located and operated within the same detention facilities where the arrested aliens are held. Such is the case in York, Pennsylvania, where a large part of the County's prison is contracted to the U.S. Immigration agency for holding arrested aliens till they are ready to be shipped back to their countries. It has been one of the major transit and detention hubs like many others operated in predominantly racially bias anti-immigrant states across the country during the Bush administration.....where aliens are held and brought to court before Immigration adjudicators to be ordered removed back to their homelands.

This detention facility, which is actually a county prison to house the county inmates from the York township, has two built-in courtrooms across from each other within the prison walls......and a third one which is squeezed into a tinny office space that could barely fit six people at a time......for immigration hearings only. This facility, among others, holds one of the largest numbers of foreign nationals picked up from the streets to be processed for deportation all year round. After the Bush administration along with his far- right Republican policymakers in Washington laid the groundwork and changed the rules of U.S. immigration enforcement and heavily funding the crackdown as well, more aliens scooped up from the streets floods this very county facility on a daily basis than even the regular county criminals brought there by the local police. It is more or less the same scenario in various other states and county jails across the country that the agency had contracts to use some of their housing space to detain these aliens.

In York, the detained aliens are brought to court with their prison-issued orange jumpsuits uniform. Thompson was very shocked on his very first court appearance that the Immigration court was inside the same jail that he was being detained. This Kangaroo Immigration courts built within prison walls where the aliens are held was intended by the Bush administration to facilitate its mission of mass-expulsion of foreign nationals from United States through the back door.....and not at all to facilitate justice nor the quality of justice being served to these aliens.

Both of the major courtrooms stays desolate of the civilians at all time. A typical setting of a Kangaroo court where any judgment, either right or wrong, can be handed down to aliens without the knowledge of the outside public. The courtrooms stays empty all the time except from the presiding judges, the government or the agency's counsels and the individual aliens whose cases are being heard at the time. Those who can afford an attorney are there with their counsels and those who can't afford one are there by themselves.

Due to the venue of the court, public's access is very limited and highly restricted during these aliens' removal hearings. The presiding judges pretty much decides if they want any of those who came to attend an alien's removal hearing to be allowed inside the courtroom or not. So whatever the judge says regarding who may be allowed to attend the court proceedings is final, regardless of how long a distance they travel to get there just to attend the hearing on behalf of their loved ones.

Only on very rare occasions that family members of detained aliens are allowed to attend their removal proceedings. To even be considered for possible clearance, family members must apply for advance clearances for at least two weeks in advance to such court date before being approved or denied pass inside the prison. In addition, such attendance arrangement must be made at least two weeks in advance with such aliens' counsel and be approved by the presiding judge who makes his or her final determination at the very last minute when the attendees have already arrived at the facility from various long distance residences.

This gives a clear picture of how secretive and ruthlessly harsh the Bush administration and the vast-right Republican faction in United States has made it a major priority to make life a living nightmare for all foreign nationals and even their American-born families.

# 06 THE FINAL PHASE OF ALIENS' REPATRIATION IN THE U.S.

A S A GOVERNMENT AGENCY CHARGED TO conduct its business civilly, the Republican administration of Mr. Bush and his right-wing faction in Washington turned the United States Immigration agency into a highly secretive agency that takes whatever arbitrary measures in dealing with foreign nationals these days in America. Very simple information that are supposed to be shared with detained aliens regarding their time of removal and progress made to speed up the removal process are withheld from these aliens by the agency.

All aliens subject to removal are basically kept in total suspense as to when their removal will be effected.

After an immigration judge enters a final order of removal, and such order was not appealed by the alien within thirty days required to follow up with unsatisfactory court decision, such order becomes final.

The U.S. Supreme court established a ruling back in 2003, permitting the agency to hold aliens with final order of removal no longer than six months under its custody before they are either deported or be afforded meaningful review for possible release on Order of Supervision only on condition that the agency is unable to secure such aliens' travel document to effect their removal within the 180 days statutory time frame. However, before then, the agency used to just hold some foreign nationals in its custody for years. Common victims of this torturous circumstances by the agency were those aliens from countries like Vietnam, Cuba, Laos, whose countries don't have much diplomatic exchange with the U.S government and therefore rarely accepts their citizen deportees back.

Within the six months period, they can be taken by surprise either by daytime or by night, or even by early dawn, straight to the airport for deportation. They are not advised or even allowed to make any form of arrangement with their families out on the streets....for those who have one......at the very least, to bring them a pair of outfit to wear on their day of returning home. That simply means that any alien subject to final order of removal are left with no other choice but to wear whatever clothing they had on when they got arrested back to their various homelands. That applies to aliens arrested at their work sites...in some cases, with their soiled work clothes.

In summer of 2006, the agency notified all aliens detained under its custody at the York, Pennsylvania detention facility, that it will no longer accept luggages brought in for aliens awaiting deportation. The best reason the agency gave was that it had no storage place to keep those luggages. Prior to that, the agency usually allow luggage drop-offs by families of aliens awaiting removal. That courtesy suddenly became too much of a burden for the agency to bear.

It would have been somewhat reasonable an excuse if the financial burden to purchase the clothing for these aliens was at the agency's expense, but none of such expenses are shouldered by the agency than just to receive the relatively small size of luggage on behalf of these aliens from their loved ones in preparation for their final departure. It is rather treated as a huge task to perform on behalf of these poor aliens facing expulsion back to their countries. What better treatment would you expect from such an administration affiliated with a national political group that harbors a deep resentment on immigrants? Their primary mission, of course, is to vanquish the growth of immigrants across America.....the land of immigrants that was built by immigrants for that matter.

If a governmental agency will go to such length as arresting civilians on the spot based on civil matters at their residences away from their little young kids, even at church or any other religious places and taking them straight to jail to be processed for deportation, it definitely could care less of the type of clothing they will be having on when they are ready to have them deported. It is another clear reflection of the level of hatred against foreign nationals that exist these days in the minds of the American right-wing policymakers in Washington and others like them across the country......a behavioral pattern championed by the Bush administration which quickly gained a lot of like-minded vast-right conservative fans during and after Mr. Bush left office.

Mr. Bush's administration's foreign and immigration policies was a reflection of his total disregard for human right as much as him condoning the practice.

Not even a final courtesy to provide these aliens with a pair of outfit each to wear on their final journey back home. Even a lot of countries that are less affluent as the U.S. do make such humanitarian provision for the aliens they are sending back to their countries. The Bush administration and its far-right Republican faction's primary goal is to have each and every removable aliens filled with so much sorrow and misery from their point of apprehension till they finally arrive at their individual homelands. Hundreds of thousands of non-criminal aliens are subjected to this type of treatment on a yearly basis these days in America. These Republican extremists in America today derives enormous pleasure devising cruel measures to be used against foreign nationals and watch them suffer in the process.

During Thompson's detainment by the agency, he had the opportunity to witness thousands of foreign nationals being repatriated. The aliens are heavily shackled with very thick metal chains around their foot, wrists, and across their waists as they are matched on a single file across the facility's hallway by the immigration officers.....ready to be loaded into the agency's standby buses idling at the back of the newly built extension of the facility intended for housing more aliens caught out there. On top of all the heavy shackles, the agency still have the K-9 Unit with at least two huge K-9 dogs on stand-by to chase down any of the aliens in the event that any of them might have the thought of escaping. And that suppose to be a civil governmental agency supposedly operated civilly.....treating non-criminal foreign nationals this way. How can any of these aliens even attempt to run in such heavily shackled condition? That is highly unconscionable.

A minimum of two full size buses drops off and loads up there at least five days a week except for Sundays. This backdoor lot is so busy dropping off and loading up aliens just like a typical Greyhound bus terminal in a big U.S. city.

This rendition process of mass-deportation of foreign nationals goes on all year round during Mr. Bush's eight years of presidency. His administration was in fact the brain child behind the draconian immigration policies and its ruthless enforcement in recent time in America.

The buses shuttles them to the airport, or to the Air Force Base where they either board commercial or chartered plane back home. The heavily shackled effect bring back to mind how the slaves were transported from Africa by boat through the Atlantic to Continental America during the slavery era. It is a very sad and disturbing process to observe non-criminal individuals being subjected to such cruel infringement of their liberty right by the government of a foreign state like United States that proclaims these rights the most to the rest of the world.

Between 100 to 150 aliens are secured this way to be deported from this York, Pennsylvania facility almost every day of the week. After being securely shackled, they are escorted out of the facility like herds of cattle into the stand-by immigration buses......with an immigration officer right behind the last man on the line and the other officer leading the line up front. This way, the aliens' dignity is reduced to zero just because the extreme-right conservative faction of the American policymakers wants them out of the country so bad.

Being guided like that in such a large number in shackles makes the aliens looks less of human being and more like herds of cattle being guided by sheapards to graze at the fields, or like cattle being guided to the slaughterhouse. It is extremely shameful for a nation like United States and its citizens to elect or allow any of its leader, after what everyone had thought was a bygone era of those slavery and the Wild-West days, to arbitrarily embolden any of its agencies to subject other human beings, foreign nationals for that matter, to such inhumane and degrading treatment in this day and age.

Being repatriating back to one's country do not necessarily have to be the worse experience like the right-wing Republican policymakers in United States has made it to become. After all, these individuals are returning to their native lands of birth. It may not be how they might have love to return, but nonetheless, there is no place like home, as the saying goes.

The point at issue is the way and manner to which the agency adopts in treating these aliens from the point of apprehension through their removal process…which tell a lot about the state of mind of those policymakers who champions such policies used against immigrants in America.

Whatever was these aliens reason for removal, the nation's Republican policymakers' authorization and the nation's Immigration agency's style of enforcing those laws towards foreign nationals is uncalled for and are way out of context from the very purpose to which repatriation was intended or should be focused by the government. As the Bush administration pushed its hardest for eight years to displace foreign nationals from America, so also has the occupation continue by his right-wing teamsters even after he left office. These category of American policymakers with extreme ideologies seem unmoved by the fact that a reciprocal effect of its hostile foreign policies may be adopted towards Americans abroad some day in the future.

Foreign nationals are increasingly getting treated so badly today in America due to the anti-immigrant policies championed by the Bush administration itself. Most of the aliens wish to have rather undergone such tormentual experiences inflicted on them by the U.S. government in their homelands by their own government rather than in a foreign state like United States.

That said, the million dollar question to all foreign nationals planning to immigrate to America some day in the future, if things still remain the same like it currently is, would be to ask oneself if it is worth going through those different forms of implicit and explicit hostilities and torments…… and even economic mobility constraints……in a foreign land like United States for that matter?

# 07

# THE U.S. PRISON MARKETPLACE

A TYPICAL PENAL INSTITUTION OF ANY SOCIETY is supposed to be operated and funded solely by the government of such state for the primary purpose of punishing and rehabilitating its citizen offenders to make them better people in their areas of weaknesses. Such governmental role in America today is almost completely diminished and seriously compromised by the government policies that condones and accommodates such counterproductive changes......the rehabilitation role in particular.

Even the agencies charged by the government to enforce and execute penal obligations for the primary interest of the public, have all been sailing towards the opposite direction for quite some time now. In effect, most penal institutions solely operated and funded by the government are run in America now like typical for-profit entities. Although there are very few privately-run penal facilities in America as well...these ones are privately owned and are strictly for-profit entities. In the cases of majority of the nation's penal institutions, which are still run by the government, the very individuals that are supposed to be rehabilitated by the government are indirectly being exploited and hustled by their custodians and it all sits well with the government.

Since the mass-sweep of foreign nationals by the Bush administration after the 9/11 incident, a lot of penal institutions, especially the County facilities like the one in York, Pennsylvania, where Thompson was held, among numerous others all across the country, are constantly flooded with foreign nationals apprehended by the United States Immigration agency. These large influx of foreign national detainees held at those contracted facilities are highly boosting the profitability of the U.S. prisons marketplace.

Some basic hygiene items and services that are funded by the government and are mandatory items to be provided for the prisoners, especially the federal immigration detainees awaiting deportation in most of the detention facilities and County prisons are now being sold for profit to local inmates as well as aliens detained there under the custody of the Immigration agency.

Items in question ranges from pillow, hygiene products items like soap, shampoo, deodorant, toothpaste and toothbrush, underwear, towel, shower shoes. These hygiene items are required to be issued to all detainees free-of-charge when the aliens are brought in by the agency. The Immigration agency is already been given enormous amount of taxpayers' money to cover the provision of these hygiene items in which most of the penal institutions turn around and sell for profit to these detained aliens.

Not only just selling these items at fairly reasonable prices, the detainees are made to purchase these hygiene items at very high prices through the institution's commissary vendors. During Thompson's period of detainment by the U.S Immigration agency at the York, Pennsylvania facility, he was subjected to this nature of exploits as well as the rest detained foreign nationals and local prisoners by the institution's administrators.

A long distance 'collect' phone call from the facility to Philadelphia, which is about two hours drive (200 kilometers) from York where the prison is located, cost Thompson about $15.00 for 20 minutes phone time. While a similar collect call from there to New York, which is about twice the distance from the facility to Philadelphia, cost detainees held there about $25.00 for the same 20 minutes call time.

Those rates are more than double the rates paid for such collect call with similar calling distance from the street. Thousands of detainees held there and in other detention facilities across the United States at any given time of the year.....awaiting deportation......are all subjected to varied outrageous rates levied by the phone service vendors permitted by the institutions' administrators to provide such service within the facilities...knowing that these detainees have to keep in touch with their loved ones out there while they await their removal which takes an average of 3 to 6 months or more.

The detainees are arrested and transported from various long distance residences across the country to be held at distant detention facilities. They are left with no choice but to use the provided phone service to stay in touch with their families and loved ones out there...especially those with families out there who wish to fight their deportation cases there in custody till they either prevail or loose. They are left with no other choice but to remain in mandatory detention under the agency's custody if they wish to fight their cases to avoid being forcefully removed back home.

A typical litigation of immigration matters with the agency, since the Bush administration changed the rules of engagement can stretch from a minimum of 4 months to a year or more, while such aliens remain indefinitely held in the agency's custody all through those lengthy period of time.

With such extremely expensive rate, the aliens' families are faced with extra financial burden on top of struggling to cater for the kids and the family members without one or, in some cases, both of the parents to the kids out there to help out. The custodians of these detainees and the private vendors, allowed to provide these services like the phone, are so hard-hearted without the least sympathy on these poor detained aliens and their struggling families out there.....indirectly putting such excessive and unjustifiable financial constraint on these families.

The aliens' families are already struggling to augment their meager and limited funds just to keep things afloat while they cope with the reality of the breadwinners of the house facing deportation back to their countries, and then comes yet another financial burden on their shoulders to carry. Yet, the government and its agencies that approves of their services and their business operation within most of the government-controlled and funded facilities are okay and well-settled with the outrageous prices of goods and services these private companies charges these detainees and regular inmates confined at these facilities who utilizes their provided goods and services.

If private citizens or foreign nationals engages in such cutthroat exploitative business practice, they will first be criminally prosecuted, and then, if they are foreigners, will be placed on deportation right after they are done serving their prison time.

Maybe half of such collect call phone rates may be somewhat reasonable, considering the critical condition of deportation the aliens are undergoing. With their unchallenged style of operation, it is well understood that these public officials and the private actors could care less of these aliens' financial situation as long as their own financial ends are in good standing and business is booming. Rather, the governmental policymakers as well as the administrators of these penal institutions and the federal government immigration agency that utilizes some o these institutional spaces to house their detainees, do not see anything wrong with this type of exploits by such business entities. Their primary motive these days is to profit from their position of authority to permits prison commerce by way of monopoly through private business entities that seem legal to hustle these poor distressed detained aliens.....by getting all they can get from them before they get kicked out of the country.

Most of these detainees' families get stuck with extremely high telephone bills that may range from several hundreds of dollars to thousands of dollars within few months just for detainees to stay connected with their spouses, kids and other loved ones out there on the streets of America. It shouldn't be this way at all. Both the governmental and the private entities involved in this prison commerce are all motivated by greed to exploit prisoners and detainees under their custody. They are indirectly using their position of authority to engage in commerce instead of the rehabilitative role which their job is only required of them.

Instead of serving the public's interest as officials in charge of public institutions funded by the public's taxpayers' money, they rather are busy cooking up marketing schemes within governmentally funded institutions to further exploit the public whose tax revenue are used by the government to fund and operate these institutions. Where is the rule of law here when elected and appointed governmental officials in charge of government agencies, charged to enforce the nation's laws in a country like United States with constitutional doctrines which clearly prohibits exploitation and injustice of any form to others, turning their legal obligations to the public into profit-making enterprise?

The very people that are supposed to be served justice in America are now, in most cases, victims of exploitation by the very administrators appointed to run these governmental agencies.....administrators delegated with the authority to enforce the nation's laws, but uses their office and authority to do the exact opposite service to the public. They have got so deep in the game to the point that it has rather become a trend in most penal institutions for quite a while now in America. The funny part is that the very same hardline Republicans in Washington and the rest across the nation, who are relentlessly behind the mass-expulsion of foreign nationals from America, have no time to be equally as forceful in cracking down on the prison commerce exploitation of prisoners and detainees by the administrators elected or appointed to administer things in these facilities as well as the private entities selling these goods and services. Their only primary goal is to continue devising draconian policies to expel foreign nationals from the country by any means necessary......both by legal and illegal means.

After so many years of excessive collect-phone call billings and unlawful windfall profiteering by the phone service provider for the state prisons in New York, a suit was filed at the state level against the phone companies by the prisoners who use the phone and their loved ones on the streets who gets stuck with the outrageous collect call phone bills. Through internal lobbying, the suit was shuttered and not allowed to proceed forward at the state court. Such blockade by the state court simply tells the public that most states within United States and their various governmental departments, including their executives or administrators running these departments, are all in this type of indirect exploitation of the public together.

The suit was subsequently re-filed at the federal level at the federal District Court in New York. This time, the presiding judge assigned to the case, however, was not swayed by the state lobbyists. The judge allowed the case to finally move forward after so many years of futile effort through the state judicial level. Evidently, this judge must have felt the pain and the mass-exploitation suffered by thousands of these New York State inmates and their loved ones out there on the streets for so many years and had decided to mandate the accused phone companies through the filed court action to finally come clear about the legality of their monopolistic business practices within these prison walls.

Not quite many judges with such moderate judgmental preferences are in the courtrooms of America these days, either in state or federal levels.

What most of the general public are not aware of about these elected public officials is that most of them get to their contested public offices through heavy campaign funding by these same private companies. In the case of the judges, such heavy campaign funding to have their favorite candidate elected to serve on the bench is an investment that finally pays off in the event of future court matters of this nature that may most likely be assigned to them to decide. That's when the companies rips the huge benefit of all the huge campaign spending they made to install such candidates into public office of authority.

To even make matters worse, the nation's highest court ruled in 2010 that it is all well for corporations to spend as much as they wish on campaign to fund the election of their favorite candidates running for public office. Such radical ruling by the conservative right-wing majority of the nation's Supreme Court is a slap in the face of all American public and a major assault to the democratic electoral process of the nation.

The whole nation was dismayed by the ruling, except for the nation's Republican right-wing faction. The Supreme Court's ruling on open-ended corporate spending on public elections in America has essentially set a very dangerous unleveled playing field for the American people to be able to elect a competent and deserving candidate for any particular public office without the influence of money corrupting the public to vote for the wrong candidate with ambiguous motives after getting elected into such office. This is one of the troubling areas where the problem lies in American politics today. And that problem is caused by the rightwing Republican faction in United States. The American public have suffered a great deal for decades because of this unrestricted influence of corporate spending to elect public officials. With Donald Trump's 2016 presidential election victory, he is pushing further to fill any vacant seat in the nation's Supreme Court with Justices who will rule on critical national matters based on the interests of their political affiliation and not necessarily by the law. His second Supreme Court Justice pick, Judge Bret Kavanaugh, will be doing just that when he joins the Bench.

The collect-call phone rates charged these aliens at the York, Pennsylvania detention facility, among numerous other detention facilities across the country, is almost three times the average fee any phone company will charge people on similar calls on the streets of America. On the streets, people can pick and choose from various phone service providers with the cheapest or fairly reasonable rates. But within the confines of a penal institutions like the one in York, the goods and services providers permitted in by the institutions' administrators, monopolize their business practice within these prison walls.....knowing that the inmates and the detainees are left with no other choice but to utilize the only source of such consumer goods and services at any cost, or do without it. The institutions provide them with no other alternatives either.

In most cases, the detainees held at such distant facilities from their original residents, who desperately needs to reach their families out there are left with no choice but to use such phone services at highly exorbitant rates set by the providers in agreement with governmental administrators of the facilities who approves of their business operation within the prisons. This setup practically leaves these detainees' families out there to foot such excessively expensive bills one way or another.

This type of exploitative business monopoly results to huge windfall profits for the concerned players at the expense of these poor detainees and their family members.

The commissary vendors adopts same price-fixing strategy in selling their food items and other consumer products. This is not a free-market system intended by the creation of capitalism. It is an outright indirect way of 'arm-twisting' or 'theft-by-deception' style of business practice. These days in America, capitalism is at its wildest state......it is becoming a business environment where most business entities are almost directly robbing their clients and the government, particularly the right-wing Republicans, does little or nothing to stop or punish the perpetrators.

A bag of noodle soup, which is one of the most consumed food items in most of the U.S. penal institutions, cost 60 cents at the York facility in Pennsylvania. That same price will buy at least six bags of the same brands of noodle soup anywhere on the streets of America. Sixty cents for the price of an item that costs five times lesser within the same geographical area might not be big of a deal for confined consumers who can afford to pay for such item at such inflated price because they are left with no other option but to buy these products. But on the flipside, those 60 cents eventually adds up pretty quickly into millions of dollars of windfall profit for the vendors and their enablers......especially at institutions that houses several thousands of inmates and detainees who are constrained to survive off these food items to augment with their often meager, or most at times, terrible institutional food rations they are usually served. The detainees and the rest inmates are continuously taken to the cleaners, while the vendors and the institutions administrators smiles to the bank.

Their actions are just as bad, if not worse, than that of some of the criminal inmates held under their watch.

In La Salle detention facility, Louisiana, one of the newly built immigration holding facilities across the country....funded by the Bush administration to enhance its mass-sweep and deportation of foreigners, a bag of the same noodle soup costs 95 cents each. That is almost a dollar for just one bag of noodle soup. That price is about ten times the price you pay for the same brands of noodle soup on the streets of America. The government has no problem whatsoever with such price gouging and such outright exploitation by these food vendors. In fact, it is actually the public officials in charge of these penal institutions that agrees to such exploitative business practices by these vendors, because they too ends up being part of the beneficiaries of the proceeds from the marketing scam.

With such remarkable windfall profiteering business activities allowed to take place within the walls of most America's taxpayers funded penal institutions, particularly the ones brought into existence by the Bush administration to detain aliens facing brutal repatriation proceedings and at the same time being bilked of their little money they have left to their names before being removed, it gets very troubling where justice really lies, or what justice really means from the right-wing Republicans point of view in American society today.

The government itself, especially the extreme-right Republican leaderships in America, condones this type of exploitative behaviors by these private business entities. The governmental agencies and the institutional administrators got no problem at all to give them the green light because they benefit immensely from these dealings and are not checked nor sanctioned by the law from the federal government itself.

There is nothing bad in making reasonable profit in legitimate business dealings, but an excessive one like this that feeds off individuals under such vulnerable circumstance is totally evil an un-American.

Since the Bush administration started the policy, foreign nationals are getting arrested by the masses on the streets of America and gets transported to these harsh and cruel detention facilities, which are nothing but real prisons where regular criminal offenders are held…..…held far away from their original places of residences.

Pending their removal proceeding, which normally takes forever, they are left with no choice but to utilize the products and services provided them at outrageous prices by their captors through these companies.

How can price of consumer-goods gets so high within penal institutions across America than what the same goods and services cost on the streets? People under governmental confinement in penal institutions are not considered to be active and productive members of the society with the liberty and choice to engage in normal economic activities to earn their livings. These confined individuals are cared for by the government through taxpayers' money and other source of governmental revenue while confined to pay their debt to the society or otherwise. They are also expected to get rehabilitated from their unlawful acts while serving such confinement time imposed by the government, but that crucial role is no longer a priority for U.S. right-wing policymakers.

These individuals should not be expected to have the same spending power like typical working-class individuals out on the streets Yet, goods and services are sold to them behind these institutional walls at much higher prices than even what similar goods and services are sold to working-class people on the streets of America. What could possibly be the logic here?…….. if any……other than insatiable greed and selfishness.

Also at the York, Pennsylvania detention facility, inmates and immigration detainees are made to pay $13.00 for an haircut, instead of the institution hiring inmate or detainees who are proficient in barbing skills just as they hire other inmates within the facility to help them perform other housekeeping and kitchen chores, to cut hair free-of-charge for other inmates and detainees. This free haircut for all has been the normal tradition in most U.S. prisons in order to afford everyone equal privilege to get their haircut done, regardless or being indigent or not.

Inmates or detainees in this facility are readily available to volunteer without being paid to give their fellow inmates or immigration detainees simple and decent haircuts as courtesy. Rather, the facility won't even make the haircut clippers available any more for such voluntary courtesies by these inmates and detainees to each other. This institution, among others, switched up from that friendly policy to a profit-making policy of taking away all the institutional barbing kits that used to be readily available for the inmates and detainees' free usage, and then sets up its own prepaid haircut service.

The institution now have a barber company come inside the facility every week to offer haircut service for only inmates and detainees who can afford to pay their fee. Any inmate or detainee who can't afford the $13.00 fee have to do without haircut pending the duration of their stay there..... including when such person might be going for court appearances. Not that the judges really cares how decent any detainee actually looks while in court in order to decide if he or she should be ordered removed or be given a little slack to remain in the country.

Speaking of price for services, $13.00 is a little too stiff for a haircut fee in prison to be paid by prisoners. There are plenty of barber shops on the streets of America that offers decent professional haircut service for just $10.00 or less, but prisoners who are not working and are confined to pay the price of their wrong-doing to the society, or in the case of foreign nationals held there to be deported, are forced to pay top dollars for their haircut in prison.

The monopoly goes on. Most of the large influx of foreign nationals detained at these facilities are awaiting removal back to their homelands and will most likely want to get an haircut to at least make them look somewhat presentable upon their arrival at their homelands. The immigration detainees are their main targets here by their custodians to patronize the prison haircut business. Since the commencement of the haircut operation in the York, Pennsylvania facility, majority of the haircut revenue is generated from the detained immigrants.

Almost every health and hygiene daily-need items that should be made available for free or at relatively low rates are being offered for sale to inmates and detainees at penal institutions at relatively inflated prices than the street prices for similar products and services.

***MISMANAGEMENT OF THE TAXPAYERS' MONEY:*** Without a doubt, the Bush administration had squandered a huge chunk of the nation's taxpayers' money in his administration's mission to hunt down, arrest, detain and deport millions of foreigners over his eight years of presidency. A policy that was continued after he left office by his far-right Republican policymakers in Washington and even at the state level like the state of Arizona. Such huge American taxpayers' money wasted year after year to deport foreigners from America by the nation's Republican leadership could have been put to much better use like providing funding for such programs like housing for indigent and homeless citizens, or for a better funding of the nation's federally subsidized housing program for low income Americans.....a program that has fallen into a very terrible financial state in many highly populated cities across America. Or even use some of such funds to create meaningful vocational and rehabilitative programs for offenders while serving time. Rather the nation's Republican leadership prefers to burn so much of the taxpayers' money to fund the arrest and detainment of so many foreign nationals who are just barely making ends meet with the low wage jobs that are even hard to come by these days in America.

The Bush administration and his extreme-right Republican bandwagon implicitly and explicitly portrayed these undocumented immigrants as financial constraint to the government, but fails to tell the same public of how important and essential these so-called undocumented immigrants' cheap labor to the nation's agricultural sector have helped eased the food price for everyone across the country.

While detained awaiting deportation, these aliens are being heavily hustled by their captors and the up-to-no-good consumer-goods and services vendors. There is no humanitarian consideration whatsoever by the agency or these facilities' administrators, nor from the vendors allowed to operate their businesses within the facilities, for the detainees who are indigent with no incoming funds from family members, or who don't even have anyone out there to send them money to pay for these services like haircut that supposed to be offered free-of-charge by the institutions for the inmates and detainees in the first place.

It is an extremely cruel and selfish motive for any governmental agency or administrators of government funded institutions charged to provide specific legal obligations on behalf of the government, capitalizing on such position of authority bestowed on them, to enrich themselves at the expense of the very people who supposed to be rehabilitated and the public who are entitled to be served justice.

It really was a hell of an experience in a country like United States for Thompson going through these series of wild capitalism, exploitation and inhumane treatment during his detainment at the York, Pennsylvania immigration detention facility. The craziest part is that these exploits are allowed and even being perpetrated on the public by the very same government officials charged to protect the public.

Even a notary service that costs $5.00 at the most on the streets of America, is done for immigration detainees, who mainly utilize the service, for a whopping $10.00 per document. A cheap battery- operated shaver that cost about $5.00 on the streets are sold by these thieves for inmates and detainees for a whopping $36.00 each. It's nothing but a direct 'theft by deception' conspiracy by public officials and privately owned business entities.

A rapidly growing multimillion dollar penal institutions enterprise is in full effect across America today. This time, prisoners, detainees and their loved ones catering for them on the streets are the victims in the hands of their custodians and the private business entities permitted to do business within these prison walls.

Like in various other locations across the country, a new expansion of the York, Pennsylvania facility was completed in 2006 to provide additional holding space to detain more foreign nationals caught on the streets. Before Mr. Bush left office, he had already allocated huge amount of taxpayers' money to build other similar facilities for detaining more foreign nationals as the administration's mass-expulsion of immigrants' policy continues even after he left office. Some were under construction or already completed at various other sites across the country before he left office.

This on-going development championed and heavily funded by the Bush administration and the rest vast-right Republicans in Washington and across the country has undoubtedly orchestrated a new wave of imperial revolution all over again.....unfortunately this time, it is targeted at victimizing foreign nationals in America. But on the flip side, the after-effect continues to take a huge toll on the nation's economy as the mass-expulsion occupation of foreigners in America continues.

And now comes Donald J. Trump.....the Anti-Immigrant In-Chief...... continuing the mass-expulsion of immigrants where Bush-Cheney had left off. doing it even more brutal than the Bush's era.

# 08

# WAR POLITICS

GEORGE W. BUSH BEGAN HIS PRESIDENCY with the worst terrorist attack on America....due in part to his reckless talk and finger-pointing of certain states as "Axis of Evil,".....and he ended it with the worst financial crisis since the Great Depression. In between, he confronted a hurricane that nearly wiped out New Orleans off the map as the administration showed ineptitude in its response.

Mr. Bush has always been recklessly confident of himself, even when the American public was sick and tired of his dysfunctional style of leadership, and never changed till his last day at the White House. Just as he remained stubbornly convinced that he did the right thing in Iraq, he was well dormantly convinced that he did the right thing on the economy that almost brought America to its knees before he left office.

The event of 9/11 is believed to have triggered the wave of hostility towards foreign nationals by the Bush administration in United States. The impact of this hostility continues to spill across America and beyond. In the administration's precautionary measure to avoid such terrible act repeating itself in the future, a lot of innocent souls have been victimized in the process.

Instead of focusing on the proven suspects connected with the terroristic incident, the administration chose to pluralize the enemies to include all the foreign nationals residing in United States......politicizing anti-immigrant sentiment among the American public.making it seem rather like all foreign nationals within the country were responsible for the 9/11 act, and in effect, must be punished for it.

Any sovereign state has the right to react and to implement measures to prevent such event that undermines the safety and security of their nation from happening again. But the government must be mindful in doing so, not to punish innocent ones for such act, or making everyone suffer in its adopted approach to stop similar act from repeating itself. This has been the exact strategy of 'punishing-both-the-innocent-and-the-guilty' approach the Bush administration had taken all along.

Only the rightful perpetrators of such acts should be hunted down and be brought to justice. Instead it appeared as if the Washington Republican hardliners along with the Bush administration rather used the opportunity provided by the event to fully come out of their closets by revealing how they have always felt towards foreign nationals. The Bush administration and his teamsters went for the cheap shot of unnecessarily turning their anguish on foreigners by making life a living hell for all foreign nationals and their loved ones in America, instead of going after only the proven suspects to the 9/11 act of terror.

As a result, foreign nationals are being harassed and arrested on a daily basis by the nation's immigration agency and detained in vast immigration detention facilities spread across the country to be deported for violations as minor as missing an official appointment with the agency, or overstay of visa, among various other bogus excuses.

Even the nation's police force was given the green light by the Bush administration to join in on the sweep whenever and wherever they come in contact with foreign nationals who are unable to produce their valid residency papers on the spot, regardless of what the cops had initially approached or stopped them for. Without such valid residency papers, the Bush administration passed an executive order known as Proposition 287(B), essentially authorizing all the Police Departments across the nation to arrest and detain such aliens and then turn them over to the nation's Immigration agency that will further detain them in its various detention facilities and process them to be deported.

The intense politics of aggression by predominantly right-wing Republican faction in America is supposedly to have stemmed from the 9/11 incident......even though it is indisputably clear to the public that less than 1 percent of those affected by the Bush administration's brutal policies against foreign nationals barely had anything to do, directly or indirectly, with the 9/11 incident itself...hundreds of thousands of foreigners are being displaced all year round since the 9/11 event.

As this arbitrary displacement went on during Mr. Bush's administration and thereon after, hundreds of thousands of immigrants have fallen victims of the mass sweep. Families and livelihoods painstakingly built and earned during their years of stay in America crumbles apart in a moments notice. Hundreds of thousands of foreign nationals who have been victimized this way can relate and attest to this fact in almost every part of the globe.

The Bush administration arrogantly defied the voice of the American people as it went head-on to implement and enforce policies to combat terrorism. The administration's level of deception got so dangerously terrible to the extent that the American public, except for the like-minded extreme-right hardliners, got so dismayed and completely lost faith over the administration's exaggerated claims of terroristic threat. Even the nation's Intelligence agencies was put on blast on so many occasions concerning their misleading information to support the administration's unilateral act of war against other nations.

Whenever some citizens happens to uncover the Bush administration's covert motives behind its arbitrary policies, they either move swiftly to silence the source, or preempt further investigation to bring the bad apples to justice.....or, attempt to put a different political spin to the scandal at issue.....trying their hardest to persuade the public, who already know the truth, to believe that what went wrong was not actually what the situation was. Deliberately giving the public a completely distorted version of the already established fact of the matter.

Even though it is often commonplace in politics to at times spin things around by most public officials, the Bush's administration spin game became too disastrous for the good of the nation. The administration was handling Washington business more or less like acted scenes from typical Hollywood movies that are just too risky to even be simulated by anyone in real life.

Nothing is more painful than being punished for something that you are not responsible for. And those bringing you to their so-called version of justice are fully aware that you were implicitly framed to carry the cross. A lot of such funny businesses were synonymous with Mr. Bush's administration and its right-wing Republican faction in Washington. The effect of the Bush-Cheney administration's toxic foreign policies continues to rub United States the wrong way till this day, even after he had left office.

All of a sudden, Immigration became the hottest issue across America during Mr. Bush's administration and thereon after.

# 09 *REFUGEE TREATMENT IN AMERICA TODAY*

IN ANY CIVIL SOCIETY, LAWS ARE made, executed and enforced by the government of such state. The citizens and residents of the society are expected to abide by such laws. Respect for the rule of law should be equally paramount for government officials as well just like it is expected of private citizens in any sovereign democratic state. Violators of the law, either in public or private domain, should be equally punished fair and square for their lawlessness relative to the offense committed.

When a particular group of people in a society becomes the government's target and gets treated like scapegoats for the least wrong they did, or didn't do......getting dealt with to the fullest extent allowed, or even at times, to the extent not allowed by the law....the very purpose of which justice was intended to serve and the punishment imposed is undoubtedly undermined. Such style of punishment is focused more to cause irreparable damage to the subjects than the primary purpose of rehabilitating such individuals from recidivism. Such excessive level of punishment fails to serve the public's interest but that of the party imposing it.

Before the 2006 U.S. Congressional election that tilted Congressional majority in both Houses towards the Democrats, the then Republicans-controlled Congress have enjoyed flexing their muscles in legislating troubling policies and seem to be above the law in whatever policy they propose and execute....either right or wrong......while the captain of their boat like Mr. Bush takes great pride in applauding their lawlessness all along.

The position of Mr. Bush's administration portraying immigrants as the major subject matter of his presidency created so much division and resentment between immigrants and the American public rather than the administration's primary role to unite America with the rest of the world.

These days across America, typical Americans who have been misinformed and misled by Mr. Bush's vague and unsubstantiated claim of on-going acts of terrorism, treats foreign nationals within the country with a great deal of hostility. Such hostility ranges from deprivation of "freedom of speech," to other various forms of governmental imposed barriers in securing jobs to make a living by these immigrants. They have put in place tougher measures and aggressively enforced policies across the country to make it very hard for the so-called undocumented immigrants to apply and obtain driver license, or to even rent a place to stay, or even to secure a job. Yet, these undocumented immigrants' hard labor has been immensely beneficial at the nation's agricultural sector and even in other sectors of the economy.

The list of hardships imposed on foreign nationals these days in America just keeps getting longer as each year unfolds. Even the U.S.-born kids of these immigrants are also faced with similar hostilities. They are being treated as subordinate who must share part of the pain and suffering inflicted on their foreign-born parents. Despite the immense contribution in all works of life by the immigrants to the growth of American society today, the Republican extremists in Washington and across the nation are defiantly bound to make them feel like they are out of place and do not belong....forgetting or seeming to forget that today's generation Americans share the same migratory lineage with the ancestral immigrant parents who gave birth to them while in America just as the cycle should have naturally been allowed to continue with today's generation of immigrants.

A public official in the state of California was working so hard to push for a bill that will exempt any benefits and even claim to citizenship to children of undocumented immigrants born in the United States, even though the 14th Amendment U.S. Constitution validates them as full naturally born U.S. citizens like anyone else who was born in the country either by U.S. or non-U.S.-born parents as far back as we can go.

However, this California state-man is not alone in such empirically biased mindset. There are a handful of U.S.-born citizens, either by immigrants or U.S.-born parents who share such twisted way of thinking and would support such move to go forward if by any chance a serious consideration for such bill was to gain some significant momentum nationwide. Even some of the same vast-right Republican policymakers in Washington like old guard Mitch McConnell of Kentucky and Linsey Graham of South Carolina along with their other buddies are bringing up the issue of strapping the provision of the nation's 14th Constitutional Amendment which gives automatic citizenship to kids born by undocumented immigrants. So the California state man who first raised the issue back in 2009 is no longer alone on this twisted mindset that feeds off the spirit of deep hatred to fellow mankind.

The late Senator, Mc. Cain who is with this bandwagon of strapping the citizenship clause in the 14th Constitutional Amendment seem to forget that he himself was not even born in United States soil. He was originally born in Panama canal when his parents were stationed there as U.S. troops in the early 1900s. A ratification put in place years later for kids born by U.S. military personnel stationed in the canal even gave Mc. Cain the chance to claim U.S. citizenship title. He should be the last person in America to support such move of hatred against immigrants in America.

But this California public official forgot to realize that if such proposition was to be taken seriously and somehow becomes federal law to be ratified across America and all its territories retroactively, himself and the rest who thinks like him that they are more of U.S.-born citizens than the U.S.-born kids by undocumented immigrants, will fall under similar category of exemption as well as almost every U.S.-born citizens except for the American Native Indians who were the original native indigenes of Continental America before the European frontiers arrives and occupied their land. His ancestral parental bloodline who eventually gave birth to him and a lot of other U.S.-born Americans today would be found also to be immigrants from somewhere else.....most likely will be found to be undocumented as well just like the U.S.-born children by the so-called undocumented immigrant parents they are trying to deprive of same opportunities that they themselves and their ancestral generations were all afforded in America.

Sadly speaking, this California public official, as well as a lot more like him that are recently coming out of their closet of hatred, are the type of individuals whose dangerously toxic ideological views about people and places, whose general views about people makes him and the rest like him very bad candidates to fill any public office in America. Yet, there are a lot of their kind in various public offices across America today screwing up both the political and the socioeconomic settings of the nation. There is no way that people with this type of mindset should be voted into public office in a democratic nation like America. Realistically speaking, there are a lot of them within the rightist conservative group today across America......particularly in Washington.

It is very sad to see or even know that such cause of action is pursued by elected public officials in today's day and age in America of the 21$^{st}$ century after everyone had thought that we have all crossed the threshold dark past of the bygone era of deep-rooted hatred and racism. Such bias mindset feeds on extreme hatred towards others, to be exact. Such evil way of thinking is out of place and should not be allowed to have any place in today's world.....especially in America of all places.

The art of new age racism and implicit hatred on mankind is becoming so prevalent within America these days as each year unfolds. It's being portrayed and used against others in so many covert ways and even through the right-wing mainstream public forums across the country like never before. Folks, particularly those associated with the so-called Republican-conservative faction in America are becoming increasingly so outspoken about their hatred towards others outside their political circle to the point that their point of views are most times considered as outright abuse of the nation's Constitutional right to 'Freedom of Speech and that of the Press,' The nation's conservative group and even the conservative owned media entities are using this freedom of press doctrine to openly spill out the deep-rooted resentment they harbor against private and public citizens outside their political circle.....foreign nationals in particular.

The issue of citizenship was made a hot button issue by the nation's bias-minded Republican faction ever since Mr. Obama presented himself as a presidential candidate back in 2007. They refuse to let the bogus issue go away even after their vague effort failed to accomplish their intended goal of weakening Mr. Obama's presidential aspiration and his unwavering leadership spirit. Mr. Obama prevailed over all the haters and won the 2008 U.S. presidential election with outstanding defeat of the Republican haters.

As the 2012 presidential election approaches, the issue of Mr. Obama's birth place resurfaced yet again. This time the drumbeat was championed by Donald Trump who is trying to grab the public and the conservatives' media attention as a candidate for the 2012 Republican presidential candidate. He likes to bluff way more than his actual financial standing. Imagine how arrogant he would have been if he was worth just a tenth of Bill Gates money. Yet Bill Gates who suppose to make the kind of noise Trump makes hardly speak a word. Trump barely worth a billion dollars and makes a lot of noise like he is five or ten billion dollars rich.

His only talking point was to come at Obama that way in a conservative public forum like he knows no better that the man is in fact a U.S.-born citizen. As usual, Mr. Obama shot him and his cheer leaders up by going on the same public forum to set the record straight once and for all for the Republican haters. In addition to clarifying to the American public and his critic's distorted fact of his official place of birth which is Hawaii, he also instructed the Hawaiian state Department of Health and Public Records, through his lawyers, to make a copy of the long version of his birth certificate available online for all to see. After Mr. Obama's public speech on this issue, Donald Trump really felt stupid and went back to the same conservative media forum, Fox News to try and tamp the huge embarrassment his public blunder has caused him.

However, none of these Republican haters raised such citizenship issue when John Mc. Cain ran for U.S. Republican presidential candidate and loss in both 2000 and in 2008. If anyone contesting for the U.S. presidency should be challenged or scrutinized of their citizenship, John Mc. Cain should have been the very first person in line to be thoroughly scrutinized that way because he was in fact born outside United States. John Mc. Cain was born in Panama Canal when his parents were stationed there as U.S. troops during the U.S. territorial control of the Canal before it was later relinquished to Panama. Donald Trump loves to dig up dirt about Obama but lacks the knowledge about the birth place of John Mc. Cain who ran against Mr. Obama in 2008. All the Republican haters attempt to make Mr. Obama looks bad and incredible has rather enhanced his report card and even played out to make him a better and efficient leader indeed. Hatred and racial bias within the right-wing faction in America is turning to a serious plague that is dragging the once great nation down instead of moving it forward in the 21st century. This is an extremely sad development in the land that love for mankind and freedom for all supposed to reign supreme.

# IMMIGRATION COURT PROCEEDINGS TO EXPEL FOREIGNERS FROM THE U.S.

THOMPSON'S LEGAL BATTLE WITH THE U.S. Immigration and Customs Enforcement (ICE) agency which is under the umbrella of the U.S. Department of Justice, is indicative of the statutory language of both the U.S. immigration law and the international law. After the 1951 Refugee treaty was enacted at the United Nation, which United States acceded in 1968, United States enacted the Refugee Act of 1980 in order to bring the country in conformity with the United Nations Convention...... relating to the status of refugees ("Refugee Convention").

Mr. Bush's administration along with his far-right conservative Congressional policymakers in Washington was so busy amending the already existing immigration laws in such a way that violates and undermines this refugee treaty which all member states are bound to uphold in regards to the treatment and protection of refugees. His administration emboldened the nation's immigration agency to undermine this valuable piece of international treaty. As a result, it's been unlawfully stripping refugees off their Geneva Convention's protection and unlawfully forcing them to return to their countries of feared persecution, which they had fled at some point in time.

Majority of these refugees forcefully kicked out of the country only committed very minor offenses that has waiver from expulsion, an authority delegated to the nation's Attorney General's office. Plus, these individuals have already been punished enough for their wrongs by the nations' judicial system. Obviously, that is not quite satisfactory for Mr. Bush and his ultra-right Republican teamsters in Washington till they have these refugees forcefully sent back to their embattled homelands to face persecution by their government or other uncontrolled groups. This constitutes a direct disregard to the International Refugee Treaty which United Sates is a member. Such lawlessness by the administration makes everyone wonder how cruel, hateful and heartless Mr. Bush's regime and his far- right Republican faction really felt towards foreign nationals living within America soil.

The Geneva Convention Refugee Protocol as well as the United States' codified Refugee Act of 1980 prohibits the repatriation of foreign nationals admitted as refugee, or most particularly, those granted asylum within its soil. Only in extremely rare circumstance should this status be disturbed. The status may be terminated if the refugee or asylee engages or commits a capital offense against another person; or such person commits a particularly serious or violent crime and deemed to pose danger to public's safety; or if such status ceases to exist due to change in such countries' condition.

None of these was the case with most of the refugees and asylees the Bush administration and the rest of his rightist Republican lawmakers in Washington are still forcefully returning back to harm's way in their homelands of feared persecution. Not that the U.S. Republican policymakers in Washington as well as most of their like-minded peers within this faction cares the least bit about what happens to these Geneva Convention refugees and asylees upon their forceful return to their homelands they had fled at some point in their life.

Thompson was admitted into the United States as an asylee after he fled his embattled oil-rich homeland of the Niger-Delta region of Nigeria. He later got in trouble with the law at the turn of the 20th century for violation of the United States Visual Arts Intellectual Property law......a relatively minor criminal offense. He was punished accordingly, followed by restitution payable to the victims.

Due to this conviction, the United States Immigration agency commenced removal proceeding against him, even though the nation's immigration law provides a waiver from removal for asylee aliens like him who committed such type of offense. The Bush Republican administration's move to deport Thompson wasn't because the agency did not recognize him as an alien admitted into the country as an asylee, but because the administration and its extremist Republican allies in Washington and across the country could care less of what happens to such refugees or asylees upon their forceful return to their various countries of feared persecution.... an outright assault to the nation's and international rule of law and a violation by the agency of its own law.

Thousands of active refugees and asylees have been violated this way in United States by the Bush administration and its rightist constituents. The arbitrary rule of the nation's immigration laws at the expense of foreign nationals became the administration's bargaining chip it used to seduce the American public to buy into its ambiguous political motive....falsely portraying foreign nationals to be the enemy that needs to be expelled from America. Over the eight years of Mr. Bush's presidency, the administration succeeded in flushing out so many foreign nationals with a total figure in the millions range. What a horrendous event unfolding in the nation of immigrants.

In Thompson's legal battle to challenge his unlawful expulsion back to harm's way, he appealed his final removal order by an Immigration Judge (IJ) to the agency's Board of Immigration Appeals (BIA). As was anticipated, knowing the Board's new unilateral style of conducting its review business to best advance the Republican administration's anti-immigrants xenophobe, Thompson's appeal at the Board was dismissed and the lower immigration court's prior ruling of removal was affirmed without opinion.

Due to huge backlog of appeals pending review at the Board, the Republican majority at the time passed a regulation which essentially allowed the agency's Appeals Board to streamline majority of the appeals filed by the aliens challenging the legality of their removal......particularly those filed by aliens held within the agency's custody for removal purpose. A regulation started under John Ashcroft, the nation's notorious Attorney General during Mr. Bush's first term in office. He was known for his extreme judicial views and rule of law, especially the laws that affects foreign nationals residing in America. The 'Streamline Regulation' basically allows the agency's Appeals Board to merely rubber-stamp majority of the appeals filed by appellant aliens contesting their final order of removal. With this authority by the Republican constituents in Washington, the Board is permitted to just merely affirm the lower immigration courts' ruling without actually reviewing the legal arguments raised by such appellant aliens, and without giving any legal analysis of the memorandum of the applicable law leading to such affirmative rulings....a completely contrary role to what the agency's Appeals Board legal obligation requires and entails.

The appeals are received and held at the Board in Virginia for a period of 4 to 6 months for appeals filed by aliens in the agency's detention.... after which most of the appeal papers gets rubber- stamped without any member of the Board's panel of judges even reading or analyzing the issues raised in most cases before it. Right after this period, the Board's streamlined order gets forwarded to the appellants, affirming the lower courts' ruling without opinion.... Stating it in just two to three lines in its decision letters reflecting the Republicans' new regulation that governs such outright assault on justice.

Most of these appeals are merely read by the Board's legal clerks and then passed on to a single member judge, instead of three, and the judge applies the streamline provision by merely rubberstamping the lower Immigration Courts' ruling without opinion and the appeals gets returned back to the sender between 4 to 6 months or more for appeals filed by aliens under the agency's custody.

The extremely troubling streamline regulation was put in place to help the Board expedite its backed-up caseloads, but it particularly has greatly undermine the very purpose of justice being served for public's interest. The result: the Bush administration and his rightist Republican faction's ambiguously intended motives are being accomplished at the peril of United States image as a nation of immigrants and at the expense of the foreign nationals who have been and still being deprived of adequate justice.

At such point in time a lot of foreign nationals with legitimate claims to their removal gets overwhelmed, tired and exhausted by the pressure and lack of justice and then succumb to getting unlawfully removed back to their countries. However, few foreign nationals like Thompson, who are fully cognizance of the fatal consequence that awaits them if forcefully returned to their homelands of feared persecution, painstakingly strives, thinking justice will eventually be served.

Within thirty (30) days of the Board's rubber-stamped ruling, Thompson followed up with a timely filed appeal of the Board's affirmative ruling to the U.S. Court of Appeals for judicial review. The appeal was sustained, but before the court entered an order to 'Stay' Thompson's removal, the agency, as usual, was moving aggressively to pre-empt the court from doing so, so that it could succeed to kick Thompson out of the country fast enough before such order was entered. But the agency's relentless attempts failed and the Federal Court of Appeals serving the District which Thompson was held by the agency ruled right on time to 'Stay' his removal till further instruction was entered by the court. The Court, from that point on, resumed full jurisdiction of the matter.

Subsequently, briefing schedule was issued for both Thompson and the government to submit their arguments supporting each party's legal position to the issue of law raised in the matter. Thompson's attorney prepared and submitted his arguing brief incorporating Thompson's position. However, when it came time for the Immigration agency, serving on behalf of the federal government, to submit its arguing brief as directed by the court, the U.S. Attorney General's office in Washington, D.C. designated to litigate immigration matters in U.S. Federal Circuit courts, representing the government, declined to submit its brief to support the government's position seeking Thompson's removal from United States as charged......as an asylum recipient.

Instead, the agency filed a motion with the court seeking "Leave Not To File Its Brief." Vaguely arguing in its motion that the filing of such brief with the court in this matter could implicate the government on its prior, present and future immigration enforcement mission in the event that the court rules on Thompson's favor. With the nature of the legal issue raised by Thompson on appeal, it would not have been a legal victory just for Thompson, but such ruling would have set a precedent and mandates the agency, serving on behalf of the U.S. government, to bring back all the unlawfully removed Geneva Convention refugees that was forcefully returned to harm's way in their various countries of feared persecution, and also affects thousands of current and future immigration matters of this nature.

At that point, it became crystal clear that the government itself, specifically the Bush administration along with its rightist Republican policymakers in Washington, was deliberately disregarding and consequentially braking the nation's laws by authorizing and arbitrarily emboldening the nation's immigration agency to forcefully and unlawfully repatriate refugees and asylees in particular, back to their homelands of feared persecution. The nation's Immigration agency under the Bush-Cheney Republican rules of engagement outright refusal to file its arguing brief with the court in Thompson's matter as directed, validated the fact that its so-called dealings with immigration matters was more like the 'Wild-West' thing, and was not at all in conformity with the nation's immigration laws and that it had some seriously unlawful dealings to hide from the higher court.

Though the agency's motion seeking 'Leave Not To File Its Brief' was not granted, due in part to Thompson's attorney's opposition. The court moved the agency once again to submit its brief on a new rescheduled date. Yet, the government continued on its defiance and contempt to the court's stipulated order. The agency relentlessly tried to divest this particular U.S. Court of Appeals for the Third Circuit, which Thompson's petition for review arose, of its jurisdiction to decide the matter. At that point, the matter has gotten very critical for the agency to defend its position.

The agency adopted yet again another tactics to avoid dealing with this very Federal Court of Appeals in Philadelphia.....knowing that this court has been one of the very few Circuit courts across the nation that reviews immigration matters as the laws are written and do not participate quite often with the nation's right-wing leadership of spinning the laws like most other Circuit courts across the country filled with predominantly extreme-right conservative judges with radical views of interpreting the nation's laws and Constitutions. This Circuit court was one of the very few that remained quite critical of the Bush administration's arbitrary treatment of foreign nationals.

As part of its maneuvering and overreaching strategy, the agency brought its Appeals Board back in the picture. The agency's Appeals Board that has already rendered its rubber-stamped ruling and was out of the picture, suddenly resurfaced with a one page '*Sua Sponte*' (meaning 'self-reopening' in legal terms) ruling, stating that Thompson's matter and the issues he had raised on appeal had suddenly become very important and that it wants to revisit those important legal issues which it ignored the first time.

As a result of the agency's Appeals Board's self-reopening of Thompson's previously dismissed appeal, it again validated the fact that the Board was in error of judgment both in fact and law on its rubber-stamped affirmative order which it had initially agreed with the lower immigration court judge's erroneous ruling to deport Thompson as charged. With this new development, the agency's attorney in Washington, D.C. tried to argue in yet another motion filed with the court, requesting this time to dismiss Thompson's petition for review, claiming that Thompson's petition is *moot* since there is no longer a final order of removal for the court to review, as the agency's Appeals Board has reopened the appeal and vacated its prior order of removal against Thompson... A petition which was at the time pending at this court for judicial review for almost two years.

Sadly, thousands of Geneva Convention refugees and asylees like Thompson have already been forcefully removed back to harm's way in their various homelands by the Bush-Cheney administration and its vast-right Republican constituents in Washington. They were all strong-armed and rendered powerless by being held for so long under the agency's detention while contesting the legality of their removal.

The whole episode for Thompson was like scenes from an action-packed movie that was so real and was so fake to have been real, but it was as real as it could possibly get. It is extremely heart-wrenching that the government of a supposedly democratic nation like United States of America will itself embolden any of its agencies to impede justice from being served to someone within its soil.

A nation that loves to proclaim itself loud and clear to the rest of the world as a pioneer and a beacon of democracy, equal justice and liberty for all. The Bush-Cheney administration did not only impede justice from being served to foreign nationals in America, the administration and its rightist Republican team was quite instrumental and crafty in devising some laws that were designed with the primary goal of causing irreparable damage to foreign nationals.

After the agency's Appeals Board had re-emerged and chose to reopen Thompson's appeal to address the legal issues he raised in his previously dismissed appeal, which the Board now suddenly acknowledge to be important, it still failed to give a legal analysis as expected upon the second time review of the appeal. It rather chose to remand the matter back to the lower court for plenary hearing in consistence with new evidence that had always been available but the agency at the time chose to ignore them.

For the meantime, the Circuit Court having jurisdiction over the matter had the matter on hold, hoping that the agency will use the opportunity to clean up its mess. The matter was never dismissed as the agency had requested, because Thompson's attorney had opposed such dismissal. Plus, the Federal Appeals court reviewing the matter is not bound by any statutory provision to oblige to either the Board or the agency's unilateral spin game. The petition was still under the Circuit court's jurisdiction pending judicial review while the agency's Appeals Board was also simultaneously revisiting the matter under the reopening move it made.

The legal saga between Thompson and the U.S. Immigration agency started under the Bush-Cheney leadership and justice, at the end, was not allowed to be served him nor to the rest of the refugees that the agency had arbitrarily repatriated and still unlawfully and forcefully repatriating back to harm's way in their various countries of feared persecution.

The gross injustice inflicted on foreign nationals has been portrayed by the administration to the American public as its effort to "drain the swamps" in its fight to combat terrorism. But the public's perception of the administration's hostile foreign policies shows that its primary intention for its chosen cause of action was highly ambiguous at best and not in conformity with the subject-matter, nor the result the public had anticipated. All through Mr. Bush's eight chaotic years in office, his administration remained defiantly unmoved by the discontent of the American public over its counterproductive style of governance.

Since Mr. Bush's first and second term in office, bloodshed, mass loss of lives, insecurities, injustice, unhappiness and oppression of the masses within America and across the globe remains the order of the day. Even the die-hard extreme-conservatives who voted Mr. Bush back in office for his second term, felt betrayed as the administration failed to live up to the promises it made to the voters who had him reelected. A large part of these promises were the politics of fear he created in the minds of most American public and how he would leave no stone unturned in hunting down theses manufactured enemies. His administration made so many American public believe the distorted impression and over-exaggeration of the extent to which the so-called potential threat posed by terrorists was after the destruction of America and its interest at home and abroad and the need for a leader like him to act fast and do it very ruthlessly.

# 11   *BACK AT THE U.S. IMMIGRATION COURT*

A COURT OF LAW IN ANY DEMOCRATIC state, be it for criminal or for civil proceedings, should be open and accessible to the general public who have the time and interest to follow up with the proceedings on such matters. It is shockingly surprising to find out that in United States, some court cases like immigration proceedings, which are regarded as civil matters, are held in some immigration courts under 'closed circuits' where everyone inside the courtroom, except the presiding judge, the prosecutor representing the government and the defendants' attorney, are ordered to leave the courtroom for a brief court session or for the entire session of some particular cases.

In one of Thompson's court appearances at the immigration building in Philadelphia, he witnessed quite a strange and incredible scenario unfolded right in front of his eyes inside the courtroom when Wati, an Indonesian woman's case was called.

As Wati was unrepresented by a counsel, she had to speak for herself. She told the court of the unfounded removal charge against her and the accompanying torment she had been subjected to for years by the agency. She sounded very pitiful indeed. But as far as the agency is concerned with its new Bush administration initiated rules of engagement, she surely was lamenting on deaf ears.

From listening to the agency's version of the case, it was just too obvious for anyone inside the courtroom at the time that the agency's case against her was without merit and unsubstantiated. Having been given so much runaround for so long over nothing, Wati spoke out in the courtroom with rage and boiling anger over the frustration, torment and injustice that the agency had put her through. The agency's attorney representing the government was left scrambling for words at that very moment to discredit Wati's assertion of facts of the matter as well as what to say to defend the agency's claim before the court of why it seeks this lady's repatriation.

Even though Wati was not professionally articulate as a lawyer to present her case before the court with fancy legal vocabularies, everyone inside the court, including the Immigration Judge (IJ), felt her troubled experience with the agency. The judge herself felt that something was terribly wrong with the agency's removal charge against her.

In an attempt to avoid such huge embarrassment on the part of the agency before the court attendees and to enable the agency to conceal its practice of injustice towards foreign nationals, the agency's counsel requested that the judge order everyone but Wati to exit the courtroom for a brief 'closed circuit' session for the court to address Wati's legal issues. Everyone, including Thompson exited the courtroom as ordered and the courtroom door was closed behind the last person that exited the court. Nobody else other than Wati, the agency's attorney and the presiding judge knew what transpired behind the closed courtroom door.

The million dollar question here is: what possibly could be so confidential in serving justice that the public are barred by the government to hear or be aware of?......that could be so confidential or so classified to the extent that everyone inside the courtroom have to be ordered to step out before the hearing can proceed? When the very public whose tax money are used by the government to fund the courts' judicial operation are barred from knowing what transpired inside the nation's courtroom of law, or what type of justice was served, the very purpose of justice itself has been seriously undermined by the very same governmental entities conferred with the judicial obligation and authority to uphold it accordingly.

Such 'behind-closed-doors' judicial dealings clearly reflects the fact that the court's judicial setting is not completely transparent in their application of the laws with the public which the courts are delegated to serve.

In Wati's case, the judge immediately seemed lost on what to do as the agency's counsel scrambled all over the place for words to make up some more vague justification for the agency to keep on tormenting this poor immigrant woman. Tens of thousands of immigrants have been and are still being victimized by this type of torment and injustice in the hands of the U.S. Immigration agency under the Bush administration and the rest of his rightist Republican constituents' established style of serving justice in recent time in America.

Most of the immigration judges appointed during Mr. Bush's presidency were undoubtedly partners with the administration's scheme to impede fair and square justice from being served to individuals from various nationalities it targeted to treat as scapegoats for no substantial reason or for some relatively minor wrongful acts they had committed at some point in time. In any democratic nation like United States as it proclaims itself to be, the courts dealings should be a public affair, and not a private affair if America wants to continue calling itself a democratic state.

The practice has essentially become more of a trend in most courtroom settings across America.....where the government's attorney convenes with the presiding judge along with his or her counsel on a brief debriefing session while the defendant just sits before the court completely dumbfounded about what form of bargain could possibly be going on between his or her counsel, the government attorney and the presiding judge. At the end of the day, the defendants come to realize, in most cases, that their counsel had just sold them out to make them accept some crazy deal that will not serve their interest, even though the final outcome might have ended up working in their favor. Or persuading them into accepting deals that will torment them right after such deal becomes final.

Such sellouts by crooked lawyers breaches attorney-client confidentiality....a violation of lawyers' code of professional ethics. This type of backdoor legal representation is usually expected from court-appointed counsels. Instead of working to advance their client's legal interest, they chose the easy way out to rather work against their clients' interest so that they can quickly get them out of the way and move to the next client. Even some privately hired attorneys treats some of their clients this way too.

However, not all of the court-appointed counsels play this type of game with their clients. Quite a few are diligent and down- to-earth in offering their best legal representation to their clients. Unfortunately, you won't find a lot of them with such loyal spirit towards their job performance to their clients anymore at least not in America....except for the litigation lawyers who don't get paid anyway till they prevail in getting money out of the defendants they are suing, usually for a nice chunk of monetary damages. In such scenario, there is every reason for such attorney to put in their best legal shot on the matter, because there is usually very lucrative monetary incentive forthcoming with little or no legal research or court representation and arguments like some other fields of law practices before the defendants, in most cases, agrees to settle the matter out of court.

What could be so secret that requires a prosecutor and a defendant's attorney whispering to the judge beside his or her desk inside the court that cannot be spoken out loud and clear for the record, to be heard by everyone inside the courtroom....including the defendant. Most government prosecutors in America carry out their governmental judicial duties with very bias spirit like they actually have real personal scores to settle with these defendants.....instead of just doing their jobs to make sure that at the end of the day justice is served accordingly to those entitled to it. They are not the only ones to blame, this abuse of authority trickles down from the highest chain of command just like it has been in the Bush- Cheney administration.

Speaking of arrogance, the new immigration rules of engagement in America, established by the Bush's Republican team, can be best described as an outright harassment of immigrants at all levels by the nation's Immigration agency's staffs......from the lowest to the highest chain of command. They are extremely rude, arrogant and ruthless when dealing with immigrants. These days, after the Bush administration and the rest Republican policymakers in Washington has arbitrarily emboldened the agency in their style of immigration enforcement, typical U.S. Immigration staffs now perform their jobs like they are some type of Gods bestowed with the highest authority. They basically act like they possesses immigrants' lives at the palm of their hands just because the Bush administration and the nation's far-right Republican faction has vested on the agency so much arbitrary latitude of authority to deal with aliens at the agency's discretion and are, in most cases immuned from prosecution or liability when the staffs or the administrators really screw things up which they do most of the time.

The indigent individuals with little or no financial resources to pay for adequate legal representation are hit the hardest with this type of legal injustice perpetrated on the public by the very government officials. The sad part is that they get away with these unlawful acts with impunity. The very same bad apples screwing things up for everyone in the U.S. government are the same ones who also create laws to immune themselves from liability or punishment, but they love to inflict maximum punishment and otherwise on others who had violated the same laws they have help created. The little men are once again being increasingly made the foot-mat to step on by the cold-hearted well-connected extreme-right conservative group in America these days. Most people outside the country have a different view of America till they find out how much things have changed for the worse in the recent decades of the the 21$^{st}$ century.

# 12

## AFTER 9/11

A MERICA EMERGED TO BECOME A GREAT society due to the founding fathers' visionary willingness in practice to settle for tolerance as a way of life.

The event of 9/11 in America was undoubtedly very horrific and coward by nature. It is deemed to have been the catalyst that had offset Mr. Bush's administration on its ruthless aggression to clamp down on domestic and global act of terror and other forms of radical acts of such nature from repeating itself.

While being mindful of the impact of such terrible event on the victims and the government as a whole as well as the government's mission to stop such coward act from repeating itself, it is also equally necessary for the government not to ignore addressing the root cause of this type of radical acts, at the least, to help address the reasons behind such line of actions by the other parties.

A diplomatic governmental approach could have paved way to the mutual and amicable resolution of things that could have led to a behavioral change between the aggrieved parties rather than the all-out military offensive adopted by the Bush administration. A hostile approach that has resulted into more loss of lives on top of those that were already lost from the incident itself.

Mr. Bush reacted to the 9/11 incident as if he took advantage of the incident itself to settle backlog of animosities he had against the targeted subjects presumed to be responsible for the act or in any way abetted its execution. The administration went extremely overboard on its mission to combat terrorism. Its approach failed to yield any tangible or worthwhile result that the American public had anticipated. Rather, the administration's approach has helped to fuel further unnecessary global reprisals......even in countries that were relatively calm before the 9/11 incident. It has created and gave rise to more harm to America and the rest of the world than good.

In the administration's inquest into the perpetrators of the 9/11 terror act on American soil, the nation's intelligence agencies feeding critical information to the federal government was found on various occasions to be deliberately flawed in their information findings shared with the public regarding the targets and those suspected to be responsible, or directly connected to the act, or the masterminds presumed to be behind the incident. Instead, the administration converges its focus and resources to punish the wrong people for the act…relentlessly persuading the general public, the American public in particular, to believe that all foreign nationals in America are responsible and therefore are guilty of the 9/11 terroristic act.

Having labeled all the foreign nationals within the country as enemies, a huge chunk of American taxpayers' money got allocated on a yearly basis by the Bush administration during his two terms in office to the nation's Immigration Enforcement agency to be used for arresting, detaining and deporting hundreds of thousands of foreign nationals who are predominantly innocent hard-working documented and undocumented immigrants living in America. Immigrants who have migrated like anyone else to America in pursuit of socioeconomic, political or religious freedom which American history represents. Through their often distorted ideologies, the rightist group in America, both in private and governmental sectors, is making the unique American values a fastly diminishing legacy. A status that was so uniquely ingrained within the country's social setting some decades back. The eight years leadership the Obama administration greatly repaired lots of damages created by the Bush- Cheney era. Sadly, Donald Trump of all people was able cajole enough American public during the 2016 presidential election to become

U.S. president after Obama.....practically taking the nation back to the bygone Wild-West of one way street mentality.

The whole operation of mass-expulsion of foreign nationals established and ruthlessly enforced by the Bush administration and continued by his fellow rightist Republican policymakers in Washington thereon after, is basically an unjust transfer of American taxpayers' funds to the wrong hands and for fruitless mission that could have been best utilized for more benefiting domestic social programs for its citizens.

# 13
# POLITICS OF GREED/SELFNESS IN AMERICA

IN MOST CIVIL SOCIETIES, PEOPLE ARE identified in accordance with the position they take on things and their general ideological perspectives on private or public issues. Such identifications are categorized under various political and social affiliations. On a political level, there are so far two major political affiliations of such in America. Anyone who is affiliated with a national political party falls under the Republican affiliation, generally identified as the conservative party by way of ideology; or the Democratic political affiliation, identified as the liberals by their ideological way of dealings.

There are those who call themselves 'Independents,' meaning that their ideologies differ from that of the conservatives or the liberals. There is also a recently emerging group who call themselves the 'Tea Party Movement' whom the conservative faction are trying to build a strong alliance with.

Also, there is another recently emerged group that surfaced right after the creation of the Tea Party Movement, called the 'Coffee Party.' Those in the Coffee party group are more liberal ideologically. The group were growing momentum in early part of 2010 in cities across the country. Growing through Face-book page, the party pledges to "support leaders who work towards positive solutions, and hold accountable those who obstruct them."

Back in February 2010, it had nearly 40,000 members, but the numbers were growing very quickly.....about 11,000 people have been signing on daily on the average since the party made itself known through the social network.

"I'm in shock, just by the level of energy here," said the founder, Annabel Park, a documentary filmmaker who lives outside Washington. "In the beginning, I was actively saying, 'get in touch with us, start a chapter.' Now I can't keep up." The party's slogan is: "Wake up and stand up." The 'Mission Statement' declares that the federal government is not the enemy of the people, but the expression of our collective will and that we must participate in the democratic process in order to address the challenges we face as Americans." The party, coffepartyusa.org., are spread nationwide with local chapters and nationwide coffeehouse gatherings to decide which issues to take on and even which candidate they want to support.

The 'Tea Party' in contrast, argues for stripping the federal government of many of its roles, and that if government have to be involved, it should be mostly state governments. The Tea party's mission is undoubtedly more in tune with the unbridled rightwing Republican style of governance, or are being seduced by the nation's rightist Republican faction to become so by luring them to join their faction a Bush/Trump-like faction with a dangerously unleavened playing field type of ideologies that almost brought the nation to its knees economically in 2008 right before Mr. Obama took office.

Born in South Korea, Ms. Park moved to Houston when she was 9 and worked in the Taco stand her parents bought there, which she said helped her understand average Americans. "We encountered racism, yes, but the majority of people were kind, they were good people, they were like our family," she said. "I understand where they are coming from."

From the time of Ms. Park's account of her childhood in America in the 1970s as an immigrant child by immigrant parents, general hospitality among Americans in most part of the country then was still within reach, compared with these days all-out hatred of different forms towards foreigners by the rightist Americans in both government and private field. Deep-rooted hatred that started reemerging from the 90's and keeps getting worse as each year unfolds till present time.

Others either just remain neutral or unaffiliated to neither of the following parties.

The conservatives, also known as the right-wingers, tends to be, in most cases, like-minded people. Not that there is anything wrong about being like-minded, but in an outstanding way and not in an outstandingly remarkable way.

Most Republicans in public office in America......not all however.....have been the co-architect and the reason behind the creation of certain policies intended to divide rather than unite America. Most of their peers in the private sector are driven by insatiable level if financial greed like Donald Trump.

Everyone loves to make money, but excessive greed at the expense of the poor is itself evil. The conservatives always thrive to have all the slices of the pie to themselves alone. Typical right-wingers are synonymous with the mindset that everyone else supposed to serve them. They see themselves as the only one, by any means necessary, who supposed to live up to their dreams to their fullest, while others were created just to serve them and help make their selfish dreams come true. What about the dreams of those they expect to serve them? Maybe they never had one or never had the time to think of one. Getting into that in details will probably take a whole new book to analyze the various mountains of both physical and abstract obstacles to overcome that lies ahead.

In the private sector, working under a typical right-wing owned enterprise means expecting to be used like a piece of rag, by way of making such employees over-earn every penny they are being paid.

Speaking of wages, most of these wages which these hardworking employees are being paid by their employers are so meager that it is barely enough to sustain them till their next paycheck.....resulting to a stagnant cycle of living basically from hand to mouth.

Having worked diligently and productively for their employers for quite a while to enhance the growth of the enterprise, one will expect such employers to reciprocate these workers' loyalty in kinds......such as affording them the opportunity with similar aspiration to one day be like their bosses. That is never in the thought process of a typical right-wing conservative boss. Rather, if any employees' job performance has been determined by the management as asset to the establishment, the boss will instead device subtle strategies to keep such employees from leaving, but not necessarily doing nothing to enhance the employees' lifestyle, to make it worth their while to continue with the good work.

Such employees are turned into slaves by their employers instead of making it a fair exchange of human resources for the right pay. These typical employers will stop at nothing to impede their employees' growth relative to their input towards the growth and success of the enterprise. They always have that selfish thinking at the back of their mind that they might lose such valued employees and their business will suffer if they get too comfortable.

In most cases, it's always about the bosses' success and never that of the employees. The employees are always treated as mere conduits to make that success a reality for their employers. A typical right-wing business owner will most likely never assist any of their loyal employees to become independent like themselves. Going that route, in their own self-centered way of thinking, will not serve much of their interest monetarily any longer.

Typical barriers imposed on employees by employers could be very devastating if one is not vigilant enough to detect the scheme at an earlier stage before their stagnating effects starts to zero in. Once these rightist employers succeeds to zero their victims in on their exploitative schemes, then the victims are really in for a long haul of hand-to-mouth lifestyle..... essentially finding oneself in a cycle of working so hard but having very little or nothing to show for all the hard work, while the employers or the behind-the-scene actors keeps smiling to the bank as well as living each day like it's always deja vu......all at these underpaid employees' expense.

This in part explains why most businesses have prospered very well on the cheap labor of the undocumented immigrants in America before the brutal crackdown by the Bush administration and thereon after.

The rightist group in America always try their hardest to dominate every scene, both at the private and the governmental sectors. Most of them have two things in common: personal greed and insatiable desire to control or dominate over the weaker species. They lobby relentlessly to legislate government and corporate policies that are in most cases designed to trap the rest of the general public to revolve around their world....in most cases, leaving no route for an exit. Yet, these are the same people who put up the coolest faces in position of authority both in the private or the governmental sectors. But deep within them, they are often time on desperate heartless mission only to alleviate their own ends and could care less about anyone outside their conservative circle.

# 14
## DISREGARD OF THE COURT ORDER IN U.S. IMMIGRATION COURTS

MOST CIVIL AND DEMOCRATIC SOCIETIES ACROSS the globe have judicial branch of their governments which are under the authority of selected or elected Justice General or Attorney General. All the judicial dealings of such state are conferred under the umbrella of the Attorney General's office. The laws of the Land are being interpreted at the courts. The courts are presided over by designated judges with judicial skills and legislative authority to preside over legal matters filed with the courts.

Judges in such civil societies are either selected or elected for the office to preside over legal matters for public's interest. The government attorneys, also known as the prosecutors or the solicitors, representing the government, are also vested with judicial authority and obligation to effectively prosecute cases and recommends punishment or recompense deem appropriate for the accused or the victims on individual cases.

The judges, being the adjudicators, have the final say in every matter. Whatever ruling the judges makes should be upheld and binding by the court until the Superior courts' judges rules otherwise in the event that either party decides to appeal the Lower courts Judges' rulings. Pending the outcome of such appeals, the judges' final ruling on any matter must be enforced and remain binding by the courts.....except in some cases where juries are involved to decide and adjudicate the verdict on such matters. Even so, after the juries' verdicts, the courtrooms' presiding judges still have the final say on the appropriate compensation or penalties the matters deserves. The courts law enforcement unit must make sure that the accused or the complainants fully comply with the judges' rulings on such cases.

In United States, it is not clear to the American public, or at least it hasn't been made public how Immigration judges gets selected or appointed to the bench to preside over immigration matters. In criminal and other civil courts in America, both in federal and in state level, judges are often times elected through electoral process by the public. It is a very different process in appointing Immigration judges who are federal judges as well.

During the Bush administration, majority of the Immigration judges appointed to the bench to serve had one similar attribute: they have been very brutal and radical in both the interpretation and the application of the immigration laws just as the Bush-Cheney administration had laid down the rules to which they must engage.

The United States Immigration authority, an agency under the judicial authority of the U.S. Department of Justice, is an exception to the other U.S. Courts' conventional judicial rules of engagement.....started during the Bush-Cheney era and there on after. The agency itself is portrayed to be civil in its dealings and are expected by the public that it's operated in such manner with less stringent treatment and handling of foreign nationals than the setting in criminal justice rules of engagement. All through Mr. Bush's tenure along with his extreme-right conservative Congressional constituents in Washington, immigration courts across the country and the immigration judges who presides over them when adjudicating immigrants' removal proceedings do not have the final say if such ruling falls short of advancing the ambiguous anti-immigrant agenda of the nation's far-right conservative administration.

It simply means that the agency will most likely disregard the judges' ruling on any removal proceedings that permits such removable aliens to remain in the country. Rather, the agency calls the shot itself on which alien it wishes to let go or deport.

Some of the immigration judges who have been on the bench for quite some time, prior to the Bush-Cheney administration, are quite liberal when exercising their vested judicial authorities, doing so fairly reasonably against or in favor of deportable aliens, while the rest of the far-right judges with extreme views in applying the laws, who, in most cases, had just got appointed to the bench by the Bush administration to help facilitate and expedite the Republican's ruthless mission of immigrants cleansing, takes enormous pleasure in spinning the wheel along with the agency to impede justice from being fairly served to aliens under removal proceedings.

It is of course an indisputable fact that the Bush-Cheney administration vested excessive authority on the agency with the arbitrary power emboldening it to hunt down foreign nationals suspected of having the slightest immigration violation, detaining them and have them deported at any means necessary......even though it means braking the nation's immigration laws or the laws and constitutions of the land itself. That is exactly what the administration was doing all through its eight horrific years of presidency anyway.

However, quite a few of the nation's immigration judges during and after the Bush administration, still gets reasonably lenient enough to grant few aliens the relief sought in order to allow them reunite with their families in America....ordering them released from the agency's custody on meritorious ground.

Having been vested with infinite authority by the Bush administration, the agency regularly flex these authorities and most at times, disregards the judges' ruling granting relief to aliens by ordering such aliens released. Instead of complying with such judge's decision, the agency rather put in an instant appeal on such judge's ruling, essentially defying the judge's order while it continue such aliens' detention as both parties awaits the agency's Appeals Board to rule on the appeal, even though such appeal often times constitutes a waste of resources and completely unnecessary.

Accordingly, the agency supposed to respect and obey the judges' ruling by releasing such aliens who were granted relief and ordered released and then proceed with the appeal of the judge's decision. If in the future its Appellate court reversed the lower courts' judges' ruling, then the agency may proceed to notify such alien and then may go ahead in the removal of such aliens if they so decide not to appeal the Appellate Board's ruling any further.

The agency's Appeals Board, in most cases, always rules in favor of the agency without any legal opinion or legal memorandum of law supporting its order of removing such aliens....or even a vague one at best. This has been the new trend of the Board when reviewing immigration appeals since Mr. Bush's presidency and thereon after.....appeasing the administration and its right-wing teamsters in Washington by helping them achieve their primary goal of mass-repatriation of foreign nationals out of the country.

The agency normally files some bogus appeals, in most cases, without legal merit in fact and law. Most of the agency's appeals opposing the relief granted to aliens by immigration judges are usually so weak and lacking any substantial laws to establish a firm legal ground or its position for appealing the judge's decision in the first place. It is one of the agency's strategies to unnecessarily prolong these aliens' detainment under its custody till they eventually become financially, physically, and mentally exhausted and succumb to the agency's unlawful removal action.

Since the Bush administration changed the rules of the agency's engagement, the Agency's Appeals Board often ends up reversing the lower immigration courts' rulings against the aliens and in favor of the agency. The agency's arbitrary styles of enforcing immigration laws established by the Bush administration is now commonly referred to as the "End Game." This simply means that the agency could care less of what the immigration laws or the laws of the land says. It pretty much does what it wants to any foreign nationals at any given time with impunity. That is exactly the way the Bush administration along with his Republican extremists in Washington had authorized the agency to operate in handling foreigners.

When the primary purpose of having judges in courtrooms is undermined by the government of the moment itself or by its agencies, justice suffers at the expense of the general public. If a government agency is excessively emboldened by the government to the extent that it feels like it is so above the law and can swing the legal pendulum to whichever direction it pleases, why in the first place does it need to bring its matters before the court to be heard and decided by judges whose rulings will not be honored?

Basically, this agency lets foreigners in America knows that it enforces the nation's immigration laws implicitly and is conferred to serve justice its own way, regardless of the immigration courts' judges' rulings on its removal charges brought against individual aliens. This style of justice is totally arbitrary and a dangerous way of any government of a democratic state to treat any human being.....either citizen or non-citizen within its jurisdictional territory.

Such judicial rules of engagement is no different from that practiced by typical dictatorship regimes......where any policy, either good or bad, that best suits the regime to remain in control, rules the day. Such outright impediment to justice by a governmental agency is worse than abuse of power. It is a symbol of cold-hardheartedness driven by spirit of hatred.

This nature of contempt of courts orders reflects how outlawed the immigration justice has gotten in United States during Mr. Bush's term in office and thereon after.

After a final hearing in some aliens' cases to determine if they merit the relief sought, at times it takes the court another month or more for some of the presiding judges to finally make their ruling on some matters..... decisions that normally should have been made the very same day after the hearing, or at the longest, few days later, or at the most, no later than a week. At the end of the day, the long anticipated wait might still end up to be negative outcome for such aliens. It's just so many devious ways the agency adopts these days to torment foreigners seeking justice in America.

Depriving aliens' their liberty interests don't seem to mean anything to either the American Republican faction in Washington, nor does it mean anything to the nation's Immigration agency that detains them under its custody for an excessively lengthy period of time before sending them home or later releasing them back to the streets. You will be quite shocked that this is happening in America of all places.....a proclaimed land of liberty.

After the 9/11 incident, almost all the immigration laws was amended by the Congressional right-wingers in Washington in such a way that it won't even matter how minor an alien' violation might be, the amended laws subjects all foreign nationals to a no-win situation when the nation's immigration agency suddenly arrest and detain them without prior notice and commence repatriation proceedings against them.

These amended immigration laws approved by the Bush administration were legislated in such ways that heavily constrain any affected foreign nationals to be at the agency's mercy. In other words, the agency calls the shot and not the immigration judges in the courtrooms......regardless of how the law might happen to work on such aliens' favor. It still won't matter if such alien hired the best lawyer in the country to represent them. The agency basically do not operate by the book. And even if it sometimes do, the amended immigration laws by the Bush-Cheney administration, are just as bad as allowing the agency to operate without laws. Either way, any alien is pretty much screwed by the agency's new style of arbitrary rules of engagement.

The agency with its outlawed style of operation, is very skilled in fomenting all types of obstacles to circumvent justice from being served accordingly, especially justice intended for foreign nationals.....making highly skilled hired attorneys by the aliens look like they are beating on dead horses to such extent that it appears as if they are not doing effective jobs in representing their clients' interest. Some of these aliens even go off on their hired lawyers that they are not putting up very good representation on their behalf as their cases most at times may remain standstill for a very long time without any progress. Some of the aliens do not understand that some of these lawyers are not to blame for the stagnation of their matters, but the agency itself frustrates the lawyers' legal efforts.......making it appear as if they are not doing enough to bring a favorable closure to their clients' cases.

The United States Immigration agency has been so arbitrarily emboldened by the Bush's rightist administration to the point that granting any alien relief from repatriation has become a discretionary thing, and not because the law said so. Technically speaking, the agency releases aliens at its sole discretion if and when it chose to do so, regardless of what the law says.

Here, foreign nationals have two odds against them: one, the new amended laws are so brutal that there is little or no form of relief from deportation made available for aliens on any type of violations which they may be eligible to apply for; second, even if aliens are somehow able or allowed to apply for a relief, the agency is equipped with all kinds of legal and non-legal tricks to give such aliens so much runaround, stalling the entire justice process till they get fed up and decide to call it quit…even though the presiding judge determines that the grant of such relief was proper in accordance with the law and merit.

The application of the nation's immigration laws by the agency since Mr. Bush established the arbitrary blueprint, has remain a one-way street thing ever since. The laws are enforced to their fullest in arresting, detaining and removing foreign nationals, but it disregards the part of the law that either waives or prohibits aliens' removal......as the case has been with some Geneva Convention refugees under the protection of international law.

95

# 15

## ALIENS' DAILY LIVES IN U.S. IMMIGRATION DETENTION

AT THE YORK, PENNSYLVANIA IMMIGRATION DETENTION facility, detainees are allowed recreation time at the facility's grass-yard playground every once a while. During such recreation time, aliens from various nationalities spread all over the grass-yard, gathering in small various groups of similar countries of origin. The setting looks more like an international camping ground of refugees from all over the world than a prison environment that it actually is.

Everyone in each group has a story slightly or completely different from the next alien to share with the next group about how they got arrested. While some of the detained aliens already had preexisting matters, others had quite a long history of unresolved matters with the nation's immigration authority that seems like a never ending saga. Some also are just freshmen in the immigration justice roller-coaster ride. Thompson interacted with his countrymen as well as folks from other nationalities.

Looking through these aliens' faces, it was not hard to tell that everyone looked pretty overwhelmed by the sudden or back-dated legal woes they were facing at the time, or had been facing for quite some time. Some had just got started not quite long, while some have been on it for years. Some have been on it ever since their arrival in the country and still are unable to see any light as they approach what evidently seems to be the end of the tunnel. Some are so overwhelmed with the grim look of things to the point that the situation got the best of them making them resort to self-imposed isolation from others and become so stressed-out that they can no longer effectively associate with their peers.

However, some were still able to socialize and engage in recreation activities out at the playground with their other fellow detainees......at least to help them temporarily stave off the thought of their current dilemma of losing all their hard-earned livelihoods behind in America.

The legal pressures on them are so huge to the extent that all their stay in America could suddenly look like it never existed just in a moment's notice....with nothing to show for all their time abroad as they face dire likelihood of being forcefully kicked out back to their homelands with everything they worked so hard for left behind in America. The U.S. government, under the Bush Republican administration, that started the "catch, detain and deport" operation of flushing out massive numbers of foreign nationals, is fully cognizance of the crushing and destructive effect of their chosen method of expulsion on the affected foreigners. But the fact of the matter is: they could care less.

Not even allowing these aliens a short grace period for them to get back out there to make some preparation to leave the country. It is not even funny how these foreign nationals feel when they suddenly get snatched up and taken away from their families and livelihood. Some are so mentally drained to the extent that they need to take some sleeping pills on a daily basis while in the agency's custody just to be able to sleep at night.

Few are strong enough to brace the rough ride and the changes they suddenly find themselves that is beyond their control. Those set of aliens nonetheless remains upbeat and realistic to the rude awakening of the moment. They just can't afford to keep themselves down by the present situation they're in. They make necessary mental, socioeconomic and physical adjustments to the current changes, strongly believing that whatever the case, life must go on. They start making plans even before they arrive home to build their lives back up again from the scratch upon their arrival in their countries.

Of course, it is much more easier said than done for some of these aliens without the will power and disposable financial and other needed logistic supports. It is much easier of course for most people to start live all over again back home if they have pretty sound financial standing. But in cases of tens of thousands of foreign nationals suddenly swept from the streets of America by the nation's Immigration agency and taken straight to custody till they get deported, and not afforded any chance to secure their belongings or any other equities of value before being kicked out of the country, it is much harder, if not impossible, for most aliens who are subjected to this type of treatment in America these days to have needed resources to start life all over when they arrive back in their various homelands.

Because of how the U.S. Republican leadership had chose to mal-handle foreign nationals in recent time in America, most aliens ends up loosing all the livelihoods they had worked so hard for in America because the Republican leadership that emboldened the nation's immigration agency would not allow them such chance to retrieve their equities before deporting them. These personal belongings and other equities of various monetary values would have been very helpful for most of the deported aliens upon their return home to help them start their lives from the scratch, instead, these personal belongings and equities ends up unlawfully becoming someone else's property when these aliens gets snatched up from the streets straight to prison and then on the flight back to their countries.

Of course, it is much easier said than done......especially when such situation are faced by aliens from certain countries whose past and present have been nothing but one rough struggle after another to finally get to where they were before getting pulled back to the crab barrel by the rightist imperialists.

Also, if aging was a factor that remain constant at all time, starting life all over again from scratch at any given time would have not been much of a stressful thing. But aging makes it impossible for certain people of certain age bracket to start certain life struggles and lifestyle all over again. As life itself do not permit us to live forever, there is time constraint to everything in life.

Some things which we might have missed out on during our prime time may never be possible to do, or revisit at later stage in our lives ever again due to aging. Some opportunities or certain lifestyle that we craved during our prime time and we had somehow missed, or was deprived of them by others, circumstances or external factors, may, in most cases, be lost forever....or, we may never have the same chance to revisit them again due to aging...or just won't be the same like the first time around, or like when they should have naturally happen.

# 16

## THE POLITICAL SWINDLE WITHIN!

IT WOULD BE A GROSS UNDERSTATEMENT to even think that any U.S. Republican administration, like that of the Bush- Cheney and Trump's cares the very least bit about what happens to the aliens after they get deported back to their homelands.....not even to mention how they fared after their arrival home......having lost all they worked so hard for in the process of their removal.

It is a very delicate and dirty politics when administrations like those of Bush and Trump creates hostile environment purposely intended to target foreign nationals residing within its soil...using toxic policies to paint a rosy picture of an outright premeditated evil to falsely gain the public's validation of its woeful job performance. These Republican administrations claimed time and time again of supposedly using such outlaw measures to improve the national security, but in actuality, the state of things rather continues to deteriorate compared to prior leaderships by Democrat presidents.

Speaking of lavish spending, Mr. Bush's administration did such a good job in squandering the American public's hard-earned taxpayers' money on counterproductive policies that plunged the nation into worse socioeconomic and political state than it was under the watch of any Democrat Leadership.

Most of these lavish spending were directed towards contracts awarded to the same Republican-run corporate entities. This means that all the huge wasteful spending directly or indirectly ends up in the pockets of

Republican corporate contractors that are usually awarded the no-bid governmental contracts. One of such Republican-controlled corporate entity is the Halliburton's KBR, a subsidiary of Halliburton Oil Exploration Service company.

After the invasion of Iraq, Halliburton's KBR was one of the select U.S. companies that was awarded very lucrative contracts in Iraq. The company was subsequently implicated for overcharging the Pentagon for every meal it was feeding the U.S. troops stationed there. The company was probed by the nation's Department of Justice and was later ordered to pay back the excessive windfall profits it made off the federal government's coffers.

Several U.S. companies that were awarded the no-bid contracts ranging from Rebuilding to feeding the troops in Iraq were all tainted with one allegation or another. They were all grabbing as much pieces of the public's pie as they are allowed to grab by the Bush administration. The public's pie was essentially made available for grabs to these U.S. Republican-run corporate entities by the Bush Republican administration. These companies were all bilking the federal government of the taxpayers' money allocated for lavish spending by Mr. Bush. They basically jacked up rates they were charging the federal government under Mr. Bush's watch for the goods and services they were providing in Iraq, while other companies of equal or relatively comparable professional capabilities that competed for the same contracts, but owned by non-Republican bosses were shot out of their fair chance to bid for these contracts in Iraq.

Such unleveled playing field culture of handling the American public's business by the U.S. far-right Republicans in Washington, reflects how divided the American society has gotten today between those associated with the Democratic left-wing and those with the Republican right-wing circles when it comes to income mobility, socioeconomic issues and their fair and balanced allocation among its citizens.

These days in America it's becoming more and more questionable if the name "United States" still signifies the unity of the country, or has it become just an empty symbol with no practicable substance attached to it. The Republican party in America is now commonly identified as the "No" party to almost every policy proposed by the Democratic ruling party..... policies intended to benefit all Americans. The Republicans come to the negotiating table on policies that only benefits the select few Americans......

particularly the select few Americans from their circle. They are essentially the nation's opposition party to any well-intended policies proposed by Democratic leadership to move the nation forward. Their stonewalling ideologies, or strategy, if you will, is sadly keeping America on standstill in the 21st century as they relentlessly refuse to compromise on the viable bi-partisan policies brought forth by the Democratic leadership.

The Republican Party has been causing so much division within America and particularly between their Democratic counterparts to the extent that it appears as if it is two nations that exist within one government.

In almost all aspects of national issues, Congressional Republican lawmakers in Washington never see eye-to-eye with the Democrat counterparts. Since Democrats took the helm of power in Washington by the election of president Obama, Republicans have been playing the role of obstructionists to any and every policy proposal brought forth by the Democrats. Republicans just won't compromise on anything that the Democrats propose if they aren't the ones who brought it to the table. Republicans rather like to deal with their Democratic counterpart as bitter rivals with serious bones to pick between themselves than seeing themselves as partners with common goals of keeping the country united and coming together to agree on what's best for all American people.

American Democratic leadership in most cases, always propose and supports policies that will be beneficial to everyone in America. Typical rightist Republicans are not always comfortable with that type of pluralistic position. But when they are campaigning for office, they keep all their vague campaign promises on a plural note just to get voted into office.

Typical Republicans with a rightist pedigree do not see their Democratic counterparts, or others, as equals. That state of mind reflects in their socioeconomic and political reasoning and behaviors towards people outside their political or social circle. However, not all Republicans or conservatives are completely alike by nature, but most are always driven by extreme greed and selfishness. That nature of desiring to have it all to oneself alone without caring about the next man is the America of the imperial era and not the one set forth by the founding fathers. Sadly, this group of vast-right conservatives in America have been overreaching for quite a while now by taking all the pie to themselves and have been getting away with a lot of such public goodies that actually belong to everyone.....

doing so with impunity. Donald Trump's dealings in private sector and now in public office is a perfect example.

In contrast, typical Democrats or 'Liberals' are usually kindhearted people who are willing to assist others in their most critical moments with no strings attached and not trying to exploit the weak because of their current vulnerabilities. Most liberals are filled with sharing spirits with no strings attached. They are usually compassionate and will not leave others stranded or pass others by in the coldest winter and allow them to freeze to death. Unlike typical Republicans or 'Conservatives', whose help, if at all they decided to offer one, will come with hidden fine-prints, ambiguous price-tags and motives. Typical Liberals will assist others in making their dreams come true, while typical Conservatives only cares about how they can exploit others to make only their own dreams come true.

Dealing with typical rightist elements requires being extra cautious as they are constantly driven by deceptive motives and schemes that may appear so convincing like the real deal, but in most cases, ends up to be nothing but a mirage at best. This nature is the result of them not having others interest at heart other than theirs. Their motives are typically driven by greed and self-interest only.... just like Trump. The very extreme-right conservatives are straight up cold-hearted by nature, who value money, power and arbitrary dealings over human lives. There are a lot of these type of so-called conservative elements serving in public office in Washington today as well as in the American private sector.

The division and indifference created by these set of people is widely growing in America as each year unfolds since the turn of the 20th century till present time. The Bush-Cheney/Trump administrations along with their rightist-wing team in Washington has been a testament to such dictatorship-like style of leadership.

The Obama administration which succeeded the unbridled 8 years of Mr. Bush's presidency, has been at work from day one to undo the entrenched Republican gridlock in America to save the nation from its demise, but the same Republicans who was screwing things up along with Mr. Bush tried their hardest to stall few of his well-intended goals for all. The Obama administration is essentially the best thing that has happened to America ever since the Bush team came on board for eight years and mess the entire country up financially, politically and otherwise.

The American public whose votes are essential to have these undesirable elements elected into public office, must take real, bold and drastic measures during election period to contain this troubling trend of Republicans' arbitrary culture of leadership in Washington and in other public offices across America, if the nation still aspires to stay relevant in the 21st century.

The United States Congress was created to establish the balance of power at the executive level. The original 13 colonies had lived under the total power of the British King. In their central government, Americans wanted to prevent the concentration of power in one government official or one office. The Constitution created three branches for the federal government so that the power would be balanced. These three branches are the: Executive, Legislative, and the Judiciary.....with separate responsibilities. It was called the system of "check and balance," No single branch of the government can become too powerful because it is balanced by the other two branches. The legislative branch, which is the Congress, is comprised of the House of Representatives and the Senate.....conferred with the responsibility of making laws for the nation.

United States being a bi-party system of government, elects people through free election to represent the general public all across America from each of the two political parties to fill in for a total of 435 seats at the House of Representative, and a total of 100 at the Senate.

Whenever laws or policies are to be made, representatives from both Houses of Congress legislate these laws and policies and cast votes on them. Whichever party with the highest vote validates such law or policy of being passed into law.

In a situation where both Houses are dominated by majority seats from one of the two national political parties, such party usually has the upper hand to have proposed laws or policies passed into law...... especially when such majority policymakers are of the same party with the elected president in office. Such has been the case in the Bush-Cheney administration whose Republican party had managed to dominate both Houses of Congress since 1994. The vast-right policymakers among these Republicans in Washington took full advantage of their majority seats to legislate unilateral laws and policies....policies that at best has been quite detrimental to the American public's interest for some decades now even when a Democrat president was in office.

With Mr. Bush declared by the nation's Supreme Court as the winner of the 2000 presidential election for the first time in the history of America, both the Republican-controlled Executive branch and the Republican majority Legislative branch of the U.S. government started to function as one branch in wielding both executive and legislative authorities conjointly. The "Check and Balances" intention created by the constitution became suddenly moot. As a result, both the executive and the Congressional majority policymakers pretty much saw eye-to-eye in executing and enforcing their ambiguously intended policies. This arbitrary rule of law continued through Mr. Bush's first and second term in office.

The executive branch of the United States government under the leadership of Mr. Bush, along with his like-minded far-right Republican teamsters, made it one of their primary mission to rewrite almost all the constitutional statutes put in place by the nation's founding fathers to best fit their ambiguous agendas as they ran United States in the 21$^{st}$ century like a typical dictatorship regime.

At the judicial branch of the government, the Bush's administration goal was to fill majority of the judges and justices at the federal courts and the nation's Supreme Court with likeminded Republicans with radical views in interpreting and applying the nation's laws like the captain of the boat himself. With such like-minded non-transparent right-wing squadron filling majority seats in all the three branches of the government, justice and equal treatment under the color of law are always far out of reach for non-Republican defendants or complainants on either civil of criminal matters. Trump's administration is now forging forward to establish similar setting across the legislative and levels......if not worse.

After Obama came and calmed the waters down for eight good years, Trump mangled his way to win the 2016 election.... sadly taking the nation's judicial system back to the Bush-Cheney era. After quite a fierce fight from Democrats, Trump's second pick for Supreme Court, Judge Brett Kavanaugh, a highly conservative individual for sure, finally got confirmed to become the ninth Justice that will be ruling over critical matters that will affect millions of lives across the nation for decades to come...criminal or civil. With the usual 5 to 4 rulings at the Court, it should be clear to anyone what direction the 5 to 4 rulings will favor when cases are decided going forward from this point on.

Those who were persuaded or impressed enough by Trump's provocative talking point went and voted for him....as well as those who never attempted to vote at all both contributed to Trump's surprise 2016 presidential election victory.

During Mr. Bush's administration, there were no balance of power among the three branches of the U.S. government as well as between the Congressional Republican and the Democrat policymakers in Washington. Mr. Bush's administration intended to take America back to the era of the original 'Thirteen Colonies' where all powers were only centralized with the colonial British Monarch. The administration's ideological reasoning intended to and has, to some extent, reversed the hands of time socioeconomically and geopolitically. Both the American public as well as the international community have been very dismayed and outraged over Mr. Bush's eight years leadership and the havoc and huge liabilities he created for all Americans to live with thereon after, to say the very least.

Even making matters worse are the roles which lobbying and public relations industry plays behind the scene to influence how laws and policies are made. The Obama administration that succeeded Mr. Bush, made it vividly clear to the American public during his presidential campaign and after he won the presidency in 2008, that his administration will quench the 'Special Interest' groups' influence-peddling culture on policy-making in Washington during his term in office.

The same Republican extremists at the Congress during the Bush-Cheney era along with the conservative justices currently serving at the nation's Supreme Court are doing everything within their power to stall Mr. Obama's effort from ending the Republican embraced culture of special interests influencing the decisions made by the Congressional Republican policymakers in Washington....a non-transparent behind-the-scene policy-making dealings influenced in large part by the conservatives in the American private sector that affects everyone within America and sometimes even beyond, when they finally push such policies into laws.

The lobbying and public relations industry influences nearly every significant decision made in Washington. Lobbyists finance campaigns, shapes proposals that becomes law, help create regulatory loopholes and tax breaks and play a key role in directing billions of dollars in government contracts to their clients.

Within 2000 to 2007, the registered lobbyists figures has more than doubled in America....from 16,342 in 2000 to 35,844 in 2007. One of such lobbying players in Washington is the WPP, with several other P.R. subsidiaries all under one roof. WPP, the U.K. marketing group is best known as a powerhouse in corporate communications business. Its Chief executive, Sir Martin Sorrel, transformed what was once a business making wire baskets into the world's largest marketing services group. However, what has received less attention is how WPP has also grown into a force in U.S. political communications.

In setting its sight on Capitol Hill, WPP has targeted one of the most promising growth industries in America....the influence peddling business. WPP is not the only company in Washington that has built up its arsenal in the U.S. lobbying industry. But it is one of the largest in revenue generations in the business.

Attempts to regulate influence peddlers in Washington have generally been feeble. While public relations outfits are not regulated at all, lobbying reforms passed by Congress in the wake of the scandal surrounding Jack Abramoff, the lobbyist convicted of corruption in 2006, are centered on relationships with lawmakers, not on duties to clients. *

# 17

## THOMPSON'S REMOVAL PROCEEDINGS CONTINUED

O N FEBRUARY OF 2004, THOMPSON'S APPEAL of his removal order entered by the immigration judge came back from the agency's Appeals Board.....with a single member judge affirming the lower court judge's erroneous reasoning without opinion. In other words, Thompson's appeal papers was merely rubber-stamped like the case of thousands of legitimate appeals filed by aliens challenging the legality of their expulsion by the agency.

In 2001, the rightist lawmakers in Washington, who were then the majority at the Congress, promulgated a provision authorizing the nation's Attorney General's office, then under Mr. John Ashcroft's leadership, to enforce the regulation known as "Streamline" provision in reviewing appeals filed by aliens at the agency's Appeals Board. A regulation which ostensibly permits a single Board member judge, instead of three-panel of judges who normally reviews aliens' appeals, to merely rubber-stamp majority of the appeals filed by aliens. It is practically a rubber-stamped affirmation of the lower immigration courts' erroneous rulings to have majority of the appellant aliens with legitimate claims unlawfully deported back to their homelands.

In enforcing this policy by the Board, aliens appeal papers merely stays at the agency's Appeals Board for an average of 3 to 4 months, then decisions are rubber-stamped by a single Board member judge.....validating the wishes of the Bush administration and that of the rest of the Republican extremists in Washington and across America who are waging war against foreign nationals living within the country. The Republican faction in Washington mandates the nation's immigration agency to operate this way against all foreigners within America.

Over 90 percent of appeals filed to this Board are treated this way to enable the agency expedite its process of removing aliens from the country. Even the single member judges who rubberstamps these appeals do not even bother to take a quick glance at the issues raised in these appeals, not even to mention taking time to read them in detail as required before rubber-stamping them.

Sadly speaking, a lot of these aliens spends a great deal of money to hire immigration attorneys to assist them prepare their appeals that was not even given any benefit of a doubt to be properly reviewed by the Board......due to the 'streamline' regulation put in place to impede justice from being served to foreign nationals. This is nothing but a cold-hearted wicked policy plotted by the extreme-right Republican policymakers in Washington, D.C. focused on tormenting foreign nationals.

The regulation, since its inception, has left tens of thousands of legitimate appeals filed by aliens unresolved…sadly leaving aliens seeking justice in suspense of not knowing what the Board considered or did not consider on legal issues raised on their appeals.

After all the slavery and the Wild West mayhem in America, this is the form of justice envisioned and condoned in the 21st century in America by the Republican policymakers in Washington and across the country. And now comes Donald Trump at the driver seat.....taking the nation back to the Wild West era rules of engagement.

They are the same Republican policymakers who were co-architects of the lawlessness that went on for eight long years under the Bush-Cheney administration. A right-wing type of justice that blatantly targets and deprives foreign nationals of the nation's Fifth Amendment's Constitutional 'Due Process' of law.

The Bush administration tried to justify this capricious "streamline" regulation by saying that the regulation will help the Board speed up huge backlog of cases and the appeal process, but serving justice which should be the government's first priority here has been taken out of the equation at the expense of these depraved aliens. This is the right-wings' style of justice today in America.

A survey by the Pew Hispanic Center, a non-partisan research group in Washington, found in December 2007 that 53 percent of the Hispanics in the United States worry that they or their loved ones could be deported. Also in a report by various scholars doing field research in Southwest and in North Carolina and other states, said that the palpable sense of fear and traumatization in immigrants communities was more intense than any other time since the mass-deportation of Mexican farm workers in 1954.

# 18 IMMIGRANTS V. U.S. MASS-DEPORTATION

AFTER AN AVERAGE OF 6 TO 8 MONTHS of severe legal battle by these detained aliens to undo the legal entrapment they have been subjected to by the U.S. Immigration authority all to no avail......at that point most of them are psychologically and financially exhausted and drained, with little or no more strength to carry on with the never-ending legal battles. Plus the agency's devious policy and regulation authorized by the Bush people of imposing mandatory detention on most of the arrested aliens has been one among many of the agency's strategies to bring these detained aliens to quick submission and make them accept being removed even though some of them actually have legitimate claims to be allowed to remain in the country.

The indefinite detention strategy implored by the agency ranges in most cases from 6 months to as long as 5 years or more of continuous detainment in the process of fighting their cases. If such remarkably lengthy period of confinement just for immigration purpose by a governmental agency for a country like United States is not evil and hateful then nothing else on earth is. And this is a governmental agency supposedly portrayed to the public as being operated civilly. These days its scope of legal engagement and particularly its treatment of aliens is far worse than the treatment one would expect from the government department handling criminal matters and individuals.

Such lengthy period of confinement of aliens in a foreign state's immigration detention is itself a crime against humanity.....particularly when it is happening right in the proclaimed 'land of the free,' If such lengthy period of detainment don't end up affecting these aliens mentally, psychologically and otherwise, then what else will.

The agency enjoys an endless advantage of taxpayers' funded government-paid attorneys to prosecute its cases on behalf of the government, while the detained foreign nationals are deprived of their Due Process of law supposedly guaranteed by the nation's Constitution which mandates the government to provide accused indigent persons who can not afford their own attorney, free legal representation. These aliens are strictly denied access to free legal counsel by the agency, while being accused of wrong doing by the U.S. government. But are provided free legal representation on criminal matters.

It is understood that the Constitution do not make it a must for the government to provide free legal representations for indigent accused persons on civil matters, but in a so-called civil situation where the accused persons are arrested from the streets and then taken straight to the same prisons where criminals who committed crimes are held, these aliens should be afforded the very same Constitutional Due Process just as the other inmates held in the same confinement area and condition. Instead, the aliens are even treated worse by the U.S. Immigration agency than typical criminals. Typical detained criminals who committed whatever type of crime are guaranteed by the nation's Constitution to request and be given bond, even though the bond might be somewhat high, but foreign nationals arrested by the nation's Immigration authority for whatever immigration-related civil violations are in most cases held by the agency under its custody indefinitely without bond to either fight their case there in detention.....no matter how long it might take.....or till they get deported back to their countries. That is extremely cold-hearted way of treating immigrants by a nation of immigrants for that matter.

Every aliens dealing with immigration issues in United States are pretty much on their own in regards to legal representations. Aliens gets heavily drained by legal fees.

In 2005, the Bush administration passed a law along with the 'Real ID Act' that specifically targeted foreign nationals, making it very hard for foreigners to obtain drivers license from any state Department of Transportation across the country. In the bill was a provision that stripped the Federal District Courts of the jurisdiction to review any final order of removal entered by the immigration agency's Appeals Board.

Such appeals, since the enactment of the bill, are to be file with the U.S. Circuit Courts of Appeals at which ever district across the country such matter was litigated.

A typical appeal of an immigration matter by any alien appellant to any of the U.S. Circuit Courts of Appeals, which, after the enactment of the Real ID Act, has been the very next stop after the agency's Appeals Board's adverse ruling on aliens, will cost such alien an average of $4,000 to $6,000 for attorney fee, because it entails a very extensive law work and research for such an attorney to effectively litigate. Such money could only be spent by aliens who can afford it. Not even to mention other money already spent for legal representations at the lower (immigration) courts.... all with no guarantee of prevailing due to how immigration laws since the start of the 21$^{st}$ century in America has been amended in such ways that the laws leaves aliens with little or no room for relief from removal. The U.S. Federal District Courts used to have jurisdiction to review appeals of immigration decisions from the agency's Appeals Board.

By the time some of these aliens are able to exhaust all their legal remedies, almost all their money is gone down the drain on legal fees...... leaving them with almost nothing to take home in the event that they still end up getting deported, which in most cases they always do.

By now, it is undoubtedly clear to the public that the Republican policymakers in America and their like-minded rightist supporters are those behind these type of brutal immigration laws and their ruthless enforcement. They are the real enemies of immigrants in America, and not the whole of the American public as they always like to pluralize the immigration issue as a problem to all American public.

Just before Thompson's appeal was rubber-stamped by the agency's Appeals Board, his attorney informed him by mail that he was taking up another job offer at another law firm in Coral Gables, Florida...an unexpected job offer, which he could not turn down. In effect, he prepared to relocate there right away from the Philadelphia law firm.

The news was quite a shock for Thompson at a very crucial point of his appeal process. This means that Thompson must secure another competent immigration attorney to proceed with the appeal in the event that the

Board rules against him.....as it indeed turned out the very following week after his lawyer moved to Florida.

However, the Board's decision did not surprise Thompson because he was already familiar with the Board's new rules of engagement of not even bothering to review most of the appeals filed by aliens to render a *De Novo*, or Board's members opinions and legal analysis leading to its decisions. The Board rather adopts the quick and the easy route of merely rubber-stamping majority of the appeals, and in most cases, affirms the lower immigration courts' erroneous rulings to have such appellant aliens removed as ordered.

Time was of essence as Thompson only had thirty days to either appeal the Board' decision, or the Board's decision becomes final when the thirty days appeal period runs out from the date of the Board's decision. Thompson tried to contact few of the attorneys recommended by his prior attorney while in the agency's custody, but was unable to receive timely response from them.

As the thirty days to file the 'Appeal Notice' with the Circuit court was fast approaching,....Thompson was left with no other choice but to file his appeal with the court *pro se,* (meaning by oneself, without attorney) within the limited time period remaining in order to preserve his appellate rights. Good thing he had few years of unfinished college education, which became very handy at the time to coordinate and raise the legal issues that needed judicial review by the court on appeal to the best of his ability.

Right after the Board's rubber-stamped decision, the agency started to move aggressively and swiftly to reach Thompson's consular in Washington, D.C. for his travel document in order to expedite and effect his removal as soon as it possibly can. Thompson's pictures were taken as well as his fingerprints in preparation for his removal from United States. All these aggressive moves by the agency was done within few weeks following Thompson's appeal of his final order of removal to the U.S. Federal Court of Appeals.

While Thompson anticipated a ruling on his requested 'Stay' order of removal from this court, which was statutorily the only remedy that could stop the agency from removing foreign nationals while their appeals remains pending with the court. All arrangement was put in place by the agency, including a set date for the mass-repatriation of Nigerians on a chartered plane or U.S. Marshal's plane.....usually every 3 to 4 months along with other Nigerian deportees from Canada.

Thompson was called to the agency's office at the detention facility in York, Pennsylvania, where he was held, to speak with his consular. He however notified his consular that he had an active appeal challenging his removal pending and a ruling on his request for 'stay' order of removal remains pending as well. The agency had also contacted the court as well to inquire about the merit to Thompson's appeal and anticipated 'STAY' order request.

After almost a month waiting for the court's ruling on Thompson's request for 'emergency stay' order of removal pending the court's review of his appeal, he inquire with the court to find out what was going on. The court responded and informed Thompson that it was aware of his anticipated removal date, and that the court will rule on his stay request prior to that date.

Approximately 4 days to the D-day that Thompson was booked by the agency to enjoin with the other Nigerians expected to be on the next mass-expulsion back to Nigeria, the court ruled with an order 'Staying' Thompson's removal. The order came right on time to change the agency's already concluded plan of unlawfully and forcefully removing Thompson back to his homeland of feared persecution which he had fled years ago.

In addition, the court directed the court's clerk to appoint him a counsel to represent him in the matter.....which the court rarely does unless such matter is found to be highly meritorious, which the court saw in Thompson's case.

Since the appointment of counsel, new light was shed on Thompsons case. Crucial facts of the matter which the agency was concealing were uncovered and brought to light by the appointed counsel.

After these relevant documentation was uncovered and filed with the court by Thompson's counsel, the court subsequently issued a briefing schedule for both parties to submit their arguing briefs. Thompson's brief was timely filed with the court. However, the government, represented by the agency, refused to file its own brief in the matter after reviewing Thompson's submitted brief by his counsel. Instead, the agency submitted a motion a day before its briefing schedule due date.....requesting "Leave Not To File Its Brief," and instead requested for the matter to be remanded back to the agency's Appeals Board. Of course, that attempt by the agency to divest the court of its jurisdiction was opposed by Thompson's counsel.

In the agency's attempt to impede justice from being served by the court having jurisdiction over Thompson's immigration matter, it went ahead to bring it Appeals Board back in the fold. The Board asserted its *Sua Sponte* (meaning self reopening of a legal matter by the court) authority to reopen Thompson's matter and essentially vacated his prior rubber-stamped order of removal, holding that it wish to reopen the appeal to consider an important point of law that Thompson had raised in his appeal, which by the way, it claimed to have ignored to address the very first time the case was before the Board for review some two years prior to that time period.

The agency then submitted with the court yet another motion. This time it submitted it along with its Appeals Board's two-page memorandum stating its intent to re-open and revisit the appeal proceeding by vacating Thompson's final order of removal which it had previously entered. This move by the agency followed after its first attempt to have the matter remanded back to its Appeals Board had failed. In its second motion, the agency this time argued that its Appeals Board has vacated its prior order of removal on its own '*Sua Sponte*' regulation and therefore Thompson was no longer on final order of removal to be reviewed by this court.

It however wasn't a surprise to Thompson neither that the agency declined to file its brief with the court to support it legal position of its relentless effort to have him deported back to his homeland of feared persecution.

The statutory language of the law argued in Thompson's brief clearly reflects the arbitrary nature of the agency's action to remove him unlawfully back to his embattled homeland like the case of thousands of refugees that the Bush administration along with his right-wing Republican policymakers in Washington had authorized the agency to forcefully return back to harm's way in their various countries.

Simply put, the fact of the matter was brought to light before an independent court where the agency's spin games wasn't going to be allowed. The agency, knowing that it has broken its own law was fearful of filing a brief in the matter that will implicate the Bush administration of its deliberate assault on the nation's immigration laws incorporating the refugee Geneva Convention statute as well as the statutory legality to seek

Thompson's removal as an alien who was admitted into the country as an asylee under international refugee law. All the agency's effort was to avoid this Circuit court from making a precedential decision in Thompson's favor in the matter. Such precedent, for which the agency knew was most likely on Thompson's favor, could have spelt a huge liability and turn very crucial on the agency.

It would have not only translate to a legal victory for Thompson, but would have also hold the agency and the Bush administration liable for all the thousands of refugees that the agency had already forcefully and unlawfully sent back to harm's way in their various homelands of feared persecution.....a direct violation of its own statutory regulations and the international refugee law.

The ruling by this particular Circuit court, where Thompson had filed his appeal for judicial review, most likely would have been justice served not only for Thompson as an asylee, but also would have meant justice for thousands of refugees and asylees who have already been kicked out of the country and unlawfully stripped of their refugee protection by the Bush administration.......and would have also change the rules of engagement with refugees currently facing similar situation like Thompson as well as the rest others who have already been victimized by the administration.

It is sad and very shameful for the United States government for that matter, under an outlawed leadership of Mr. Bush's administration, a president who was presumably elected into office through public voting system by the American public, to have arrogantly ran this great nation in such a recklessly brutal way like a typical military dictatorship government along with his outlawed like-minded right-wing Congressional policymakers......camouflaging his evil actions under the pretense of securing the homeland against terror...while arbitrarily emboldening its various Security and Intelligence agencies to enforce evil policies against humanity....foreign nationals in particular.

# 19

## JUDICIAL ENTRAPMENT

GONE ARE THOSE DAYS WHEN LEGAL system in America was allowed to serve the very purpose of fair and balanced justice which the system was intended for. These days, most of the rules of engagement at the judicial arm of the government......especially under the temperamental conservative leaderships.....are implied and applied to essentially bully the very citizens and the general public which these laws were meant to protect. Most people within America have become marginalized and entrapped by some of these draconian laws relentlessly lobbied and legislated by these temperamental U.S. right-wing lawmakers.

In some cases, it takes the victims a lifetime of legal battle with the government to finally undo the injustices that was forced upon them. Some individuals' quest for justice took them all the way to the nation's Supreme Court....with very slim chance of fair justice, as most of the justices appointed there by the prior Republican administrations are filled with radical views in interpreting the nation's laws and constitutions and are temperamental conservatives by nature as well. They take political spin in most cases when rendering legal opinions on judicial matters that affects millions of people in America at times the Supreme court's majority decisions has a legal impact on the entire nation as a whole.

However, some of the laws from federal to the local level adequately serves their legitimate purpose, while others put in place at various levels of the U.S. government serves the complete opposite. Those other set of laws are purposely designed to entrap the violators into a never-ending spiral of woes. Part of the motives to these draconian laws are intended to subject the victims to socially and financially stagnant state once caught in the web. The beneficiaries are the so-called 'Free Market Conservatives' who build creed around freedom and capitalism.....with the help of the temperamental conservatives whose ideologies does not see a nation composed of individuals who should be given maximum liberty to make choices.

Some of these laws designed to entrap the public are so sleekly and artfully crafted to the extent that majority of the violators don't even know these laws existed, or are totally ignorant of their terrible consequences. Before the victims fully comprehend and digest what they had got into, they slowly start to realize that they are not only being punished for their violations of these laws, but also are in for a long treat of new age imperial entrapment. From that point on, their whole being will either gradually deplete, or just remain stagnant, or swing back and forth like a roller-coaster ride.

The American society has got so deep into the implicit judicial business to the extent that various professions have sprung up as a result to cater to the victims of this new age debacle in America. Some of these new-born professions are even making fortunes at the expense of these individuals victimized by the judicial system. The American legal system today, especially under the Republican leaderships is just such a joke and a shame to a nation like United States. It is more like a cat and mouse business these days....where the cat waits patiently for the mouse to slip up and then make the mouse its prey. The Republican leaderships' ideology today in America is more geared towards being an accessory to peoples' failure and misery rather than helping to make people better citizens of the society. failure and misery rather than helping to make people better citizens of the society.

No society is perfect in its rules of engagement, or governmental businesses, but a distinct line must be drawn between honest mistakes and deliberate intention of government representatives in public office acting under color of state law. When ugly things happens where the public expects better rules of engagement, people are bound to be shocked by such unprecedented performance. A democratic state like United States should live up to the pledges its elected leaders made to the citizens before being voted into office, instead of becoming unbridled leaders who does what they pleases as opposed to the public's wishes after having gained the same public's votes to get elected into office.

If an elected leaders' job performance turns contrary to their earlier pledges after getting elected, the citizens of such society has the absolute right to challenge the legitimacy of such governance. The citizens who voted such leaders into office are also part of the government and deserve to know how their elected leaders are utilizing their tax money, or other sources of national revenues. Instead, certain policies are put in place in America these days by the temperamental conservative policymakers that silences the majority taxpayers and treat them rather like slaves to the government......whose jobs and obligations are only to pay their taxes to the government, and don't deserve to know what their elected leaders do with their money.

# 20 *HOSTILITY TO THE REST OF THE WORLD*

SPEAKING OF WORLD INSTABILITY, THE BUSH- Cheney's administration alone has contributed immensely to the global instability through his first and second term in office as the president of the world's most influential nation. His administration relentlessly embarked on failed domestic and foreign policies. The administration stayed preoccupied in implementing covert policies with ambiguous motives......to the extent that even some of its Republican high-ranking officials were often under one conflict of interest or another among themselves over strategic issues concerning the non-transparency of their often distorted visions of directing the nation.

In effect to this conflicted power struggles, there were more fall-outs in the Bush administration than any other administration in the U.S. history. Without a doubt, America has not been the same nation that everyone once knew and identified with by Americans themselves and the rest of the world as the symbol and beacon of justice, liberty for all, and respect for human dignity.

After Obama came and restored most of Bush-Cheney's mess, Trump suprisingly got elected in 2016. And sadly for the nation, he has been busy undoing all the progress Obama made for eight good years. Thanks to those who went and vote for him....including women for that matter.... and those who never went to vote at all. Trump believes in America of the Wild-West days. He envision taking the nation back to that era along with his angry and hateful crowds.

A provision was struck down in early 2006 when the Bush administration pushed to legislate into law a bill that will empower his administration as well as his predecessor, to try terror suspects captured and detained by the administration in military- style tribunals instead of trying them in conventional courts. This type of cruel bill is not only unlawful in a democratic society like America, but also a violation of the Article 3 of the Geneva Convention provision to protect captured enemy combatant prisoners of war (P.O.W.). Such bill will allow the military tribunal to utilize information obtained from detained suspects through coercion in court against such suspects, among other measures. This brings forth a serious question to ask oneself where justice has gone in America when its leaders personally recommend and push hard for a provision of law that will permit the administration to try foreign national terror suspects, or enemy combatant prisoners of war in military tribunal courts with evidence obtained from such suspects through forced admission of guilt.

Not only that such evidence obtained through coercion will be used against the suspect in the military courts, but also the suspects, including their counsels would be barred from any access to review the evidence mounted against them in preparation of their defense...as the administration intended to keep such information obtained through coercion classified.

Mr. Bush and his vice Cheney approved and condoned the enforcement of such evil policy during their leadership against foreign nationals, and at the same time wants to advocate and promote democracy...or at least pretending to do so, while using the same double standard politics to condemn communist and dictatorship regimes like N. Korea, Cuba, Iraq and Afghanistan, among others. An administration implementing and executing just as cruel style and policies of governance, if not worse than that of the regimes it accuses and waging war against.

It just don't sit right when correcting the next man of his flaws while the corrector himself is doing the exact same things, or even worse than the person he is trying to correct. Ruthless masters always love to intimidate the weak-spirited ones so that they can occupy the playing field all to themselves. Bullying the little men just don't work all the time these days anymore. Sometimes the oppressed have no other choice but to stand their grounds and defend their own interest as well after having been pushed around so much for so long.

Before it was even brought to the public's attention, the highly criticized court marshal military style tribunal proposed to be used on captured enemy combatants had already been secretly authorized by the Bush-Cheney team to be used against the captured combatants in Afghanistan, held in the Bagram military base, 40 miles North of Kabul, and those held in Guantanamo Bay in Cuba. The Obama administration is attempted to set the record straight by bringing these so-called captured terror suspects held in these detention facilities for years without charges to justice in the U.S. civilian court with the proper provision of the Due Process of the law in consistent with the U.S. constitution. But the right-wing Republican Congressional policymakers in Washington, part of the Bush-Cheney administration teamsters, continues to circumvent this effort by the new administration to serve justice the right way to these accused individuals. Now Donald Trump wants the rest of the accused prisoners to remain detained there forever without trial.

This covert treatment was brought to the public's attention when a court action was filed by the American Civil Liberties Union (ACLU) to challenge the constitutional legality of the administration's cause of action towards foreign nationals for that matter. Similar treatment were applied to the prisoners of war (P.O.W.) detained in Abu Ghraib prison during and after the invasion of Iraq.

In one of his draconian policies, Mr. Bush declared that those detainees "are not entitled to the protection of the Geneva Convention's Article 3 clause, and should not be treated as one." That said, it simply means that these captured prisoners of war, according to Mr. Bush and his vice, Dick Cheney, who is believed to be the mastermind and main architect of these policies, can be subjected to any type of cruel and inhumane form of torture by American military personnel and other U.S. national security agencies and Intelligence operatives in coercing them to false admission of guilt over unfounded accusation of rabid acts as a result of their religion or geographical orientations. When people are accused by the government of any given society, the government must have enough evidence beyond reasonable doubt before the court in order to establish justified guilt. Such evidence must outweigh the innocence claim presented by the accused person to the extent that any reasonable fact-finder, who is not in any way influenced by governmental double standard, will adjudicate the matter in favor of the party with preponderance of factual evidence to establish guilt or innocence.....rather than making summary findings to establish guilt based on evidence obtained by the government through coercion or through some deceptive or fabricated means.....which would be more or less like a manufactured evidence.

While the U.S. -led war in Afghanistan and in Iraq went on and the enemy combatants in these regions are detained under the watchdog of the Bush-Cheney administration within their own countries and elsewhere across the globe, so also are the random and simultaneous mass-arrest of foreign nationals being aggressively enforced in United States by the nation's Immigration and Customs Enforcement and the Homeland Security agencies......enforcement policy started by Bush-Cheney and now continued in the worse way by Trump. Tens of thousands of foreign nationals residing in America are being arrested on a daily basis, detained and subsequently processed for removal back to their individual countries over relatively minor criminal or civil offenses, or no offenses at all. Majority of these type of offenses are categorized under summary infractions that are punishable by mere payment of fines and do not rise to the offense categories that should trigger these aliens being forcefully kicked out of the country just to satisfy the twisted egos of the nation's temperamental right-wing conservatives. The Republicans are going somewhere with this anti-immigrants crusade, but the actual reason behind their actions against immigrants remains a best kept secret from the American public.

The sad news is the fact that most of these victimized foreign nationals have already been well established as permanent residents with family ties, tangible equities and the like. None of these factors are considered by the agency, whose job these days entails a mandate by the Bush-Cheney era... and now Trump, to prey on well-intended foreign nationals residing in America. As a result, tens of thousands of families have been broken, lives shattered, hard- earned equities displaced and lost. Victims spirits have been crushed along with those of their loved ones left in America after their forceful removal. Not that the administration cares about the effect of their policies on the victims anyway.

Not quite much has been said or heard about the cruel and inhumane treatment of foreign nationals indefinitely detained till their forceful removal under the custody of the U.S. Immigration authority during Mr.

Bush's administration and thereon after. As the case has been, Mr. Bush's administration arbitrarily empowered the nation's immigration agency to arrest any foreign nationals within the country without prior 'Notice to Show Cause', or arrest warrant. They get picked up on the spot and detained indefinitely in jails without bond. In most cases, they are held and detained in prison in such manner over relatively minor immigration violations. Yet, the agency is portrayed to the public to be civilly operated, but the Bush-Cheney right-wing Republican administration had turned the agency's prior civil rules of engagement into a military style justice......far worse now than going through any typical criminal proceedings. At least in any criminal proceedings the accused are entitled the constitutional right to be given bond and upon posting such bond they would be released from custody on that ground to proceed on the charges against them on the streets.

As a foreign national during Mr. Bush's Republican administration... and now that of Donald Trump, your fundamental human rights, which are supposed to be protected by the nation's constitutions, are extremely restricted and constantly infringed upon...not to even mention an alien's liberty interest. After being arrested and detained in jail by the immigration authority, the next phase is being processed and scheduled to see an immigration judge who will determine such alien's fate of either getting kicked out or allowed the chance to remain in the country. Even if the agency decides to give such alien another shot to remain in the country, the torment and run-around they subject such aliens to seem not worth it anymore. The agency's legal spin game begins during the court proceedings.

For some aliens whose removal charges are based on convictions of either major or minor offenses and are subject to removal as a result, the immigration agency normally retrieve such aliens' record of conviction from the criminal courts where their criminal charges were prosecuted, and file them with the Immigration court as evidence to establish such aliens' ground for excludability before the immigration adjudicators that such aliens are removable as charged by the agency.

However, some of these aliens' criminal convictions are just so weak that the agency even finds it hard to make its case that the government is really seeking to deport them based on such charges. Just to portray the exact picture of how critical and heartless the agency had become under the Bush-Cheney/Trump administrations new rules of engagement, some of the cases are evidently so weak and without merit to successfully argue by the agency before the adjudicator. Instead of dismissing such removal proceedings as moot, the agency will rather request the court to give it more time hoping to uncover some more smoking guns that it can use to enhance its already weak case against such aliens in court.

The agency these days go to such aggressive length of retrieving the police report and discoveries to some extremely weak cases and try to exaggerate the severity of the obviously minor offenses to which such aliens were alleged to have committed along with the ones they were actually convicted of. Next time in court, the agency will proceed to admit all the frivolous police reports and discoveries of such aliens' criminal activities into record. Most of the like-minded Bush-Cheney era immigration judges who presides over such matters will gladly admit them into the court record, even though such biased adjudicators undoubtedly knows that those new submitted evidences are totally frivolous in fact and law.

Next follows an extensive cross-examination and drilling of the aliens on a witness stand by the prosecutors in respect to the various analysis to the supposedly new evidences freshly admitted into the courts record. At such point, it is very crucial for such aliens to be represented by very effective counsels, and hope that the presiding adjudicators are not among those judges who engage in judicial double standard in serving justice...... those who plays the role of both the judge and the prosecutor at the same time. Only then that the defense counsels for the aliens might be able to successfully sustain their clients' rebuttal of the new unsubstantiated evidences admitted in court by the agency in its relentless attempt to make the aliens look worse than they really are before the court.

Even though the conviction record clearly indicated that the rest other charges which the agency tries to elaborate upon were already dismissed at the criminal court, the agency still persists in trying every tricks in and off the book just to fulfill its ruthless mission of repatriating all foreign nationals from the country by any and every means necessary.

Very few repatriation cases of this nature get successfully argued and won by very competent and aggressive immigration lawyers before the agency's courts. Even in some cases where the presiding immigration judge agreed that such aliens merit the applicable waiver from removal and grant their relieve and release from the agency's custody, the agency blatantly disregards the judges' order and continue such aliens detention while it proceeds to appeal the judge's rulings. All that just to further stretch the aliens period of torment by arbitrarily prolonging their already lengthy period of confinement. Only when the agency's Appeals Board, which now operates just like the agency in its scope of judicial review of appeals and its rulings, especially the appeals filed by aliens, finally rules and affirms the lower courts' judges' decision, then the agency will finally back down and release such aliens. Not even releasing them immediately but at its own convenient time and date. Such release may be further delayed by the agency from at least a week up to several months. The level of frustration imposed on foreign nationals by the U.S. Immigration agency these days is just remarkably evil. It is compelled by deep-rooted unsubstantiated degree of hatred by the nation's right-wing Republican faction.

In most cases, when the agency appeals the judges ruling that was in favor of aliens, the agency's Appeals Board usually end up ruling in favor of the agency by reversing the lower immigration court judges' ruling, even though such lower court judges' ruling on the matter might have been legally appropriate in fact and law.

Before such aliens finally attain that type of legal victory against the agency, they must have been through a hell of legal saga with the government and a fortune expended to retain the service of aggressively effective counsels. To some aliens, going through this supposedly legal saga with the Republican-led immigration enforcement mission, the time and money expended, when it's all said and done, seem just not worth the mental and socioeconomic torment these aliens endure during such lengthy process. But for aliens with strong family ties, sizable equities in the country and the like, it somewhat seem more like a dedicated battle and a painstaking sacrifice to try and prevail at all cost on their cases, regardless of how long it might take and the open-ended sacrifices involved for the sake of reuniting with their loved ones, and to secure their unattended equities and other livelihoods out there.....if only such equities are not already claimed by others or by the government itself by the time such aliens finally get through with their immigration nightmare.

Never was it necessary when the agency used to run its immigration business civilly, for the agency, in any of its removal proceedings against any alien, to go that unnecessary extra mile in obtaining additional police records leading to aliens' convictions. The certified court record verifying specific convictions was all the agency needed and required by its operational laws to file with the court to establish its case before an immigration adjudicator. If the crimes committed by the aliens falls under the category of particularly serious offense, only then will orders of removal be inevitably entered against such aliens and their removal henceforth be effected.

The agency's new position of going to any length to repatriate any foreign nationals back to their homelands have turned into a governmental agency that violates its own laws and regulations......all for the appeasement of the biased-minded Republican conservatives in America today.

When faced with the agency's extra-judicial prosecution, some of these aliens unfortunately can not afford their own lawyers to represent them during their individual removal hearings in court. In such situation, when additional evidences and charges are introduced and admitted in court, pro-se aliens are professionally unable to effectively rebut those type of frivolous evidences. The agency normally take full advantage of such situation to slam-dunk such aliens by erroneously swaying the presiding judges hearing such cases that, such aliens are in fact removable as charged. And with immigration judges who are typically inclined in politicizing justice and the rule of law like the rest right-wing conservatives, they will most likely side with the agency with its frivolous evidence admitted with bias as part of the record, to have such aliens wrongfully removed from the country as charged. Such frivolous evidences by the government are best suppressed and rebutted professionally by effective counsels. Thompson's matter with the agency serve as a perfect example of such cruel and arbitrary style of justice practiced by the Bush-Cheney/Trump administrations against foreign nationals.

Some of the aliens held under immigration custody are indigent. But they are not entitled to lawyers provided by the government. A person accused of shoplifting gets an appointed attorney, but someone who fled persecution and may be tortured or killed if forced to go back to their home country does not. That means asylum applicants may get only the justice they can afford.

# 21 MISPLACEMENT OF JUSTICE IN AMERICA

BEFORE THE BUSH-CHENEY ADMINISTRATION, TO SAY the least, the outside world could hardly imagine or think of United States, widely portrayed as the beacon of liberty, democracy, fair and square style of justice for all, to also engage in the art of judicial politics to the very public its obligation is to serve and protect. Through the 8 years of the Bush Cheney era, it was a heart-wrenching experience for the general public, mostly for foreign nationals, to discover for themselves first-hand during their legal encounter with the nation's judicial system, that justice served, in most cases, do not really imply the essence of justice, but rather a politicized justice specifically intended for the entrenched governmental interest, and not necessarily for public's interest as the case should be, or portrayed to be. And now comes Trump implementing policies that intends to take the nation way back to the Wild-West bygone era once again.

In some of the judicial levels of the nation's Justice Department, like the one overseeing immigration matters, the rules of engagement are purely political. To average aliens being subjected to removal back to their countries, they view it as the government serving justice against them to justify their prior wrongful actions, or for having been in the country without papers. It is true in some few cases, but not so in majority of the cases. Majority of the aliens being arrested and removed from the country never committed any crime in the country in the first place, but they still end up being detained in jail with criminals who actually committed crimes and later gets deported anyway. Regardless of the adverse impact which the politicized justice is having on the general public, for the extreme-right-wing leaderships in America like that of the Bush- Cheney/ Trump administrations, it is always business as usual.

Speaking of justice, most of the so-called legal actions taken against foreign nationals, and even citizens, by the Bush's 8 years' presidency were no way in conformity with the justice the administration portrayed and proclaimed to provide the American public. The only promise he lived up to was the abuse of his executive authority to torment foreign nationals within America and across the globe. Trump is going down similar path with immigrants.... and enjoys boasting about how ruthless he'll be man-handling them before and after he got elected in 2016 After their unilateral judicial missions are accomplished, the nation's conservative media networks helps these administrations in rose-painting the awful look of things...portraying the oppressed groups rather as the menace to society just as the oppressors had wanted them to be portrayed before the public, rather than identifying them to the public as the actual oppressed ones which is the relative truth.

It is very delicate to either condone nor accept such skewed governmental stigma, while the real story has been left untold to the public by the same media that has served as the administration's mouthpiece. It is impossible for any fact-finder to make sound assessment of any event or incident when the facts leading to such events has either been altered, impaired, or inaccurately presented to the fact-finder. Such practice was synonymous of the Bush-Cheney era... and now that of Trump.

Even some of the nation's mainstream media networks which most of the American public rely heavily on for accurate and independent news and information on private or governmental issues......to which their practice of journalistic independence is protected by the nation's constitutional provisions of the "Freedom of Speech", and the "Freedom of Press" are highly restricted these days in America, particularly during the Bush-Cheney Republican administration along with their temperamental right-wing conservative constituents in Washington and across the country.

Control has been prevalent with the Republican administrations in America as to the authenticity, in-depth analysis of the relative truth of things, and the extent to which sensitive news information journalists and news information networks can publish or broadcast, and the ones that may not be shared with the general public, or the ones that must be approved by such Republican administration of the moment, for censorship before they can either be published or broadcasted to the general public. Such freedom of press are increasingly been infringed upon legitimate journalists by both the temperamental conservatives in public office and the free-market conservative corporate executives and the owners of some of these mainstream media entities...impeding such diligent journalists from presenting the actual facts of things and events without spin to the general public. At the end of the day, crucial news and information that matters to the public are highly distorted, edited and censored to conform with what the administration wants the public to hear, as opposed to the actual facts of things.

Consider how Mr. Bush has degraded the office of the Attorney General during his eight years tenure as the U.S. President. His first choice, John Ashcroft, helped railroad undue restrictions of civil liberties through Congress after the 9/11 attacks. Mr. Ashcroft clearly had some red lines and later rebuffed the White House when it pushed him to endorse illegal wiretapping. Then came Alberto Gonzales who, while he was White House counsel, helped to redefine torture, repudiate the Geneva Conventions and create illegal detention camps. As Attorney General, Mr. Gonzales helped cover up the administration's lawless behavior in anti-terrorism operations, helped revoke fundamental human rights for foreigners and turned the Justice Department into a branch of the Republican National Committee.

Mr. Gonzales resigned after his extraordinary incompetence became too much for even loyal Republicans. Then came Michael Mukasey, a well respected trial judge in New York who stunned the public during his confirmation process by saying he believes the president has the power to negate laws and by not committing himself to enforcing Congressional subpoenas. He also suggested that he will not uphold standards of decency during war time recognized by the civilized world for generations.

Following a Senate Judiciary Committee hearing in which Mr. Mukasey refused to detail his views on torture, he submitted answers to senators' questions that were worse than his testimony. They suggest that he, like Mr. Gonzales, would enable Mr. Bush's lawless behavior and his imperial attitude towards Congress and the courts. In a letter to 10 Democrats on the Committee, Mr. Mukasey refused to say whether he considered water-boarding....a method of extracting information by making a prisoner believe he is about to be drowned....to be torture. He said he found it "repugnant", but could not say whether it was illegal until he has been briefed on the interrogation programs that Mr. Bush authorized at Central Intelligence Agency prisons.

Water-boarding is torture and was prosecuted as such as far back as 1902 by the United States military when used in a slightly different form on insurgents in Philippines. It meets the definition of torture that existed in American law and international treaties until Mr. Bush changed those rules. Thanks to the succeeding Obama administration that had strapped most of those torturous Bush- Cheney policies. Even the awful laws on the treatment of detainees that were passed in 2006 prohibited the use of water-boarding by the American military. And yet the third attorney general under Mr. Bush's presidency had no view whether it would be legal for an employee of the United States government to subject a prisoner to that treatment? The only information Mr. Mukasey could possibly be lacking at the time was whether Mr. Bush broke the law by authorizing the C.I.A. to use water-boarding.......a judgment that the White House would not want him to render in public because it could expose a host of officials to criminal accountability.

Mr. Mukasey's letter to the Senate Committee accepted the administration's use of the so-called shocks-the-conscience test to determine the legality of interrogation methods, rather than the clear and specific prohibitions against torture, humiliation and cruel treatment embedded in American and international law. The administration's standard was dangerously vague...which invited abuse and amounted to a unilateral reinterpretation of the Geneva Conventions. Would Mr. Mukasey or any U.S. attorney general approve of any foreign jailer using water-boarding on American soldier? Mr. Bush's policies had paved the way and increases the danger of that happening.

Mr. Bush's administration fell short all through its two term 8 years tenure in White House to appoint the sort of attorney generals that the nation needed, a job that includes enforcing voting rights laws and civil rights laws and ensuring that criminal prosecutions are done fairly.*

Extreme abuse of executive authority became so prevalent during Mr. Bush's administration to the point that anyone, particularly foreigners could easily be labeled or framed as a terror suspect, or affiliated with one, or even branded as rabid fundamentalist just for voicing his or her liberal opinion about the administration's failed and counter-productive domestic or foreign policies and its covert and deceptive style of governance.

Here we are into a fresh millennium in a nation that has been placed in such a high pedestal by the outside world due to it adherent to unique constitutional principles set forth by the founding fathers......and in fact has reflected those unique values in the past, gradually going down in history as an outlaw nation by and through the actions and the toxic ideological influences of the free- market conservatives and that of the temperamental conservatives in public offices.....trying their hardest to amend and re-write almost all the well codified fundamental federal constitutional statutes put in place by the founding fathers....turning the historic nation of liberty and respect for humanity into a den of outlaw right-wing leaders.

22

# SOUTH-AMERICA BORDER CROSSING ODYSSEY INTO THE U.S.

F ROM DELAWARE TO OREGON TO GEORGIA, the so- called "browning" of America is once again forcing America to reexamine their definition of citizenship and the very meaning of being an American. The explosive growth of Americas Latino has shifted immigration.... particularly illegal immigration....to the forefront of the national debate.

According to the government's data, there are still anywhere from 8 to 12 million undocumented aliens residing in the United States. Primarily from Mexico, but increasingly from Central and South America. The influx has somewhat receded since the 200708 U.S. economic downturn and the extremely harsh sanctions and hostilities imposed on these immigrants by the Bush administration. They cross the border from Mexico and end up in places like North Carolina, Ohio and Idaho in search for work. While some are naturalized or natural born citizens, the open secret is that the majority are recent immigrants who have entered the country without authorization. These workers are so integral to the country's service economy that there is a thriving black market in fraudulent identification for illegals. Although the Bush administration's 2005 Real ID Act imposed criminal penalty for any alien in possession of fraudulent identification either for work or for any other purposes.

As the forces of globalization compel corporations to maximize profit at the expense of labor, the number of undocumented immigrants flowing into United States seeking relatively higher wages for work will only increase, which in a way is quite healthy for the overall economic growth of the country.....if only the policies of the entrenched conservatives in the corporate America and that of the vast-right conservative policymakers in Washington and their skewed ideologies will allow the economy to recoup back to its hey days. Also rising, however, is the wave of anti-immigrant sentiment, particularly within the border communities which are literally at the center of the immigration issue.

In early 2011, an American civilian from the state of Arizona was charged in the cold-blooded murder of two Mexican immigrants along the Arizona-Mexico border. This American individual deliberately opened fire and killed a Mexican immigrant and his wife while attempting to cross the border. His best line of defense in court was that his life was being threatened by these immigrants, so he shot and killed them for self-defense. What an incredible line of defense indeed. However, subsequent investigation found that these poor immigrants were totally harmless and had no deadly weapons on them in the first place. The American fellow's motive, like many others with bias mindset about foreigners like him, was based purely on hatred of immigrants. He was later sentenced to death.

Although the issue of the illegal immigration clearly must be addressed, its impact is typically overstated, and radically overreaching steps that the nation's right-wing extremists advocates will likely only further complicate the matter. Pundits from the American conservative Talk Shows like Luo Dobbs of CNN, Glenn Beck, Sean Hanity and the defunct Bill O'Reiley of the Fox News network, whose nightly rants against illegal aliens portray the issue as a crisis that threatens to destroy America itself, often attempt to paint immigration as a national security issue instead of an economic one. The point that none of the 9/11 attackers snuck in through Mexico and were, in fact, all in the country legally is rarely raised. Meanwhile several glaring economic truths are overlooked. The $600 million in federal taxes the Mexican immigrants paid in 2006 and the $ 1.5 billion paid annually in rent and mortgages rarely garner a mention. When these numbers are compared to the roughly $250 million in social services that these illegal immigrants use, the argument that they are depleting precious public resources appears specious at best.

**- *DEATH ON THE BORDER:*** Historians will write about how a lax America let its unique and coveted form of government sink into a quagmire of mutual acrimony among the various subnations that will comprise the new self-destructing America.

These words are from the mission statement of the Minutemen, a group of private citizens unaffiliated with any law enforcement agency who took it upon themselves to police the Arizona-Mexico border, looking for Mexicans who are trying to cross over to the U.S. illegally. For the duration of their 30-day "awareness campaign" in early 2005, the Minute men patrolled part of the same area as the 11,000 federally authorized agents of the U.S. Border Patrol. While later on declared their operation a success, roughly one million unauthorized foreign-born Hispanics successfully cross the Mexican border annually. Between 1990 and 2000, the number of foreign-born Mexicans in the United States more than doubled. Even so, foreign-born Mexicans represent only 3% of the total U.S. population.

To make the modern day vigilantism of the Minutemen more disturbing, there were reports of men, women, and children across the border being detained at gun-point by these self-styled defenders of American sovereignty. California governor at the time, Arnold Schwarzenegger, himself a celebrated immigrant from Austria, publicly endorsed the actions of the Minutemen and similar groups. For any public figure to openly applaud this blatant contravention of U.S. laws is bad enough, but that a state governor.....of California, no less.....to do so is even more egregious. Most troubling is the acceptance of the notion that illegal immigrants constitute a great threat to the American way of life. This is an untenable position for even the most casual student of American history, as it is common knowledge that America is a nation built on the backs of immigrants, willing and otherwise.

Furthermore, instead of deterring the illicit border crossings, Washington ultra-right policymakers have only shifted the flow of immigrants' traditional crossing points like San Diego into more remote parts of the Arizona desert, where hundreds of immigrants die every year from exposure. The desperate poverty they seek to escape leaves them ill-equipped for the arduous days-long trek from Mexico into tiny towns like Alta, Arizona. Towns like Alta have entire economies that exist to provide border crossers with meager, sometimes worthless supplies.

Most Mexicans are smuggled into the U.S. through Arizona.....from a Mexico border town, Naco to Way stations mainly in Western Phoenix...

where increasing number of drop-houses are found and occupied by human smugglers and these undocumented immigrants as they awaits to be transported to destinations across the country. The rates for the Naco-Phoenix transportation ranges between $1,000 to $1,500, while the transport fare for smuggling people across borders through the San Pedro River Riparian National Conservation Area, a remote desert site, is about $2,500.

One of the major smuggling ring is based in Naco, Mexico. The group typically transports two to four loads of six to ten a day mainly using rental cars...adding up to several hundred people in all a day. The rings are estimated to making between $100,000 to $ 130,000 a week from this operation which seem pretty lucrative.

One group that profits from the desperation of these illegal immigrants other than the businesses that employ their cheap labor, are those in the bustling smuggling trade. There are also dozens of "Coyote" operations which charge up to $1,200 a head to sneak people from as far away as Guatemala into the U.S... These job seekers are often stuffed by the score into big rigs, vans, and SUVs, then spirited across the border as far as Ohio where an underground railroad scatters them across the Midwest and rural South. Many times these illegals are abandoned mid-trip at the first sign of border patrol, or by less scrupulous smugglers, once they get their payment. Worse, desperate coyotes often flee the authorities. These high-speed pursuit sometimes result in terrible accidents, as the dangerously loaded vehicles are susceptible to rollovers.

What's being ignored in this debate is the vital role that the undocumented workers play in American agricultural and service economies. It is the refusal of hardcore immigration policymakers to acknowledge this truth that represent the biggest challenge to formulating a responsible immigration policy in United States of today.

*- HAVE JOB, WILL TRAVEL:* A staggering number of undocumented workers from Latin America form the backbone of California economy. Cooks, valets, maids, nannies, and gardeners in overwhelming majority of households...particularly among California's moneyed entertainment industry professionals......are non-native Spanish speakers. Most employers neither know nor care about the legal status of their employees. They simply benefit from the cheap labor that makes their lives easier.

Drive past any Home Depot home improvement and construction tools outlets from L.A. to Richmond, and you will likely find dozens of Latinos hoping to be hired as day laborers. There is no form of regulations overseeing these workers who simply do the job and hope to be paid. The fact remains that despite public sentiment, there is no indication that people in need of cheap labor will ever stop hiring them, even though anyone with an ounce of common sense would suspect that they are in the country illegally.

Even if employers wanted to comply, current immigration laws actually provide a disincentive for them to do so. Employers must prove that no qualified citizens could be found to do the job. They must then find, transport, feed and house the workers and return them to their point of origin after the completion of the job. What business would go through all that trouble when there are endless supply of workers whom he is under no obligation to feed, house or pay benefits?

Those seeking to work legally in the U.S. by obtaining a H-1B work Visa fare no better. They can only be in the country for a limited period of time only for the employer who initially hired them and at that person's discretion. In other words, they are at the whim of an employer who has the option of deporting his employees should there be any dispute or if he simply doesn't want to pay them.

So the dance continues. The aggressive immigration raid scatter workers and those caught. Whether 10 or 1,000 are repatriated, only to cross the border again at the first opportunity, often with their minimum wage…or less….waiting for them when they get back. However, that holds true when the country's economy was in healthy state. Since the massive economic crunch that started back in late 2007 up until present time, job security in America have become a far fetch expectation for even the American citizens, talk less of undocumented immigrants. The job situation has deteriorated so bad to the point that most of the work force now in America will be glad to even have a part-time job that will hire them for a mere 3 to 4 days a week just to make enough to provide them sustenance allowance. This applies to both citizens and noncitizens alike as well as undocumented immigrants.

This border crossing odyssey should not be taken lightly neither. To some of these migrants, it is a life or death ordeal. Regardless of arrest, deportation, and the near certainty of being taken advantage of, the risk is never too high to prevent Mexicans and what the border patrol call OTM's (other than Mexicans) from making their way into the U.S in search for better life....even though such better life is becoming far-fetch in America these days.

   - ***FACING THE FUTURE:*** In 2006, the U.S. government spent $30 million on seismic sensors, night vision cameras, hundreds of new border agents, and a small fleet of Apache helicopters in the hopes of intercepting immigrants before they cross the border. This effort has succeeded only in proving that no amount of money or technology can stop people who need work from getting to people who need work done. Policies that ignore the circumstance that compel millions of people to risk life and limb for $7.25 per hour do little more than put Band-Aid on the problem. Whether the immigration lawmakers like it or not, a nice chunk of Hispanics are working and living in the United States, and with one in four Americans projected to be Latinos by 2050, they aren't the only ones who will need to assimilate. Absent a clear voting majority and in the face of the expanding political power of Latino strongholds like Miami, San Antonio, New York, and Los Angeles, the reality that the sociopolitical landscape in United States is about to change for ever. Even though the right-wing policymakers in Washington are stopping at nothing to root out immigrants, particularly the Hispanics, from the country in a very ruthlessly alarming rate. The question now is: will America remain true to its founding ideals and step into the future with openness and tolerance, or will it retreat out of fear and ignorance? We'll see...and soon. One of the key reasons for the aggressive mass-expulsion of foreign nationals, particularly the Mexicans and other Hispanic migrants, has not yet been clearly narrated to the American public. There is an underlying political motive behind the U.S. conservatives' anti-immigrant aggression.

# 23. A VIETNAMESE WAR VETERAN'S REPATRIATION SAGA

ONE WOULD EXPECT THE GOVERNMENT OF any civilized, and most of all, democratic state, to not discount the invaluable contribution of a foreign national who joined force at some point in time with such nation's military, particularly at the time of war, to fight against his own country and was later resettled in the U.S. after the war. Decades later, through the nation's immigration authority, the U.S. government under the conservative leadership of the Bush administration sought his forceful expulsion back to his homeland.

And not just a mere repatriation, but an expulsion back to the very country of his birth which he had joined force with a foreign state to wage a brutal war several decades back in time. Not only has he taken such a fatal risk against his own country of birth along with a foreign state, he had barely survived the battle which later rendered him permanently disabled.

Sung Nguyen, a Vietnamese citizen who fought for the United States government against his own country during the Vietnam war, and in the battle field, lost his left arm and right limb, was arrested and indefinitely detained for almost two years at the immigration detention facility in York, Pennsylvania.....all over relatively minor domestic violent offense which at the time of his arrest by the agency the matter was already resolved and quashed.

Sung was rendered disabled by the war he narrowly survived in Vietnam. Decades after the war, this poor war veteran who, after the war, has become permanently wheelchair-bound, was faced with the threat of being forcefully expelled back to his native Vietnam.

Sung's case was a typical case in point which warrants and mandated special waiver from expulsion. But nonetheless, the immigration agency did not see it that way, or at least did not act like it saw it that way, for having held this handicap man under its custody without offering him a chance to post bond, at the very least, for the sake of his disabled physical condition. He was forced to remain in custody fighting for his life for a very lengthy period of time.

His permanent disability resulting from his service to the U.S. military was more than enough to warrant prompt clemency from expulsion by the government of a nation he has provided such invaluable service at the time of war. After all, Sung's offense was not a capital offense or any particular serious crime that would subject him to be perceived as danger to public safety if released back to the street of America. Instead, this poor wheel-chair ridden war veteran was made to languish indefinitely at the agency's custody.....fighting yet another battle.....this time inside the courtroom..... trying hard to stop the Bush administration from removing him back to harm's way where his country's government will undoubtedly persecute him to the fullest if not even kill him upon his arrival there.

Thompson met with this pitiful elderly war veteran in 2007 at the York, Pennsylvania immigration detention facility......one of the numerous immigration detention facilities spread across the country...holding facilities funded by the Bush-Cheney administration for detaining and processing tens of thousands of foreign nationals subject to be deported back to their various homelands.

It would be extremely troubling for anyone with any humanitarian feelings for others, knowing Sung's past service to the U.S. government and then seeing him in such terrible physical condition languishing in the U.S. Immigration custody, fighting his hardest and pleading to be spared from expulsion under such condition, and above all, for the fear of becoming a subject of reprisal upon his arrival by the government of his original country of birth.

Sung's domestic-related offense did not in any way rose to the level of offenses which the government will consider him or categorize him as a danger to society, or to public's safety to the extent that the United States government wanted to expel him at all cost. Even if he was removable as charged, weighing in on the military service he rendered for the country during the war is more than enough reason for the Bush administration to have waived his deportation for humanitarian reason and for public's interest, considering the relatively minor criminal infraction that triggered his expulsion proceedings in the first place. Considering his physical condition, he should have been afforded bond right away and have him proceed with his case out on the street instead of the indefinite detention policy of arrested aliens often adopted by the agency.

With such life-threatening type of immigration policies enacted and aggressively enforced all through Mr. Bush's tenure, it got the whole world in a state of absolute shock and in total dismay on what "justice" actually implies in recent time's right-wing leadership reasoning in America. The Bush administration was practicing the exact opposite of the true meaning of justice all through his 8 years in office, especially in the administration's foreign policies which specifically targeted foreign states and foreign nationals.

In effect, the Bush- Cheney administration's legislated policies were not designed to afford the public at large any chance to rehabilitate from their lapses, but to ruin them completely in the process of them serving the punishments. A fair and balanced justice in a democratic society is required to not only enforce laws and punishment on the culprits, or recompense for the victims, but also make simultaneously effective provisions for rehabilitation to cure future recidivism. The so-called extreme-right policymakers in Washington along with the Bush-Cheney Republican administration were basically turning the nation's judicial system into a "cat and mouse" business.....the law enforcers being the cat and the general public being the mouse. Donald Trump and his like-minded team are sadly setting the stage towards that direction again after Obama's tenure of repair work of the nation's image.

Most of the new and amended laws under Mr. Bush Republican leadership differ in applicability from the conventional laws that was intended to serve the purpose of recompense to victims while it punish and rehabilitates the violators. The laws are covertly enacted and are rarely made public or heard of by the general public. Most were laws that lacks majority or public's approval. These are laws and policies covertly legislated by unilateral consensus of the temperamental conservatives whose motives are primarily intended to target and cripple specific people of special interest and potential.

The typical targets are usually resourceful and enterprising whom the temperamental and the free-market conservatives perceives as threats. Threats that are, in most cases, to their financial interests.....whatever that may be. The same free-market conservatives are usually behind the indirect lobbying and sponsorship of these bills to be passed to protect both their private or corporate interests......and not necessarily laws made to serve public's interest.

The message usually gets across to these policymakers through the messengers known as the "special interest influence peddlers" without the public's knowledge of what is brewing behind the scene. When its all said and done, these private actors ends up being the beneficiaries to these ambiguously legislated laws. This explains why corporate politics in America continue to influence the decision and actions of the nation's policymakers. To be exact, those of the right-wing conservative leaderships.

* Recalling America's greatest historical shames, majority have involved the singling out of groups of people for abuse. Based on distinguishing features like skin color, religion, nationality, language. It is undoubtedly factual in recent time that people......particularly foreign nationals...within America have suffered unjustly for it, either through freelance hatred of the citizens or aliens or as a matter of official government policy. The right-wing leadership in America has been heading down this road again...for quite some time now. United States as an historical nation of immigrants needs to have working immigration policy, one that corresponds with economic realities and is based on good sense and fairness. Sadly it doesn't. Driven by the nation's right-wing conservative inertia and a rising immigrant tide, and an outrageous conservative instigated national mood of frustration and anxiety that is slipping, as it has so many times before, into hatred and fear. Hostilities against immigrants falls disproportionately on an entire population of people, documented or not. The administration

of Mr. Bush's hostile immigration policy, that has been followed up by the rest of his right-wing constituents in Washington and across the country after he left office, has harmed everyone.

The evidence and the impact can be seen and felt in any state or town that has passed constitutionally dubious laws to deny undocumented immigrants the basics of living, like housing or the right to gather or seek employment. The crackdown on the so- called undocumented immigrants during Mr. Bush's administration and thereon after has become so prevalent to the point that a neighbor citizen now turns in neighbor immigrants. It is on talk radio and blogs. It is on campaign trails where candidates are pressed to disown moderate positions. And of course it can be heard nearly every night on CNN, in the nativist drumming of Lou Dobbs, for which immigration is an obsessive cause.

Lets concede an indisputable point: The new temperamental conservative demagogues are united in their zeal to uproot the illegal population. In doing so they do not discriminate between the criminals and the much larger group of strivers. They champion misguided policies, like a mythically air-tight border fence and a reckless campaign of home invasions. Worse of all, they summon the worst of America's past by treating a hidden group of vulnerable people as an enemy to be hated and vanquished and not as part of the problem to be managed.

The case of Sung, an handicapped Vietnamese war veteran who was detained by the United States Immigration agency under the Bush administration......faced with the threat of being repatriated back to his native Vietnam after joining force with the U.S. government to fight against his own country, lost his right arm and left limb during the war, is more than enough to puzzle anyone with a sound mind to wonder how brutal an administration can get to even attempt to repatriate a lawful permanent resident alien who fought against his own country on behalf of the same country that now wants to deport him so bad back to his own native land that he fought against several decades later...all over a relatively minor domestic dispute offense that has long been resolved before he was even arrested and detained by the Immigration authority. As a matter of fact, he was residing within the same household which the very domestic dispute at issue had occurred with the family member who were the alleged victim of the incident.

The very incident that triggered Sung's removal action by the U.S. Immigration authorities has long been amicably resolved within the family members, and everyone had since then been living under the same roof thereon after before the immigration authorities came and got him to send him home. So it wasn't an issue that Sung could be a potential harm or danger to his family or others out there that compelled the agency to be so ruthlessly aggressive in getting rid of him. Sung never had any prior record of being abusive to his family or others, or others complaining of his violent nature to the authorities. What happened was just a situation of a typical isolated incident. But with the Bush-Cheney administration's established style of immigration justice, the agency now could care less of how the incident happened or how minor or how severe it was. As long as a record of guilt was established in the criminal court, there is a very strong likelihood of any alien being kicked out of the country just for that.

These days, the agency basically adopts the strategy of capitalizing on any alien's least infractions as enough reason for it to initiate its removal proceedings on such aliens and move aggressively to kick them out of the country. But the main political reason behind this ruthless mass-immigrants expulsion started by the Bush administration in America.... an historic nation of immigrants......has been left untold to the American public and the rest of the world.

This, among other ruthless rules of engagement, has been the type of troubling legacy Mr. Bush and his team intended to establish and leave behind for the next president to emulate.as well as other like-minded administrations across the globe that his administration's xenophobic pedigree was able to influence during his passage as the Republican president of United States.

Mr. Obama who succeeded Mr. Bush is a complete opposite character from the Bush-Cheney's ways of dealing. He has a sound and incorruptible mind of his own. He did not continue the anti-immigrants policy started by Mr. Bush. He refuse to be pressured or wrongly influenced by the right-wing Republican policymakers in Washington who have been the primary architect to the recent time laws and policies aggressively enforced to root out foreign nationals from the country.

Also, another foreign national, Jindal, from Cashmere, a long time troubled enclave between India and Pakistan, was also detained in 2008 at the same York, Pennsylvania detention facility by the agency to be sent back to his country by the U.S. Immigration agency enforcing the Bush administration-led immigration policies.

Jindal signed on and went to fight in Iraq on behalf of the U.S. government under the Bush-Cheney war. He was lucky to have made it back home to the U.S. after surviving a deadly roadside explosion planted by the insurgents. The explosion led to the death of two of his fellow comrades. He survived but he was left brutally wounded on one arm and leg. Just seeing those scars on his left arm and leg which is so huge and stretches almost all the way through his whole arm and leg, anyone will instantly know that Jindal must have narrowly survived a deadly incident. Yet the Bush administration who sent him to fight unjustified war in Iraq found it quite appropriate to have him kicked out back to his native Cashmere for having got in trouble with the law on relatively minor offenses of possession of small amount of 'Controlled Substance' and for 'Simple Assault' offenses.

Since Jindal was a 'lawful permanent resident' alien at the time, the presiding immigration judge finds it appropriate by law and discretion to grant him a relief, canceling his removal and reinstating his green card status. The agency, however, finds the judge's ruling inappropriate and chose to further appeal the ruling while Jindal continue to languish much longer in the agency's custody pending the appeal's outcome which could takes between 3 to 6 months for a ruling by the agency's Appeals Board, after having been detained there for over a year fighting the matter.

This, among many other heart-wrenching scenarios, are among the various torturous schemes designed by the Bush-Cheney team and the rest of the nation's vast-right Congressional lawmakers in Washington have been using to inflict irreparable pain and suffering on foreign nationals who have served the U.S. government in private and governmental sectors. That was the kind of reward you get or should expect to get during the Bush administration, or when dealing with the rightist conservative leadership in America today for your past service to the nation.

# 24 ETHICAL MISCONDUCTS OF JUDGES IN COURTROOMS ACROSS AMERICA

A "JUDGE" OR AN "ADJUDICATOR" IS AN individual with independent and sound mind with capability of entering impartial decision; an advocate of 'fair and balance' justice in resolving differences between two or more beefing parties......one whose decision would be widely viewed and accepted by majority of the public as rational, fair and reasonable.

Speaking of justice and the rule of law, judicial ethics and the rule of law adopted by the politically influenced judges across the courthouses in America. has never got as troubling and capricious in this new age than it has been during the Republican leadership of the Bush-Cheney administration. Judges, especially those at the federal level affiliated with the ultra-right-conservative fold, has literally turned the courtrooms into a political playground, instead of serving justice to the public. The states' judiciary politics is an entire theatrical episode on its own.

A Republican administration with Republican legislated laws, executed and enforced by Republican dominated judiciary that treats the rest of the public outside their ultra-right Republican circle like scapegoats....regardless of whose side the law favors, or otherwise. The new age conservative style of serving justice to the general public in America is disturbingly being switched into a no-win system of justice for both the victims and the culprits alike.

It is just too much odds against the average general public to be served justice these days in America without some level of profiling and a substantial degree of partiality. Odds as having politically influenced judges presiding over courtrooms of law, playing the part of a prosecutor and an adjudicator at the same time. In such judicial setting, typical of the Bush-Cheney administration, justice will never be allowed to prevail regardless of how competent and effective such defense team might have been in presenting and arguing such matter. It is a sad judicial evolution starting to take a deep foothold in American judicial system. The ethical lapses has got so remarkable across America among some typical old-guards and new-age conservatives and ideologically biased judges to the extent that they have shifted the judicial obligations to that of serving the ambiguous motives of their rightist conservative pairs in Congress whose judicial interest reflects that of their free-market conservative colleagues at the private sector. If such terrible trend is allowed to continue for the next decade or so in America, the extreme-conservatives' plan of taking the world back to the colonial era in this 21$^{st}$ century will surely be allowed to become a reality.

In an attempt to reverse this ugly trend of judicial double standards and ethical misconducts by these type of judges at the nation's high courts, some sound-minded Congressional Senate Democrats from various states across America, in late 2006, made a proposition to push for creation of an independent oversight "Inspector General,"...a department that will oversee, check and scrutinize judicial lapses of these type of judges that connives with the nation's policymakers to undermine and pre-empt the true function of the judicial setting in America. Such an oversight would have been very instrumental in curbing the growing misgivings and ethical lapses transpiring in most courtrooms across the country.

It will also be a major milestone and a sigh of relief for tens of millions of America public as well as foreign nationals who have been victimized by such ambiguously legislated laws and arbitrarily applied by the judicial arm of the U.S. government.

The effect of such judicial lapses deliberately condoned by the Bush-Cheney/Trump administrations, have and still causing irreparable havoc to millions of live across America and beyond. Even some of those who voted Mr. Bush into office for the second term came to realize a little too late the terrible mistake they have made, as they themselves were also affected by some of the draconian policies the administration has implemented......and what a monster of a leader they voted for to run the country.

Most of Mr. Bush's supporters later came to express bitter regrets that if they knew what they later came to know about him, his vice and his other vast-right conservative teamsters' covert and deceptive style of governance, they definitely would have had second thought before casting their votes for him to lead America towards such a destructive path he chose after getting elected into office.

 *- SELLING OF THE JUDICIARY:* "We put cash in the courtrooms and it is just wrong", Sandra Day O' Connor, the former Supreme court justice, declared at the start of a conference in New York on April 2008, on a growing trend to judicial independence and integrity: the escalating millions that special interests are pouring into state judicial elections in an effort to buy favorable rulings. The substance of her remarks was no surprise. Since retiring in 2006, justice O' Connor has devoted herself to spreading the word about assaults on judicial independence and the bedrock principle of impartial justice....including from big-money judicial campaigns. Still, it was startling to hear from a former member of the nation's highest court speak about the problem in such stark terms.

Thirty-nine states in the U.S. elect at least some of their judges. On top of the inappropriate judicial involvement in partisan politics, recent years into the 21st century have seen the dawn of a grubby new era of multimillion dollar campaigns for important state judgeships. These include 15- and 30 -second attack ads, a staple of competitive races for top executive and legislative posts. Those slug fests are largely underwritten by well-heeled interest groups.... including insurance companies, tobacco firms, the building and healthcare industries, unions and trial lawyers that have seized upon judicial contests as a promising avenue for influence-peddling.

The perception that money is corrupting the courts would be damaging enough. But often, it seems, special interests are finding that buying up judges likely to side with them in big dollar cases is good investment....the real-life grist for John Grisham's new fictional legal thriller, "The Appeal,"

Events on April, 2008 in Wisconsin and West Virginia only deepens this concerns. On April 1, the first and only African- American member of the Wisconsin Supreme court, Louis Butler, lost his seat after a nasty, racially charged campaign in which his opponent, Michael Gableman, was aided by a barrage of TV advertising, paid for by the state's largest business lobby.

In West Virginia, meanwhile, the state Supreme court's handling of a case involving a large coal company, Massey Energy, took on a decidedly farcical flavor. For the second time, the appellate court threw out a $50 million verdict against Massey.

The court decided to rehear the case after photographs publicly surfaced of it chief justice, Elliot Maynard, vacating in Monte Carlo with Massey's chief executive, Don Blankenship, in 2006, while the matter was pending in the Supreme Court. The chief justice disqualified himself from the rehearing. So did another justice, Larry Starcher, because he had publicly criticized Blankenship and his company. The 3-to-2 outcome in favor of Massey was unchanged from the first round, which might not have been noteworthy except that the deciding vote was cast by the third justice, Brent Benjamin, who declined to recuse himself despite owing his election to the court to more than $3 million dollars spent by Mr. Blankenship.

In response to such travesties, judicial reformers have stepped up their call for public financing and strict fund raising rules for state judicial contests or a switch to a non-elective merit selection system. Surely, special interests would be less inclined to invest so heavily in judicial elections if they knew the recipients of their largess would be barred from sitting on their case.

In a January 2010 U.S. Supreme court ruling on a campaign finance matter filed by the Citizens United v. Federal Electoral Commission (FEC), the court struck down a century old ban on corporate spending to influence elections outcome in support of candidates running for public office. The justices, in a 5 to 4 majority ruling, held that corporations have a constitutional right to spend millions of dollars on public election campaigns that attacks or support particular candidates. The court established a very troubling precedent that opens an infinite floodgate of private or corporate campaign spending for or against state or federal candidates running for public offices. In the majority ruling, the court reversed a long standing provision that previously put certain limit on the amount of money which private or corporate entities are allowed to spend in funding the election of their supported candidates running for public office in America. Now, with this Supreme court ruling, private or corporate entities are given the green light to spend as much as they wish on campaigns to help push their supported candidates to the finish line....including spending heavily on attack ads against such candidates' opponents. The ruling basically nullified restrictions on corporate spending to influence elections.

Sadly, this Supreme Court's ruling will definitely pave way for very unleveled playing field in the country's electoral process. The Decision did not sit well with the Obama administration. It stifles one of the administration's campaign pledges to the American public that promises to put brakes on the influence of the lobbying industry in his administration..... the influence peddlers known as the "special interest" groups who influences almost every major judicial decision-makings championed mainly by the rightwing Congressional lawmakers in Washington. Everyone but the Republicans was dismayed by this ruling. The American public calls the Supreme Court's ruling " a major blow to democracy in America and an assault on the rule of law and on the nation's electoral process,"The rightist Republicans saw it rather as a victory and a move in the right direction. Of course, anything that favors only very select few people at the expense of the masses is always a move at the right direction for the vast-right conservatives in America.......either the ones in the private sector or those in public office alike.

Since 1907, the U.S. Congress banned all corporate campaign financing....radical departure from a hundred year old law, said justice Ginsburg. The ruling is referred to as a disaster to the American people. It is also referred to as a deregulation of the nation's political process. It has serious potential to distort and corrupt the nation's political system.... an earthquake in the law. It is like the umpires canceling the game itself and making up the scores. That is the extreme-conservatives style of governance... the arm-twisting style that later always brings forth huge adverse consequence for everyone else to bear.

To be exact, such terrible ruling, simply tells the American public that the conservative justices at the nation's highest court had just put American public offices for sale for the highest bidders. Those private or corporate entities, foreign and domestic, with the deepest pockets gets to buy the candidate of their choice, while the other potential opponents with much less power of the purse will have to concede defeat and essentially bow out. That is exactly what the ruling translates to the American public. The Obama administration intends to try and put in place provisions through the Congress that will circumvent and minimize the full exposure of this ruling as well as its devastating effect during the election time.

In yet another sad twist of unconscionable act of corruption by judges in America, especially those affiliated with the nation's rightwing Republican Party, in 2009 a sitting judge handling municipal cases in Luzerne County, Pennsylvania, was eventually busted after taking millions of dollars in kickbacks over some period of time from the owners of then a newly opened privately owned prison in the locale. The millions of dollars in kickback to this judge is intended to have him unlawfully convict and sentence juvenile offenders and send them to serve their time in this privately owned jail. Essentially, the kickback paid this judge was to help the owners of this private jail bring in clients to fill the newly opened facility to enhance their prison business operation.

If a judge in a courtroom of law in a country like United States of all places could be so corrupt to allow his love of personal gains trump the rule of law as a judge for that matter, what worst case scenario are we yet to find out that is still ongoing within the judicial system in America in this current day and age of the 21ˢᵗ century. Yet, the American media are always the first to raise their drumbeats out loud portraying similar lawlessness going on in other people's countries.

The former juvenile court judge, Mark Ciaverella, was later charged and convicted on February 2011 for the "kids for cash" scheme he willfully partook with the owners of the for-profit prison. This judicial fraud, presumed to be one of the biggest courtroom fraud, if not the biggest in U.S. history, made national news after the cover-up all unraveled. Sadly, he is definitely not the only judge across the courtrooms in American engaging in such unconscionable act of lawlessness. He just happens to be one of those who got caught in the act.

These days, new jails are now built across America by both the government and private entities more like typical business enterprises that are intended by their owners to be profitable by any means necessary, rather than their true purpose to be used by the government only for punishing offenders accordingly and for rehabilitation purposes. Once money has been invested to build these prisons, they must be filled up one way or another.....either by folks actually guilty of breaking the law or by the relatively innocent ones. Majority of the prisons in America are now run with the mindset of return-on-investment mentality by the government and the private entities alike. That is the judicial setting in America today going forward into the 21st century.

*- EFFECT OF INJUSTICE:* When laws are ambiguously enacted, erroneously or arbitrarily applied and enforced on the public, justice has been preempted from serving its intended purpose. The innocent or the weak ones are often made the scapegoats. In such scenario, punishment is usually not proportionate to the offense. It is very usual in this type of setting that some people gets very bad breaks while some people enjoy undesirable easy rides. Essentially, some people always suffers unduly, while others enjoys undue free rides. The effect of injustice and governmental lawlessness is very damaging to the soul of the victims and to the society as a whole.

Sung, the embattled Vietnamese national whom the Bush administration sought to repatriate after he almost lost his life fighting with the U.S. government against his country....a war that rendered him permanently disabled. Around four decades later after the war, the Bush-Cheney administration moves to kick him out of the U.S. back to his homeland...knowing quite well that things definitely won't sit well with him upon his arrival in Vietnam... being forcefully sent back home after such a long time after the war with evidence of the war written all over his body. The question is: do the Bush-Cheney administration cares about what might possibly happen to him upon his arrival home? Of course not. His situation and the ones imposed on many others exemplifies the Bush administration language and doctrine of governance, which clearly implies that those considered as outsiders, both citizens or non-citizens, are as good as their most recent good deeds to such administration's entrenched interest......whatever that may happen to be. Once they fall short of that instant significance, the rightist administration in America today do not accommodate nor condone giving others second chances, even for the sake of their prior service to the nation. These days, they preys on peoples' least infractions and capitalize on them to the fullest as ground to reign down and inflict irreparable torment and havoc on their lives. Such style of governance is not typical of a democratic government. Most American public as well as the outside world have come to grip that America has deviated from democratic governance during the Bush-Cheney's eight years reign. Obama came and included everyone in his governance...

Republicans stood in his way all along. Trump got elected in 2016 and started running the nation with Wild-West mentality along with his base who went and voted him into office.

With the Bush-Cheney/Trump style of governance, you are merely as good as whatever these administrations can get out of you at that moment. When such usefulness subsequently becomes obsolete, then you too becomes obsolete and irrelevant as well... regardless of the history of your past good track record. At that point, such typical rightist type of administration will device all types of conniving tactics to dump you at the back burner. You won't even be allowed to stick around to even enjoy the fruit of your prior good deeds. Once you outlived your usefulness, the Bush-Cheney/Trump neo-cons style of governance capitalizes on your least infractions as ground to treat you like an outcast who is out of place that needs to be discarded. Such style of governance is synonymous of a typical dictatorship regime.

Sung served the U.S. government during the Vietnam war against his very own country. In the process he lost his right limb and left arm. Four decades back in time, the Bush-Cheney Republican administration moved to get rid of the rest of him after the nation got the best of him....a man who, after the war, has made United States his permanent place of residence.

# 25

## LOCAL AND STATE AUTHORITIES' ENFORCEMENT OF FEDERAL IMMIGRATION LAWS...FIRST TIME EVER..... DURING THE BUSH-CHENEY/TRUMP ADMINISTRATIONS

NEVER IN AMERICA HISTORY HAS IMMIGRANTS become such hard targets like it has been during the eight years Republican leadership of the Bush-Cheney administration......and now followed by Trump. Immigrants have become so hard pressed in America to the extent that not just the Federal Immigration agency alone has been handling immigration-related operations. The administration made it such a forefront national issue to the point that even local police departments across the nation were given the green light to join in on the crack down… under a federal proposition put in place by the Bush-Cheney administration called 'Proposition 287G,'

Even the local government administrators in a handful of counties across the country took the federal immigration law enforcement into their own hands as well….enacting local ordinances targeting undocumented immigrants living within their locales. All in their relentless attempt to make life a living hell for these so-called undocumented migrants and even the documented ones alike.

Such ordinances are aimed at chasing away immigrants living within these communities by imposing harsh penalties on businesses caught hiring undocumented immigrants, or home owners, with either private or commercial properties, found renting any part of their properties to undocumented immigrants or even harboring them. The penalties ranges from the revocation of their operating licenses, to the imposition of huge fines on them for such violation. And even a threat of criminal prosecution.

Such was the case of a small rural township of Hazleton, a former coal town in Luzerne County, Pennsylvania. A township of total population of about 31,000 residents......one-third (1/3) of whom were of Spanish dissent before the hostility started.

In mid 2006, the township mayor at the time publicly declared his intention to take the federal immigration laws into his own hands under his municipal jurisdiction without permission or first seeking leave to do so from the federal government. He boldly joined in with the Bush administration's anti-immigrant crusade and relentlessly pushed for such local ordinances aimed at making life a living hell for any undocumented immigrants living in that town. Since almost half of the residents of this little town are of Spanish dissent, it made the Spanish-Americans living there perceive such hostile move by the town's heads as being directed towards the Spanish people in particular. A spokesperson on behalf of the Spanish community in the town responded to the mayor's cause of action on a public news report...declaring that "these same so-called undocumented Spanish immigrants whom the town mayor is trying so hard to kick out of the country are the same ones whose cheap labor have helped revived this once economically crushed former coal town," The spokesperson said. As a long time resident there, she further noted in her public news conference that "This little town was like a ghost town in about a decade or so ago till the recent influx of migrant workers came and revive the town's depleted economy. The industrial sectors in this town have benefited immensely from the cheap labor of these undocumented immigrants, boosting the economic growth of this once ghost town", she added.

Like other typical vast-right conservatives in public office in America, the mayor was more than pleased to give Mr. Bush's administration a helping hand, without even an official invitation, to help kick these undocumented migrants out of the country after their cheap hard labor helped to revamp the town's previously crushed economy. That has been the reward given them for the years of hard labor they have contributed to the growth of the township.

It is becoming more and more so that if things are not one way or another associated with exploitative motives, they just don't sit well with the rightist group in America today.

The 'Hispanic' group and the America Civil Liberties Union (A.C.L.U.) in fall of 2006, filed a suit against the County, principally to overturn the laws and ordinances......contending that the local ordinances against undocumented immigrants are discriminatory and unconstitutional. In the mayor's account to justify his antiimmigrants stance, he contended publicly that the undocumented immigrants in his township are in fact the ones responsible for the most heinous crimes committed in the town...of course without any concrete proof to substantiate his vaguely asserted speculation. In other words, this mayor tried to justify his unsubstantiated claim of enacting anti-immigrants local ordinances against the undocumented migrants living in this township by rather labeling them as the root cause of all the public nuances that ever occurred in that town...to help him rally public support for his xenophobic motives.

This widely unpopular cause of action by Hazleton former mayor made national news across America in the fall of 2006... all due to the Bush-Cheney's administration being the advocate-in-chief for the anti-immigrant sentiment. The claims made by this town's mayor against foreign nationals, documented or not, were just as flawed as those proclaimed by Mr. Bush to the American public. The mayor's position as a typical ultra-right conservative, is not to assist these poor undocumented migrants, who have been very productive members of the town, to the path of becoming documented aliens, but rather to exploit and dump them after they outlive their usefulness....a typical right-wing conservative style.

Even the sitting state governor at the time, Ed Rendell, in a public speech following this ugly development, broadly denounced this mayor's anti-immigrant ideological cause of action. He called the mayor's action "cruel, evil, counter-productive and un-American. Such action is mean-spirited and feeds off hatred and divisiveness," The governor said in 2006 news conference shortly after the mayor's anti-immigrants local ordinance was made public.

During the fall of 2006 as well, the township Committee of a factory town of Riverside became the first municipality in New Jersey to enact legislation penalizing anyone who employ or rent to illegals, or otherwise known as 'undocumented' immigrants. Within months, hundreds, if not thousands of recent migrants from Brazil and other Latin American countries had fled. The noise, crowding and traffic that had accompanied their arrival over the past decade from the time of this municipal action abated. With the departure of so many people, the local economy suffered.

Shortly after the enactment of the ordinance, the town was hit with two lawsuits challenging the law. Legal bills began to pile up, straining the town's already tight budget. All for the sake of showing how resentful some Americans in public office feels about foreign nationals living within their midst. Suddenly, many people.... including some who originally favored the law...started having second thoughts.

Following a federal court's adverse ruling against similar ordinance started by Hazleton township in Pennsylvania in July 2007, Riverside rescinded the ordinance two months later, joining a small but a growing list of municipalities nationwide that have begun rethinking such laws as their legal and economic consequences have become clearer. The town's former mayor, George Conrad, who voted unanimously for the original ordinance, sounded regretful to the town's anti-immigrants cause of action....saying that "I don't think people knew there would be such an economic burden. A lot of people did not look three years out," The American public and the international community awaits the Bush-Cheney administration...even though they had left office while the problem the administration created still looms.....to someday publicly express deep and profound apology for the consequences of their immigration policies, like this municipal township mayor had did after their actions backfired.

Between 2006 and 2007, more than 30 towns nationwide have enacted laws intended to foment problems attributed to illegal immigration, from overcrowded housing and schools to over-extended police forces. Most of those laws like Riverside's calls for fines and even jail sentence for people who knowingly rented apartments to illegal immigrants, or who gave them jobs. In some places like California, Texas, among others, business owners have objected to crackdowns that have driven away immigrant customers. And in many, ordinances have come under legal assault by immigrants groups and the American Civil Liberties Union.

In June 2007, following a court action challenging these local immigration ordinances, a federal judge issued a preliminary injunction against a housing ordinance in Farmers Branch, Texas, that would have imposed fines against landlords who rented to illegal immigrants. The following month, the city of Valley Park, Missouri, repealed a similar ordinance, after an earlier one was struck down by a state judge and a revision brought new challenges. A week later, a federal judge struck down ordinances in Hazleton, Pennsylvania, the first town to enact laws barring illegal immigrants from working or renting homes there.

Some residents who backed the ban when it was initially started in late 2006, were reluctant to discuss their stances after various adverse courts' rulings in 2007. Though they uniformly blamed outsiders for misrepresenting their motives. By and large, they regretfully said that the ordinance was a success because it drove out illegal immigrants even if it hurts the town's economy.

"It changed the face of Riverside a little bit", said Charles Hilton, the former mayor who voted for the ordinance. He was voted out of office at fall of 2006, during when the town's administrators embarked on this local immigration ordinance saga, but said it was not because he had supported the law.

Such resentful behaviors by American publicly elected officials towards foreigners living amongst them stemmed in great part from the gestures and policies advocated and championed by the very person running the country. The local ordinances implemented against undocumented migrants residing within United States are reflective of how the leader of the country at the time feels about foreign nationals in general. The lower level officials were merely following Bush and now Trump's lead on the nationwide war being waged by their administrations against foreign nationals living in America.

# 26 ARREST, DETAIN AND REMOVAL PROCEDURES OF FOREIGN NATIONALS IN THE U.S.

B ACK INTHE DAYS, A COMMONLY USED term to describe aliens subject to be kicked out of a typical Western country like the U.S. was the word "Repatriation," As time went by, the action word was modified to "Deportation," At the turn of the 20th century, the action word has further been modified into a more subtle verb now known as "Removal,"

The United States Immigration agency now works hand-in-hand with the newly created agency during the Bush administration, U.S. Department of Homeland Security (DHS)......created after the 9/11 incident to enforce immigration laws and national security.

When aliens are found deportable, charges are initiated and served upon such aliens and arrested through a combined operation by both agencies. Removal proceedings, as it is now called, commenced when such charging documents are filed with the Executive Office of Immigration Review (EOIR), a separate immigration judiciary arm that reviews and adjudicate the cases. These agencies all operates under the judicial capacity of the office of the U.S Department of Justice. The Executive Office of Immigration Review is presided over by immigration judges who are conferred with judicial authority to adjudicate immigration cases filed by the agency with the immigration courts. The agency of course is represented by the prosecuting attorneys at the federal government's expense, while the embattled aliens are either represented by themselves or by accredited immigration counsels at their own expense.

Just like in criminal matters, aliens subject to deportation are required to enter their pleadings in regards to the excludable charges levied against them....either in person or through their counsels, if they can afford one.

Uncontested pleadings takes an average of 3 weeks to 90 days to conclude for aliens held in detention...either such aliens are afforded relief from removal or not. While contested pleadings for aliens detained in the agency's custody may drag for as long as 6 months to a year, or even years to resolve. This is due to, often times, cosmetic delays and continuances and unnecessarily delayed appeal process that typically takes forever in some highly contested cases like that of Thompson.

Ever since the Bush administration turned the U.S. immigration enforcement into an all out politicized war against all immigrants living in the country, and turned immigration justice and its enforcement into a discretionary business instead of the statutory standard of justice that is required by law, most aliens contesting their removal charges are subject to remain detained under the agency's custody all through such lengthy appeal period. Very few deportable aliens held at the agency's detention are afforded the privilege to remain at large by granting them bond while contesting their removal charges. After such lengthy years in the U.S immigration custody, some of these aliens still end up getting being removed back to their countries any way. Quite a few usually end up with their case on a good note after all the torment they have been subjected to by the agency.

Being forcefully returned to one's country is not necessarily the worse experience for some aliens. Some aliens are relatively okay socioeconomically and otherwise upon their arrival back home. It has definitely been a heck of a nightmare for majority of foreigners going through deportation process under very harsh confinement condition in a foreign state like United States while awaiting removal. Repatriating foreign nationals back to their countries for whatever offenses they might have committed, which fairly justifies such expulsion from such foreign states, is itself not such a terrible thing or the worse form of punishment, but the troubling part is the manner to which the aliens are being treated in their removal process by the government of some foreign states......the

U.S. Bush-Cheney/Trump administrations and the nation's right-wing Republican faction, to be more specific.

The Bush administration made it seem like the foreigners residing in America are America's biggest problem that not only needs to be kicked out, but needs to be tormented first before they get kicked out of the country.

The manner to which the Bush/Trump administrations along with their Republican policymakers in Washington had mandated the nation's immigration agency to apprehend, detain and repatriate foreign nationals back to their individual countries has been very cruel, disgraceful, degrading and shameful way of returning foreigners back to their countries of origin. American born citizens have not always been so law abiding while abroad either. They engage in all forms of unlawful acts that you can possibly imagine while temporarily or permanently residing abroad as well. They break laws while in foreign states just like the foreign nationals the American government accuses of breaking its laws in America.....may be even worse.

However though, no country across the globe known to have ever subjected any American citizens who broke the laws of a sovereign state to such a cruel and inhumane repatriation treatment like the Bush/Trump administrations had done to aliens subject to removal back to their homelands. One good turn, or a bad one, deserves another.

Whichever way you treat someone is the same way you should expect to be treated in return.

When its all said and done, the aliens who still ends up with a final order of removal, as the agency now calls it, are passed on to the agency's designated Deportation Officers (D.O.) whose job is to make the necessary request and contacts to secure travel documents from such aliens' individual Consular offices in Washington, D.C., or in other U.S. cities, to effect their removal. Some Embassies are more responsive in issuing travel documents to deport their citizens than some. While some Embassies just flat out declines to do so. Reasons are: some of these countries do not have diplomatic ties with the U.S. government. So their Embassies do not exist in the U.S......like the case of Cuba, N. Korea, Laos and others. Some have very minimal diplomatic standings with the United States and therefore feels very reluctant to issue travel documents to deport their citizens back home. These diplomatic disparities among these nations goes way back in time. Vietnam, for example, is just recently slowly transcending those old wounds with United States. Its president visited Washington in 2006 for the first time since the Vietnam war.

Some former communist states like China, some former Yugoslavia Balkan states, Ukraine and others, takes quite a while before they finally issue travel document to deport their citizens. So also is India. These nations that do not accept their deportee citizens back, or at least are somewhat reluctant in doing so initially before they might later accept them, have legitimate reasons in some situations not to do so. While the U.S. government feels like it has its justified reason to remove these foreigners from its territorial soil. The nations that have not been quite friendly with the United States for quite some time feels that they are not obligated to accept United States liabilities....even though the deportees aliens are undoubtedly nationals of those countries.

Like India for example, if any of its citizens are found deportable from United States and lived in the country continuously for 10 years or more, it reasons that such Indian deportees have become pretty much integrated to American society and would be socioeconomically detrimental to such individuals to be forced back to a country they have left for that long and suddenly be forced to start afresh to acclimate with things...regardless of the reason behind such removal. India government reasons that this will best serve both the interest of the deportees and that of its government... allowing those who do not want to be forcefully removed to remain in the repatriating nation and be afforded the opportunity to somewhat recoup their lives and may return on their own accord in the near future. This line of diplomatic reasoning is much better for these embattled deportees than the method and policy preferred by the U.S. Immigration agency to strip the deportees naked and be kicked out without being afforded any chance to secure their equities on the streets of America before being kicked out for whatever reason that might have been.

China also share similar reasoning. Holding to such humanitarian reasoning on behalf of their embattled citizens subject to expulsion in a foreign state like America. India, China, among other nations, normally declines to issue travel documents for their deportee citizens, if they have continuously resided in foreign states for at least 10 years, or a relatively reasonable period of time. In the case of China, its government usually declines, in most cases, to accept its deportee citizens from United States, whom, prior to such removal proceedings, were U.S. permanent residents for 10 years or more... regardless of the fact that they might have committed whatever offenses in United States that made them subject to removal.

In Chinese government's reasoning, it contends that if any of its citizens who have been lawful permanent residents for 10 years or more, is believed to have fully integrated into the America society, and later on the line commits crimes that subjects them deportable, the United States should deal with such liability. China holds that its U.S. permanent resident citizens who committed crimes in America should be punished accordingly in America for their offenses and afterwards remain there in America. Holding that it is in fact the America society that turned them into criminals and not China. Since they were not criminals before they left China, Chinese government feels like they are not obliged to accommodate such liabilities from the American government....even though it is indisputable fact that these individuals are its citizens.

The American society bred them to become criminal-minded individuals and should be dealt with solely by such society that made them what they have become.....and not passing such liabilities to their countries of birth that did not have any part in what their foreign-based citizens have become in foreign countries. After all, American government never sought to expel those foreign-born celebrities or those foreigners considered an asset to the nation's economy....like all the international brains providing invaluable intellectual skills for the day-to-day operation of U.S. Tech. sector like Google, Face Book, Microsoft, among others.

Just a visit to the headquarters of any of these tech companies in the U.S will amaze anyone the vast number of foreign brains from various countries dispensing their intellects necessary for the daily running of these companies. Those sets of foreign nationals are regarded by the companies they serve as well as the U.S. government as very valued and indispensable asset to the company and to the country. As it accommodates the good ones, so also should it accommodate the ones who fell short. Sadly, that is not even the underlying reason for the nation's right-wing Republicans relentless pursuit to expel foreign nationals from America.

Anyone with a bilaterally sound sense of judgment can see that these countries that exercise some level of caution before deciding either to accept their deportee citizens or not, in fact, have a valid point here.... that they are doing what best serves the interest of their nations and that of their prosecuted foreign-based citizens. It is of course a different story when foreign nationals are found deportable abroad without any legal status in such countries. In such situation, if the deportee aliens can be identified by their consul abroad that they are in fact citizens of the countries they are claiming, then such states would have no choice but to accept their deportee citizens...like the case of most of the Mexicans who are predominantly undocumented residents in the U.S... Still, diplomatic reservations are always best by every consulates to exercise before taking either action on that ground.

There is just no legal justification to explain away the draconian laws put in place by the Bush/Trump administrations and their fellow vast-right conservative policymakers in Washington to strip permanent resident aliens from their permanent residency status. As soon as they commit the very least crimes, the government is ready and waiting to capitalize on the offense to subject them removable from the country right after they finish serving the punishment for their offenses. Punishment already served by the offense committed by such permanent resident aliens should be more than enough and not to further subject them to deportation on top of their already served punishment.

What the Bush/Trump administrations has championed and condoned on immigration policies in America amounts to double jeopardy. Foreign nationals, particularly legal resident aliens, are being made to pay twice for one offense committed. That is not justice, it is rather an outright strong-arming of the law and of these foreign nationals by the entrenched conservative policymakers in America.

More nations are also catching on to the repatriation schemes of the United States championed by the same rightist Republican leaderships...... as well as those adopted by other Western nations. More nations are becoming increasingly unwilling to accept their foreign-based citizens subject to deportation by some Western states like United States. They have started to realize the socioeconomic consequences those liabilities are causing their government. Regardless of what the Bush/Trump administrations and their right-wingers have been telling the public, repatriation of foreign nationals for whatever reason back to their native countries, is strictly political and in most cases are not on the strength of serving justice as most of the Western nations like the U.S. makes it seem it is to the public.

Of course, nobody wants to hold on to liabilities. That said, you can not always want to select the good at all times and discard the bad. Some bad should be managed and not discarded...because the bad have not always been bad all their lives. Their prior good deeds should not be ignored as well. Sadly, that is the style of the rightist leadership in America today. Life is made up of the good, the bad, and the ugly. There are good and bad people among all people. We all must learn to live with them all.

Most so-called developed Western states like the U.S. are deep in the business of implicit geopolitical and socioeconomic profiling of foreign nationals that hails from certain geographical parts of the world. At the same time some are afforded certain preferential treatments due to their geographical and socioeconomic orientations. It all boils down to survival of the fittest for those being stereotyped this way to do what they got to do to change that stigma. It is largely up to individual foreign states to adopt policies that will best suit its government's interest and the interest of its citizens. It would be unrealistic for any nation to think or assume that another nation would care more about the next man's sovereign state's interests than the owners of the states themselves.

In today's day and age, nations got to do what they got to do to protect the interest of their people.....regardless of how the next nation might want to perceive such move.

It is very reasonable for some of these nations to consider several factor to determine if it is in their best interest, holding to case by case circumstances, to accept back all their foreign-based deportee citizens or not because most repatriations, especially from the so-called Western nations, is nothing but an indirect way of shifting burdens or liabilities from one party to the other party. While some repatriations are legitimate, most are outright the opposite and unlawful.

Despite the remarkable criticism of the Bush/Trump administrations' anti-immigrant policies, every sovereign nation has the absolute right to regulate the influx of foreigners into its territorial land....to make sure the nation's socioeconomic resources can adequately sustain its population. But in such nation like United States where almost everybody's lineage can be traced back in time to that of immigrant ancestors, and in fact has been and still remain the cornerstone of its strength, such increased migrants influx is needed to further expand the nations' population and its economic strength. Such a massive expulsion of these group of people by the nation's right-wing conservative leaderships is gravely a major blunder and a counterproductive one for sure. Sadly for America, those foreign nationals being ruthlessly flushed out of the country are essentially part of the equation to put the country back to its prior economic state.

To be clear, it is unmistakably and equally reasonable to root out any undesirable foreign elements that are more of economic impediment and liabilities to such nations than being part of the growth. But the Trump administration's immigration enforcement policy conferred upon the nation's immigration agency, have been busy year on out since he took office in 2017.....even more ruthless than Bush-Cheney who started these brutal raids. in rooting out both the undesirable as well as the desirable foreigners out of the country by any and every means necessary...... including the use of lawful and unlawful means.

The so-called undocumented aliens caught by the local Sheriff Chief, Joe Arpaio in Phoenix, Arizona during the Bush-Cheney era were housed in an open desert land under tents till they are subsequently processed and deported. Some are even punished to serve jail term there for up to 6 months or more for unlawful entry before getting deported. Such open field tent in Phoenix holds up to 2,000 detainees in a fenced open land either during the hottest summer or at the coldest winter season. The detainees' complaint over their cruel and unusual confinement condition fell on deaf ears all year round on a yearly basis. This is just one of the detention camps used by the Bush and now Trump administrations' immigration agency to enforce their brutal immigration policies towards foreigners. Other ones are in Texas, California, among other states.

Donald Trump has sadly taken up the mantle where Bush left off... this time, parents and their little kids and babies are apprehended along the U.S. Mexico border and held in these open field/warehouse-like spaces indefinitely till they are forcefully kicked out of the country... including families from Central America who fled danger of persecution in their countries. The most cruel part of it is when these babies are being forcefully separated and taken away from their parents at these detentions.

It's extremely heartbreaking and quite emotional scenario to watch these kids cry for their parents while being tricked away to undisclosed location by U.S. government Immigration officials. This events took place in Texas after Trump took office in 2017. This is nothing short of child kidnapping offense if this act was performed by any private individual or an entity…but the U.S. government officials has gotten away perpetrating such horrifying crime against minors with impunity.

# 27

# PRICE TAGS FACED BY MIGRANTS JUST TO REACH AMERICA

THE PRICE PAID BY MIGRANTS FROM various parts of the world to migrate either temporarily or permanently to typical Western nations like the United States are relatively varied....depending of the immigrants' socioeconomic or political circumstances. A case in point is the price associated with recent time migration to America for whatever that reason might be by foreign nationals across the globe.

Some people sacrificed little to nothing to come to America. Some are sponsored by parents or other family members. Some are sent through government sponsored programs; some are even brought to America by the American government itself, or through private interests; while some sacrificed their entire livelihoods just to make it to America. It cost some immigrants arms and legs, while it cost some absolutely nothing to reach America.

Whatever the case, life in America, particularly since the nineties ('90s) through the turn of the 20th century, has not quite measured up to most economic migrants' expectations of what America used to be. Some immigrants have sacrificed a little too much to relocate to America in recent time, but came to find out that the anticipated high expectations they looked forward to has drastically changed and is no longer holding up to the impression and image of the country which it once was known to be by the outside world. Or perhaps the new wave of immigrants have failed to acknowledge the reality that America has in fact been slowly drifting away from its "milk and honey" hey days since the late '80s, and those high expectations for good life and all the likes have also been diminishing thereon after.

These days, upon some immigrants long anticipated arrival in the so-called land of infinite opportunities, they are instantly faced with the rude awakening....discovering that the price tags they have put in line to seek better life in America was either too much, or not quite worth the headache. Most migrants these days are faced with the actual reality of things after a short stay in America that they have actually sacrificed a relatively stable and predictable life back home for an unstable and unpredictable one in America. There are quite a lot of sad odysseys of this nature among a huge number of foreigners living in America today... especial among those who came under the impression of securing a better life, thinking America is still what it used to be.

After having sacrificed so much to get so little, they feel stuck on the struggle...hoping to someday strike that depraved balance that looks like a mirage. They hope to at least recapture that back home nostalgic flavor which has long been compromised ever since their departure from their homelands. Forever daydreaming and anticipating for the so-called better life in America. Quite a lot of foreigners have found themselves caught up in this awkward situation...not only those who came to America. It applies to folks who migrated to other parts of the world as well. The struggle to some of these migrants has got to a 'no retreat-no surrender' type of situation. Why? Because so much has been put at stake with almost nothing back in return. A small loss has been allowed to escalate into a huge one...with so much time expended to arrive at something lesser than what was sacrificed to get there in the first place.

Some immigrants' ordeal in America is like being stuck at the point of no return. They have come to discover the real deal to the so-called better life they came to seek in America. Better life which to a lot of immigrants seem more like an illusion than what they had anticipated of experiencing upon their arrival in America.

It is often very easy to get fooled by the American media networks when viewed abroad, especially in one's own country......conveying relatively hyperbolic impressions of the glitters and the good life in America like no other place...cravingly making these outsiders have distorted impressions, thinking that America is undoubtedly the only promise land for all and nowhere else. A land supposedly filled all over the place with milk, bread and butter, and even honey...a universal symbol of good living, an utopia setting.

In other words, America was once that relevant land during its hey days when freedom and opportunity reigned for all... when immigrants were not being harassed and deprived of their freedom by the rightist faction of the nation. Those who migrated to America then were living those realities. In contrast with today's America, those milky days have long become a bygone era. America still continues to be misconstrued by some outsiders as still that land of the good old days where everything flourishes. It is still being showcased that way to the rest of the world today. The vast-right conservatives who always cajole their way into national policy making, have sadly turned America that was once the land of the free and that of opportunities for all into a land of 'pies in the sky,'...pies that can only be seen from a distance, but not close enough for grabs. America in its hey days was commonly identified everywhere as the "God's own country",...which symbolizes how great God was actually blessing and watching over the nation. Those were the days when the fear of God, moral conducts and respect for humanity were everyone's utmost priority. God was very pleased with America in those days. Once its temperamental conservative leaders and the so-called free-market conservative corporate players allowed greed and love of money to trump their love for God, America started to deteriorate from its bestowed glory and grace days.

## (a)   The Migratory Odyssey

-- ***THE MIGRATORY ODYSSEY:*** Undoubtedly, America has wielded enormous impression in the minds of the outside world to the extent that people still continue to risk their lives by taking dangerous back door routes just to make it to the so-called promised land. Some even lose their lives in the process. Thousands of Mexicans and other Central American citizens venture into America through the Arizona, Texas, New Mexico and California border states between United States and Mexico. While majority of these Spanish migrants survives this odyssey, some never made it.

Jose Pedro, one of the thousands of Mexican migrants who survived several days of trekking across the blazing hot Arizona desert from Mexico, shared a heart-felt narrative of how he made it through the vast Arizona desert into the U.S. from Mexico, with fellow migrants held at theYork, Pennsylvania immigration detention facility. Thompson met with Pedro while at this facility. "Along this vast Arizona desert, we came across the remains of fallen fellow migrants who either lost their lives due to dehydration, or might have ran out of food they needed to sustain them through the long stretch of desert land we journey to America", Pedro recounted. He went further on to narrate how life —threatening this long crucial expedition in pursuit of better life and economic opportunity in America could turn for those who are not extremely brave to endure thirst and hunger, not even to mention being attacked by wild desert snakes and other deadly reptiles in the desert when they resort to take short rests at night to recoup some of their depleted strength before they resume their journey the next day.

They also have to be mindful of the U.S. patrol helicopters hovering across the desert, hunting to zero in on them while they are trying hard to sneak into the country. Once they see or hear the sound of an helicopter approaching, they must immediately duck under cover to avoid being spotted. Some get spotted just like that and get sent home before they even make it across the desert. These are risks taken by individuals as young as 13 years of age and adults alike. Even migrants from other far countries like China, India, Brazil, Egypt, Pakistan, among other countries also ply this back door routes of land and water along these border states with U.S. and Mexico.

Pedro said that "It is common to get bitten by snakes while migrants tries to catch a little sleep. The only way to guard against this is if anyone among the entourage was mindful enough to carry a particular chemical compound with pungent and irritating smell that keeps the snakes away from getting close and biting them while they are asleep", he added. Some of these migrants lose their lives just like that at this desert from snake bites and never made it to their destination. Nonetheless, these predominantly Hispanic migrants never stop crossing these dangerous borders to enter America......thinking it's still worth the risk.

The Bush administration, before leaving office commenced a 700 mile, 50 feet high fence across the Arizona border with Mexico. Part of the administration's effort to deter the influx of illegal immigrants, specifically the Mexicans, from sneaking into the country. The nation's agricultural sector, and a wide range of other businesses have been badly affected as a result. Some states were hit so hard by the Bush-Cheney administration's mass-expulsion of immigrants. This led in part to serious economic downturn across the nation in late 2007. Most businesses, particularly the agricultural sector were so badly affected with workforce shortages at some point during this period of reckless immigration sweep. The sweep started to have very major impact on workforce shortages mainly at the nation's agricultural sector to the extent that state governments in various states have to lend some helping hands to assist these businesses push for an expedited workers program that could allow foreign workers to come in the country under a H-1-6 Guest-Worker visa on a temporary basis to fill in for these labor shortages.

How awkward that is when the same workforce are being kicked out of the country at a very alarming rate, while arrangement is also being put in place to bring in more workforces to fill in for the nation's labor shortfall in some industrial sectors of the economy. Those already in the country are being kicked out by the administration and at the same time making provision to bring in new foreign workers to fill in for these jobs.

Obama came in 2009 and did all he could to minimize the reckless raids and mass-deportation for 8 years while Republicans were trying their hardest to keep it 'business as usual' as Bush-Cheney had left it. Fast-forward to 2017, Donald Trump of all people won the 2016 presidential election. Prior to the election, he has been ranting all along about his hatred towards immigrants......particularly the Mexicans and those from Central American countries. Since he got in office he has kept the main promise that got him enough votes to get elected...hunting down and deporting immigrants by any means necessary...legal or illegal. Those who went and voted for him feels the very same way he feels towards immigrant.....hatred. There is no other mild way to put it. Trump's words and actions clearly shows his level of resentment towards immigrants from particular regions of the globe.

Manuel Cruz, another Mexican migrant held at the York facility also shared his own version of backdoor crossing through the Mexico-Texas border. The Texas border crossing is by water. This means that such contestants attempting to cross through the Texas area must have some swimming skills to make it across the water. The river is as deep as 7 feet and takes an average of 10 to 15 minutes to swim across. "The worse part in the river crossing is that the river looks pretty calm on the surface, but there are sometimes strong under-current strong enough to sweep away the swimmers' foot underneath. Some of these immigrants crossing this Texas river have minimal swimming skills to withstand such undercurrent tides. As a result, some end up getting swept under by the strong tide and drown inside the river", Cruz shared. He further added that, "some of the migrants just don't have enough strength to swim through the width of the river to reach the opposite end of its bank. They end up drowning at the middle of the river. Only the brave and the very skilled ones survives this Texas river crossing," The coyotes can pilot them safely across the river, but for those who can not afford the fee they charge, they have no other choice but to attempt the crossing on their own.

Some of the coyotes even use an inflated tire-shaped latex tubes for this crossing. The latex tubes are inflated and up to three people who are not very good swimmers are tightly fitted half way to their shoulders within the donut-like hole, while two proficient coyote swimmers pilots the tube from the opposite end. Each of the pilot coyotes lock in one elbow with one of the guys fitted within the tube, while they use their other arm to swim, piloting along the non-swimmers with the tube across the river. This strategy gives the rest non-proficient swimmers a level of assurance that, if anything, they at least will not end up drowning while attempting to cross the river into Texas. Such coyote border crossing service is widely used by most Brazilian and Venezuelan migrants who come to the U.S. through the backdoor. This odyssey is not cheap either. Such coyote-assisted river crossing through the Mexico-Texas border cost an average of $7,000 to $10,000 per person to arrive in U.S. if such pilot escort deal is struck from the migrants' country of origin. But the coyote fee just to cross someone across the river from the Mexico border town to Texas is between $1,500 to $3,000. The fee is fully earned when the coyote succeeds to get the migrants through into the U.S. territory and even lodge them in some cheap motel for a night or two before they finally split to their various destinations thereon after. A Brazilian migrant, Batista, gave this narrative of how he came to the U.S. and how much he had paid for the Mexican coyote service through the Texas river crossing.

Pedro, Cruz and Batista all met with Thompson at the immigration detention facility in York, Pennsylvania back in 2008. Pedro and Cruz both got scooped up at a meat processing plant in Dallas, Texas as undocumented immigrants. Batista was first apprehended by the Immigration authorities while he was traveling on a Greyhound bus from Dallas en route to New York after he had successfully got into the country, but was processed and luckily paroled and required to report to the agency on a later date which he never went. He was stopped by a Philadelphia cop 4 years later and was turned over to the immigration authorities who identified him as a fugitive alien. He was apprehended and detained in York facility and subsequently sent back to Brazil.

Pedro also elaborated on how some of these migrant border crossers across the Arizona desert sometimes get robbed by other fellow stranded migrants of their only food and water they desperately relied upon, or just basically become physically unfit to survive the horrific nights and days of trekking through the desert heat.

For those who survives the border crossing ordeals, their next hurdle is to hope and pray that their suffering through the border do not end up in vain. While quite a lot made it through, some unfortunately get caught by the U.S. Border Patrol right at their point of entering into America. Those caught are immediately handed over to the Immigration agency and get sent back home. When this happens, such setback means that they either have to try their luck all over again across these dangerously rough borders...... hoping that they get lucky and make it through on their second try.

Some even attempt these delicate border crossing up to 3 or 4 times before they finally get successful to enter and take their survival chances in America.....hoping to offset the deadly migratory risk.....they took in search for better life abroad.

The obsession of high expectation of better life in America has pushed some of these migrants way overboard to the extent that some even risk being put in jail for reentry after having been deported for the first or second time and have been barred not to reenter the country legally or illegally for a given probationary period of time.

The so-called American dream continue to seem more like an illusion than reality in recent time, and getting even worse as each year unfolds. Today in America, the American dream is more of a nightmare due to the various obstacles put in place by the rightist Americans. The drive to pursue a better life in America by foreigners these days, weighing in on the open-ended sacrifice at stake and the inevitable torments they face or look forward to face from the hands of the nation's ultra-right leaderships, makes such drive and mission seem somewhat unrealistic compared with America during its hey days.

## (b)    The Caribbean Migrants

**--- *THE CARIBBEAN MIGRANTS:*** Most of the citizens from the Caribbean Islands like Haiti, Cuba, and Dominican Republic, among others, also set sail with undersized and overcrowded boats through the Caribbean waters to enter United States via Miami, Florida. Most of the boats they use are relatively small to the number of occupants and the size of the water they navigate. The small boats are just unfit to safely navigate the Caribbean waters en route to the Florida keys. Some of the boats never made it safely across the waters.

Whenever the waters becomes rough and the small boats' relatively light weight are unable to offset the tide, such boats suddenly flips over with all the crowded occupants dumped in the water.

Whenever incidents like this happens, it becomes the survival of the fittest for those who can really stay afloat on the salty water.....hopefully long enough till the U.S. Coast Guards' boat or helicopter is able to spot them and pull them to safety. Such rescues might not come along for hours or even for a whole day, which sometimes might be a little too late to save the life of some of these migrants who were not brave enough like the few others who managed to stay afloat on the sea for that long. Sadly, many of such Caribbean migrants have lost their lives just like that on the high sea, especially the Haitians and the Cubans, on their attempt to reach America to pursue better lives.

Sometimes these boats are spotted by the U.S. Coast Guards who immediately go to their rescue and bring them to safety before the small overcrowded boats end up capsizing and sink. The lucky ones who gets rescued usually gets processed and resettled in Florida. Those were the good old days of the '80s and the early '90s. Such good Samaritan role by the U.S. government, at least by the Republican conservative leadership, is long gone. When Mr. Bush took office in 2001 through his 8 years presidency, his administration abolished such humanitarianism and resettlement policy for the Caribbean boat migrants, particularly the

Haitians rescued at the high sea heading to Miami. Before he left office, Mr. Bush himself authorized the nation's immigration agency to repatriate the Haitians and other Caribbean migrants, rescued from the Caribbean waters, immediately back to their homelands......regardless of their reasons for such risky odyssey.

During the '90s there have been several instances of mid-size boats packed with Caribbean migrants anchoring at mid-water to the Florida shores to discharge their occupants at about 400 to 500 meters away from the Miami shore. These smuggled migrants have to dive into the water and swim the rest of the distance to reach the shore. Such evacuation of the boats must be done very swiftly by the boats' owners to avoid being spotted by the U.S. Coast Guards and be charged for unlawful human smuggling into the country.

Some of the occupants of the human smuggling boats are not quite skilled in swimming, or at least have never swum on huge water of such magnitude, but the blend of urge and fatal excitement in them at that very moment makes them ignore the underlying risk of drowning upon their desperate attempt to swim their way to the promised land.

Jean Baptiste, an Haitian immigrant who entered the United States through one of these human smuggling boats back in 1993, shared an exclusive account of his voyage from Port O' Prince harbor to Miami shore. "While on the high sea, the high tides threatens to overturn our mid-size passenger boat as we navigated our way across the Caribbean waters en route to the Florida keys. After surviving the wicked tidal twist and turns that almost flipped the boat, myself and the rest occupants of the boat were made to dive into the water to swim our way to the Miami shore......a stretch of about 500 meters of salty water to swim", Baptiste narrated. He said he was pretty proficient with swimming, even though he never finished swimming the 500 meters water distance to the shore before the Coast Guard spotted them and came to their rescue. "Not everyone made it to safety. Unfortunately, some of the boat's occupants that was instructed by the boat owner to dive in the water and swim to the shore along with me had drowned before the Coast Guard boat arrived. The swimming distance appeared shorter till after we all jumped in the water...plus some of the boat's occupants jumped in the water purely out of the rush and desperation to finally reach the so-called land of opportunity. But shortly afterwards, they discover that they were not skilled enough or physically fit to swim such long stretch of deep water. A lot of Caribbean boat migrants have lost their lives this way before they could make it to America....the dream land", Baptiste added.

In some of these nations, it is understandable that most of their citizens are facing grinding state of poverty and feels that they rather die in the process of trying to better their lives elsewhere than staying stuck at home within the same cycle of bellow zero socioeconomic mobility. Survival in some third-world struggling countries could be quite hectic and critical to prompt some of their citizens taking certain deadly risks to try and escape such cycle of economic hardship to where the grass is presumably greener. Nonetheless, most people fail to be equally mindful that some grasses that looks greener might not necessarily taste relatively as good as they look from a distance. This has been the case with most migrants who came to America in recent decade under the impression that America is still that place where its grasses continues to remain green at all time...the land of immense opportunity like it was during the '70s and the '80s.

Upon their arrival, they are faced with the rude awakening that those grasses that appears greener was in fact not as delicious as they look from the distance, that those high expectation of better life was in fact no longer in existence, or not a plural affairs as they had thought, and to some, not worth the sacrifice and the risks they had subjected themselves to.

However, to some migrants from nations that are relatively okay and above average economically, undergoing such risks, and the endless torment imposed by the nation's right-wing leaderships, in pursuit of better life in America, is uncalled for and just seem not worth it at all for them these days.

The recent migrants who arrived America after the good old days are discovering that what some people have risked or sacrificed in pursuit of better life in America these days are, in most cases, unrealistic and not worth it upon their final arrival there. The so- called American dream are barely there anymore.

## (c)   The.U.S./Canada Border Crossing

--- ***THE U.S/CANADA BORDER CROSSING:*** The backdoor border crossing from Canada into the U.S. has been in existence also for quite a while, but those who sneak into the U.S. through Canada are not Canadian citizens but citizens of other countries who, in most cases, flew in to Canada and then mangle their way by road, some through the Niagara river via Buffalo, into the U.S... Indians, Pakistanis, Moroccans, Egyptians, Nigerians, migrants from the European countries, among other nationalities ply this U.S/ Canadian border route. The traffic, however is nowhere near that of the Mexican and Central American migrants flowing through the Arizona, Texas, New Mexico and California border states with Mexico.

Navid Khan, a Pakistani citizen whose dream was to join his older brother at the 'Big Apple', the other name for New York city, took off from Islamabad to Montreal. Even though he had some chance to remain in Canada and eventually acquire his legal residency there, but he just could not settle for anything less than joining his brother at the Big Apple. That relentless desire drove him to abandon his pending application for legal residency with the Canadian government and embarked on plans to take backdoor route to sneak into the United States. His master-plan was to board an 18 wheeler cargo truck en route from Canada to the U.S. along with 5 other migrants of his Pakistani descent.

Navid's older brother, Sahid, who lives in New York, has been very supportive of him financially in sponsoring him to come to the U.S. and join him in New York. Navid tried for two years to no avail to secure U.S. travel document till he finally resorted to obtain a Canadian visa instead, which landed him in Montreal. According to Navid, Sahid have sent him money close to $20,000 just for travel document-related expenses over a 3- year period. Upon reaching Canada, he applied for political asylum in his attempt to establish his legal status there......even though he knew he was an economic migrant. Maybe he would have succeeded in his asylum claim or not, his patience ran out just 6 months into the waiting process. He then embarked on a backdoor mission that he thinks will finally get him to his dream destination...the U.S of A.

As typical of most Western nations today, refugee applications takes quite a while to get processed...but at least Navid was allowed to remain at large on the streets of Canada while his asylum application was pending...unlike the case in United States and Australia that holds refugees in detention for at least a year or more pending the processing of their asylum claim.

In Navid's desperate attempt to maneuver his way into the U.S. to evade the U.S Immigration authorities, he got busted anyway by the U.S. Border Patrol and Customs Enforcement along with his other 5 accomplices inside the tractor trailer cargo vehicle they had hid themselves en route to United States.

Of course this was not a free ride even though they had got busted along the way. Navid and these 5 other accomplices agreed to pay the truck driver $3,000 per person to smuggle them along with his cargo from Canada across to the U.S. The truck driver pockets a cool extra $18,000 for less than a day's truck driving in addition to his original truck driving wage which is nowhere near that. Unfortunately for Navid, his backdoor expedition into America was after the 9/11 incident. The incident has resulted to heightened border security across the country. High security surveillances were put in place at all ports of entries and border crossings into United States since the 9/11 incident. This means that whatever moves or crosses into United States was being thoroughly checked before being green-lighted to proceed into the country....including cars, private and commercial trucks of all sizes.

Navid's luck once again ran aground when this truck they were smuggled in got stopped at the border crossing between Canada and United States' territory by the U.S. Customs and Border Protection agency.

As the truck search ensued, one of the custom officers came across a white transparent plastic container, half filled with a yellowish-brown looking fluid upon walking into the narrow unloaded space of the truck's cargo section. This finding aroused the custom officers to persist in their search further into the rest of the cargo space which was loosely packed with boxes of goods stacked to the truck's roof. One of the officers opened the container containing the urine-looking substance and suspected the smell to be human urine. That further indicated to them that some human beings were possibly hidden somewhere inside the cargo trailer. The search continued till one of the custom officers eventually discovered Navid and his rest accomplices well tucked inside various plastic lockers that look very identical to the rest other cargoes en route to the U.S.....stacked at the front-end of the truck's cargo space.

Navid and Co. were all standing inside these lockers which were large and tall enough to fit their bodies individually...with the doors slightly cracked open for air and to enable them squeeze in and out to urinate inside the plastic container situated at relatively distant end of the truck, away from their hide out spot. It seemed like a pretty smooth and a well orchestrated hide out strategy. But the urine container gave them away to be discovered by the U.S. Immigration authorities, which Navid, in particular, was trying to avoid.

The bust consequently ended Navid's and his companions' anticipated trip to America. The setback dealt a major blow to Navid's odyssey to get to the land of his dreams....after all his efforts. He of course was apprehended along with the five other accomplices and they all end up at the same immigration detention facility in York, Pennsylvania, where Thompson was held. At this detention facility, like various others across the country, every detained immigrant has a unique and an intriguing story to share with their fellow detainees.

After his failed attempt to make it to his dream destination....the Big Apple......and the money that has gone to waste in the process, Navid felt like he is once again back to square zero. This means that he would be sent back to his native Pakistan. He was 29 years old then in 2007. Thompson inquired about his prospects upon his return back home...if he would give it another shot to attempt coming back to America, or go elsewhere when he gets home. "I want to get myself situated once I get home and get married and move on with my life in Pakistan. I have wasted enough time and my brother's hard-earned money on my obsession to reach America. Despite all the time and money sacrificed, here I am in prison waiting to get deported after getting caught trying to sneak into another man's country with no proper travel document. A lot of people made it through, but I guess I was not as fortunate as them. When I get home this time. I shall learn to be content with my country." Navid asserted.

## (d)   After-effects and Reality Check

   *--- **AFTER EFFECTS AND REALITY CHECK:*** In some cases, experience is the best and only teacher, and seeing is believing. Some people are just persistently hard-headed and loves to learn their lessons the hard way, while some people learn their valuable lessons from the experience of others and avoid being victims of similar pitfalls...as well as learning to be sometimes content with what they have, instead of trying

too hard to reach for a goal that comes with unreasonable and excessive price tag. It is in fact a very painful feeling to endure when people come to discover much too late that they have expended way too much resources and time on a mission that was not even worth such price tag. As a result of such irreversible sacrifices, they become stuck and complacent with the dead-end struggle that continues to stifle their growth and that has, in most cases, cost them the most valuable prime time of their lives......like someone pursuing an illusive goal.

Thousands of foreign nationals from various countries like India, China, Russia, Brazil, and those from certain African countries like Nigeria, Ghana, South Africa, among many other countries nationals who were residing in the U.S. as legal or non- legal residents continue to pack their bags on their own accord and return to their various countries to resettle. They finally came to grip with the economic and other reality of things in America of the 21$^{st}$ century. In fact, life in general and the economic mobility for average citizens in most of these countries mentioned are now much better for them than the lifestyle lived by their peers in the U.S. these days.

Living condition has drastically changed in America for worse in recent decade and seem to be getting worse as each year unfolds. Those returning home on their own accord like the Indians, Brazilians, Nigerians, among others, are making much better lives for themselves back home than the 'pie-in-the-sky' lifestyle they were living back in America after the toxic policies of the nation's vast-right group continues to drag the once outstanding nation towards the path of doom.

A case in point is the Brazilians returning home in recent years in the thousands from the U.S., due in part to the nation's ever harsher immigration policies put in place and aggressively enforced by the Bush-Cheney/Trump administrations. Such trend has been noticed in states like Florida and New Jersey where a large number of Brazilians have settled.

Speaking of obtaining their so-called legal residency status in the U.S., it has basically become impractical and untenable for the Brazilians as well as millions of such undocumented foreign nationals these days in America. Their best bet is to leave all the undue headache, stress and all other baggage behind, which these days seem not worth it anymore, to go and start a new and fresh life back in their countries, which in most cases have changed economically and otherwise for better in recent time of this 21$^{st}$ century.

It is however a different story in the case of true political migrants who was forced to flee their homelands to escape persecution....seeking refuge protection in a foreign state. These category of migrants, by international law, are and should be exempt from forceful expulsion back to the countries which they had fled persecution. This exemption does not necessarily mean that they are also immuned or precluded from punishment if they broke the law of such foreign states that granted them the refuge protection. But such punishment goes overboard and inhumane when any foreign state that is a signatory to the Geneva Convention Treaty, forcefully removes or attempts to repatriate Geneva Convention refugees back to their homelands of feared persecution for having committed and already been punished for relatively non-violent or particularly non-serious offenses...knowing that it is a violation of the Convention's protocol and a human right violation as well.

For refugees who fled their homelands due to genuine threat of persecution, they have no choice but to put up with whatever torments they are subjected to in foreign states....all because such refugees are afraid to be returned home where they may lose their lives. All the countries that are signatories to the Convention's protocol are prohibited of taking advantage of such refugees' fearful situation of being forcefully returned back to their countries of feared persecution to torment their lives instead in indefinite immigration detention. The law prohibits the signatory states of forcefully repatriating refugees. This type of torment is a form of mental torture and was widely okayed and approved by the Bush- Cheney administration to be inflicted on Geneva convention foreign nationals held under the nation's immigration custody.

A lot of foreign national who was admitted as Geneva Convention refugees in United States have been forcefully removed back to their countries of feared persecution during and by the Bush-Cheney's administration as a result of his approved immigration policy......for these refugees having committed relatively minor offenses that are waivable by certain immigration provision already codified in the immigration law by the U.S Congress. The same treatment continues now with Trump in office.

As a refugee, when you challenge the legality of your removal, like the case of Thompson, the Bush/Trump administrations leaves you to languish indefinitely at the agency's various immigration detention facilities across the country till you eventually get exhausted and give in to be sent back home. This has been the Bush-Cheney/Trump administrations' approved style of justice for foreigners today in America.

## (e)   The Golden Venture Odyssey

*--- **THE GOLDEN VENTURE ODYSSEY:** In* 1993, a small mid-size passenger boat, 'Golden Venture', packed with about 400 Chinese migrants from China, ran aground in Long Island, New York. All the occupants were instructed by the boat owner to jump overboard and swim their way to the Long Island shore. Some who were not very skilled in such huge and deep water swimming ended up drowning. However, majority of them were rescued by the U.S. Coast Guard and subsequently held in detention pending their ostensible claim of asylum. Even though it was apparently clear that most of them were economic migrants. They were all detained at the same immigration detention facility in York, Pennsylvania. In fact, these Chinese migrants were the very first set of immigration detainees ever detained at this county prison by the Immigration authority before the prison got expanded years later to accommodate more undocumented or deportable aliens to be processed for deportation. Bill Clinton was the president at that time. Even though a Democrat president was running the country at the time, the nation's immigration laws was predominantly underwritten by the right-wing Republican Congressional policymakers who were the majority at both Houses of Congress at the time.

Quite a few of these Chinese migrants were able to secure bond to be released to the custody of their relatives or countrymen residing in United States pending the decision on their asylum applications. The rest of them had no other choice but to remain in detention pending the outcome of their asylum claims. This particular incident aroused both national and international attention, because it was one of the largest, if not the largest, one trip mass-smuggling of migrants into America in such a manner. Plus, some lives were lost in the process.

The U.S. Coast Guard's surveillance camera captured the whole event as it unfolds. Some of them unfortunately drowned while the rest got rescued to jail.

Of course, no one is suggesting that the U.S. government, or any other government should just allow such large number of smuggled aliens into their soil if it's not an extremely life-threatening situation. At least the U.S. government could have held them at a civil camp like those typically used to accommodate refugees, instead of detaining them among criminals in jail. About 300 of this 'Golden Venture' smuggled entourage was detained at this York, Pa. facility for at least 2 years, during which some of them gave up and requested to be returned to China. China at that time was still a relatively communist setting. China, like most other countries, do not condone any of its citizens abroad ridiculing its internal affairs and human right flaws with foreign governments. Such sense of disloyalty of one's sovereign country to other sovereign states is taken very seriously by China and most nations across the globe.... especially communist or dictatorship regimes.

To establish their claim for asylum, they had to divulge their nation's harsh communist style of governance and the various forms of human right abuses they claimed to have suffered in the hands of their government human right conditions in which China today has impressively improved on in comparison to the Bush-Cheney administration's human right abuse record over their 8 years of leadership in America. And now comes Trump detaining migrant parents indefinitely while their kids/babies are being separated and forcefully taken away from them to undisclosed locations.

As the news of this Golden Venture Chinese migrants spreads across the globe at the time, the Chinese government was also aware of the stories its detained citizens in America was sharing with the U.S government regarding China's human rights lapses towards its citizens.

With the international coverage of the incident surrounding their voyage and the loss of lives in Long Island coastline, coupled with their troubling account of things about their government to establish their asylum claim with the U.S. authorities, it was undoubtedly a very tough decision for some of these Chinese detainees to decide being sent back home after having waited in detention for over a year and their asylum claims were still pending.... knowing the type of treatment and punishment they may be subjected to by their government upon their arrival home.

With the exponential level of economic growth in China today, life now may have turn up for good for those set of Golden Venture crews who, after a very lengthy period of detainment by the American Immigration authority, decided to be sent back home to face the music rather than to languish in U.S. Immigration custody fighting to stay in America. With the economic state of things in China these days, there is definitely no Chinese person who will undertake such risky odyssey any more just to come to America in search of better life. In fact, they are making life much better for themselves these days in China than even some of their peers who are in America. It's quite funny how things could change sometimes for the better over time.

Also, China's respect for human right has change significantly since the start of the 21st century and has been far better than the United States' Bush-Cheney administration's....according to International Human Rights Organizations' human rights report ratings conducted during Mr. Bush's eight years tenure as the U.S. president.

The very same vast-right conservative Republican policymakers in Washington are the same ones who drafted the 1996 immigration bill and persuaded Mr. Clinton to sign it into law. However, Mr. Clinton should have vetoed the bill, but he didn't. A lot of people, including most immigrants blamed Mr. Clinton as the bad guy who started and supported the anti-immigrant policies, instead of blaming the temperamental conservative masterminds at both Houses of Congress who drafted the bill and relentlessly pushed for its enactment.

In 1996, president Clinton signed an order for the release of the rest of the Golden Venture's Chinese detainees held at the York County prison, Pennsylvania, where these smuggled Chinese migrants were detained after 3 years of their crucial expedition to America. If it was a Republican leadership sitting in office at the time, and was only up to the ultra-right conservative leadership in Washington, those Chinese detainees may still be held at the immigration custody till this day, or held there till they all submit to be returned home to face their demise.

The big question is: how much punishment and deprivation to foreigners would be considered, or would be justifiable to the rightist factions in America before they can have a change of heart from their counter-productive hateful nature towards foreign nationals living within their midst? Or does it even worth it anymore for foreigners to endure needless pain and suffering in anticipation for the so-called American dream.....a dream that is increasingly becoming so far-fetch and unrealistic for most American-born citizens and immigrants alike as the years goes by. Immigrants might need to start reflecting on such question before they embark on their trip to America or other supposedly developed countries in search for better life. Maybe they can start somewhere in getting their own domain in order instead of sacrificing too much just to be integrated into a society that would stop at nothing in inflicting their hatefulness in so many ways to make life a living hell on them.

# 28

## THE TORTURE POLICY-ON FOREIGNERS

HAVING ESTABLISHED A FLAWED SENSE OF resentment about foreigners in the minds of most American public including typical ones who already possess such sense of xenophobia for no justifiable reason.....the Bush-Cheney's administration had deceptively impaired the thoughts of most America public to think that all foreign nationals in America were responsible for the 9/11 event and, in effect, should be served their own share of punishment for their role in the incident. The administration's treatment of foreign nationals from all parts of the world through its 8 years leadership in America was unmistakably indicative of that message.....especially right after the 9/11 episode.

Hundreds of thousands of foreign nationals have been embroiled in the administration's amended and the newly added immigration laws. The Laws that were craftily drafted by the rightist faction of the nation's Republican policymakers and signed into law by Mr. Bush, the Enabler-In-Chief himself.......toxic laws that was specifically legislated and intended for causing irreparable damage on foreign nationals within the country. By harming foreigners this way, Mr. Bush, along with his vast-right teamsters still in the helm of policy-making in Washington today after he left office, continues to be very delighted to see foreigners suffer and be subjected to shameful and tormentual situations for no justifiable cause. These rightist factions across America today fails to realize, or cares less to recall that they themselves, going few generations back, were sons and daughters of immigrant parents who came to America from another part of the world as well.

The Bush administration's policy of forceful mass-deportation of foreigners have not only been detrimental to the lives of the deportees, but also have taken terrible tolls in the lives of their American-born kids and families. To be exact, it adds a great deal of socioeconomic strain on the government and the citizens of the countries of which these aliens are designated to be returned. The adverse effect of this ruthless immigration policy championed by the vast-right Republican extremists in America is equally as devastating to America as a nation as much as it has been on foreigners. The government, especially the Republican leaderships, will be the last group of people to admit to the crushing economic impact the anti-immigrants policy they champion is causing the nation as a whole. Either the American government, Democrats or Republicans, wish to come to grip with the reality associated with this anti-immigrants policy and the ensuing consequences, or just wants to remain in denial. Continuous aggression of this nature towards foreigners in America is bad business for the country all across the spectrum. Economically speaking, the American free- market conservatives in the corporate sector knows and feels the diminishing economic impact of the nation's policy of the mass-expulsion of immigrants and the adverse toll it has taken on the various economic sectors across America. It has been a major contributing factor plaguing the nation's economy since 2007 till present time.

Such cold-hearted immigration policies has left most affected immigrants with chilled sense of emptiness like they had just got robbed by thieves in broad day light.

Janet Napolitano, the former Democrat governor of the state of Arizona and a former federal prosecutor who prosecuted hundreds of illegals before she moved to the state house, and in 2009 was appointed to serve as DHS secretary under the Obama's administration, signed a strict law in January 2008 with some regret, forcing any business that knowingly hire undocumented workers to loose its license after two offenses. Thus far, there have been thousands of tips about people who look like illegal workers prompting police to chase innumerable bogus complaints. But so far, not a single citation. Not even from Phoenix, home of Maricopa

County Sheriff Joe Arpaio, the self-proclaimed toughest lawman in the West, part of the Lou Dobbs Gasbag Hall of Fame.

Arizona, with an estimated 500,000 illegal immigrants...a state that boast being the nation's busiest gateway for illegal crossing.

The U.S. Immigration agency under the Bush-Cheney administration.....ever since the enactment of the nation's most aggressive immigration policies.....have been engaging in various forms of arrest tactics that have led to outright harassment of foreigners and even citizens on the streets of America.

One case in point occurred in New Haven, Connecticut on June 2007, where the city's administrators was cajoled to be a party to the agency's covert plan to round up undocumented immigrants within the city.

The operation started two days after the city's Board of Alderman had approved plan to offer municipal identification cards to all residents, including an estimated 15,000 illegal immigrants settled in this city of 125,000. The sweep began on June 6 and ended on June 11, 2007.and those arrested by the Immigration and Customs Enforcement (ICE) agency around the New Haven area were scattered to jails in Rhode Island, Massachusetts, and Maine. Following a widespread condemnation of such hostile measure in apprehending the so-called undocumented and fugitive aliens, the then former Homeland Security secretary, Michael Chertoff defended the agency's extreme style of operation as part of a year old "nationwide interior initiative" called "Operation Return to Sender" that applies an organized and methodical approach to the identification, location and arrest of fugitive aliens......immigrants with outstanding orders of deportation.

In response to pointed questions from Connecticut's two senators, Joseph I. Lieberman and Christopher J. Dodd, and Representative Rosa L. De Lawro, whose district includes New Haven, Mr. Chertoff wrote "once intelligence is gathered on several fugitives located within the same general vicinity" a team "will develop an operational plan for the swift and safe arrest of the fugitive aliens in the most fiscally efficient way," According to the agency's policy, wrote Mr. Chertoff, "the team prioritize their effort in the following order: 1). Fugitives who are threat to national security; 2). Fugitives who pose a threat to the community; 3). Fugitives who were convicted of violent crimes; 4). Fugitives who have criminal records; 5).

Non-criminal fugitives." Yet, by Mr. Chertoff's count, only 5 of the 29 arrest in New Haven fits the priorities…apparently the lowest.

Following series of such open-ended harassment of foreigners across the country, several lawsuits were filed against the agency. One of such lawsuits was brought by lawyers at the Center for Social Justice at Seton Hall Law School in Newark, New Jersey, in April 2008 at the federal district court in New Jersey, against officials of Immigration and Customs Enforcement, or ICE, on behalf of 10 plaintiffs, including two United States citizens. The suit contends that teams of ICE agents used "deceit or in some cases, raw force" to gain "unlawful entry" into homes and made arrests without proper warrants during raids to round up immigration fugitives…like the case in New Jersey and several other states across the country. Agents sometimes misrepresent themselves as local police hunting for criminals, entering houses where fugitives being sought were present and detain residents without showing any legal cause.

Immigration agents have broad authority to question foreigners about their immigration status, but they may not enter a home without either a warrant or consent.

These victimized immigrants who have been wronged by the Bush-Cheney and now Trump's anti-immigrant policies and their ruthless enforcement of these policies, might choose to put such crushing experience behind them and move on with their lives, but that does not necessarily imply that they will completely forget about the wrong and the pain associated with such experience they have been subjected to in a foreign land. Any way we choose to look at it, everyone's individual experiences in life inevitably affects and reflects on our future lifestyles to some variable degree on individual basis. Such experience which might have been constructive or counter-productive, will affect us either to become reactive or proactive individuals, or just outright dormant characters.

Whichever way such experience might have impacted these individuals, it is best for the affected individuals to thrive and allow such experience to bring out the proactive futuristic nature out of them. This is a productive mindset that turns ugly experiences into stepping stones, instead of the reactive instinct that arouses reprisal for the wrong suffered.

Nonetheless, it might take some time before America starts to see the adverse effects brought about by the foreign policies championed by the Bush-Cheney/Trump administrations.

## (a)   The Torture Policy

-- ***THE TORTURE POLICY:*** You can tell if someone understands how wrong their actions are by the length to which they go to rationalize them. It took 81 pages of twisted legal reasoning to justify president Bush's decision to ignore federal law and international treaties and authorize the abuse and torture of prisoners. Eighty-one spine-crawling pages in a memo that might have been unearthed from the dusty archives of some authoritarian regime and has no place in the annals of the United States. It is a must read for anyone who still doubts whether the abuse of prisoners were rogue acts rather than calculated policy.

The March 14, 2003 memo was written by John C. Yoo, then a Pentagon lawyer. He later helped draft a memo that redefined torture to justify repugnant, clearly illegal acts against Al Qaeda and Taliban prisoners. The purpose of the March 14 memo was equally insidious: to make sure that the policymakers who carried out those orders, or the subordinates who carried out the orders, were not convicted of any crime. The list of laws that Mr. Yoo sought to circumvent is long: federal laws against assault, maiming, interstate stalking, war crimes and torture; international laws against torture and cruel, inhuman or degrading treatment; and the Geneva Conventions.

Mr. Yoo, who, inexplicably teaches law at the university of California, Berkeley, never directly argue that it is legal to chain prisoners to the ceiling for days, sexually abuse them or subject them to water-boarding...... all things done by American jailers. His primary argument, in which he reaches back to the 19th century legal opinions justifying the execution of Indians who rejected the reservation, is that the law did not apply to Mr. Bush because he is Commander-In-Chief. He cited an earlier opinion from Bush administration lawyers that Al Qaeda and Taliban were not covered by the Geneva Conventions...a decision that puts every captured American soldiers at grave risk. Then, should someone reject his legal reasoning and decided to file charges, Mr. Yoo offered a detailed blueprint for escaping accountability. Sounds quite familiar with what Trump has been pulling since he got elected?

American and international laws prohibits making a prisoner fear "imminent death,' For most people, water-boarding…making a prisoner feel as if he is about to drown….would fit. Mr. Yoo argues that the statutes apply if the interrogators actually intended to kill the prisoner. Since water-boarding simulates drowning, there is no "threat of imminent death."

After the memo's general content were first reported, the Pentagon said in early 2004 that it was "no longer operative," Reading the full text release on April 2008 makes it startlingly clear how deep the Bush-Cheney administration corrupted the law and the role of lawyers to give cover to existing and plainly illegal policies. The memo is also a reminder of how many secrets about the administration's cynical and abusive policies still needs to be revealed. As late Senator Edward Kennedy noted, "the release of the Yoo memo is a reminder that neither Congress nor the American people have seen the policy memos that govern interrogations during the Bush-Cheney reign." Some know of at least two being kept secret for supposed reason of national security, including one authorizing water-boarding.

When the abuses at Abu Ghraib became public, we were told these were depraved actions of few soldiers. The Yoo memo makes it chillingly apparent that senior officials authorized unspeakable acts and went to great lengths to shield themselves from prosecution.

During his November 2010 book tour, promoting his new memoir, "Decision Points", in the book and on tour, Mr. Bush continued to validate the use of "water-boarding" and other forms of torturous measures which he authorized to be used on captured Al Qaeda or Taliban militants as being legal and acceptable. His re-emergence through this memoir promotion, after almost two years of leaving office, did not sit well at all with the rest of the world as the mess he created still continue to torment millions of lives thereon after…especially for him publicly reasserting that those evil measures that him and his vice, Dick Cheney, authorized and used on captured foreign nationals by the C.I.A. operatives were perfectly okay. They is a strong call by the United Nations'

Criminal Court Tribunal in Europe to have him arrested if he travel to certain countries and be charged and tried for war crimes and all the atrocious acts he authorized during his presidency.

After Barrack Obama took office on January 20, 2009, few months into his administration, some attention was focused on the inner workings of the Bush-Cheney administration's dark pasts. On April 16, 2009, the Obama administration released the memos detailing the troubling interrogation techniques approved by the Bush-Cheney administration back in 2002 by the administration's Justice Department.

These Interrogation methods are as follows:

***ATTENTION GRASP:*** "Grasping the individual with both hands, one hand on each side of the collar opening, in a controlled and quick motion."

***WALLING:*** A fake flexible wall is built, and then the suspect is forward and "then quickly and firmly" pushed against the wall. "The idea is to create a sound that will make the impact seem far worse than it is."

***FACIAL GRASP:*** "Used to hold the head immobile. One open part is placed on either side of the individual's face."

***INSULT SLAPPING:*** "The purpose of the facial slap is to induce shock surprise and /or humiliation."

***CRAMPED CONFINEMENT:*** The suspect is placed in a confined place that "is usually dark," Some spaces only allow a subject to sit down; confinement in those spaces "lasts no more than two hours."

***WALL STANDING:*** Subjects are forced to lean with only their fingers for support against a wall 4 to 5 feet away from their bodies in a tactic "used to induce muscle fatigue."

***STRESS POSITIONS:*** They include "kneeling on the floor while leaning back at a 45-degree angle" and "sitting on the floor with legs extended out in front of him with his arms raised above his head."

***SLEEP DEPRIVATION:*** This is meant to "reduce the individual's ability to think on his feet and, through the discomfort associated with lack of sleep, to motivate him to corporate."

***INSECTS PLACED IN A CONFINEMENT BOX:*** The subject is placed in "a cramped confinement box" and told a stinging insect will be placed in the box with him. Instead, a harmless insect, "such as caterpillar," is placed inside.

***WATER BOARDING:*** The subject is placed on a board with a cloth covering his nose and mouth. The cloth is saturated with water to simulate drowning. It creates "the perception of suffocation and incipient panic."

## (b)   Assault on the Rule of Law

-- ***ASSAULT ON THE RULE OF LAW:*** Under the Bush-Cheney administration, the nation's Constitution, the Bill of Rights, the nation's justice system and the Separation of Power came under relentless attack. Mr. Bush chose to exploit the tragedy of Sept. 11, 2001, the moment he looked like the president of a unified nation, to try to place himself along with his vice, Dick Cheney, above the law.

Mr. Bush abrogated the power to imprison men (foreign nationals) without charges and brow-beat Congress, which at the time the Republican party has the majority seat, into granting an unfettered authority to spy on Americans. He created untold numbers of "black" programs, including secret prisons and outsourced torture. He issued hundreds, if not thousands, of secret orders. Even as a new president took office on January 2009, the new administration found it extremely troubling disclosing to the public concealed proofs of some of the atrocious acts ordered and executed by the administration over its 8 years tenure at the White House. Facts continue to unfold after Mr. Bush left office as to the extent of havoc the administration have caused America and the world as a whole. His Vice, Dick Cheney, believed to be the key architect who devised and drafted about all of these lawless acts for Bush's approval, had spoke more often within the very first year he left office than the entire 8 years of his vice presidency....trying his hardest to deflect the accusations of all the Bush administration lawlessness pointing towards him.

The American public fear it will take years of forensic research to discover how many basic rights have been violated by the Bush- Cheney administration.

On August 24, 2009, the Obama administration ordered the release of some of the intensely controversial and highly concealed CIA memos relating to the Bush-Cheney torture policy executed by the CIA operatives on captured foreign nationals suspected of terroristic acts.

In the memos, which was hundreds of pages of documents, about forty-something pages of the memos that was believed to have contained very troubling narratives to some of the cruel and most gruesome torturous acts inflicted on these captured terror suspects by the CIA was deliberately redacted and rendered unreadable. Among the readable ones were yet some shocking revelations of torture acts carried out by the CIA operatives, which till then, the public was unaware of, or would have never thought any American government security agency would dare inflict on others...foreign nationals for that matter. All approved by the Bush-Cheney administration.

Torturous acts like coercing suspects into false confession under gun point, threatening to blow their brains out if the suspects refuse to agree to doing what the CIA operatives wanted them to falsely and forcefully confess to being accused of. Also, among others, are threats made to the suspects that the rest of their families out there would be arrested as well and be brought there at the secret cells to face similar torments like them if they refuse to comply with the false confession.

On top of all these shocking new revelations from the released memos, there were still more photo clips of the horrendous acts perpetrated against these so-called terror suspects by the CIA operatives....all approved and directed by the Bush-Cheney administration. Photo clips which was yet to be made public due to the troubling graphic nature of the pictures and the damaging repercussion their release may cause to United States reputation and its image which by the way the Bush-Cheney administration had already tarnished across the globe.

Some of the former world leaders already or currently facing international tribunal in the Hague for atrocities committed during their watch against their citizens and others did not even do half of the heinous acts done by Mr. Bush and his vice, Cheney, and have or in the process of being handed down sever judgment for their crimes against humanity, but shockingly to the whole world that Mr. Bush and Cheney have not been brought before the same international court that they have played an instrumental role in the capture and prosecution of some former world leaders for similar crimes they were alleged to have committed while in public office.

John Mc Cain, the late former Republican Congressional Senator for the state of Arizona, who meddled twice for the Republican presidential ticket in 2000 and 2008 and lost on both occasions, ostensibly improved protection for detainees during Mr. Bush's administration. But then helped the White House push through the appalling Military Commission Act of 2006, which denied detainees (foreign nationals) the right to a hearing in a real court and put Washington in conflict with the Geneva

Conventions, greatly increasing the risk to American troops. In his political calculation for a chance to get reelected on November 2010 Congressional election, he switched gears once again and teamed up with the Arizona state Republican conservative faction to pledge his full support for yet another tough immigration law enacted within the state and signed into law on April 2010 by the sitting Republican governor, Jan Brewer.

In it, the law authorize all state law enforcement officers to stop any individual within the state that fit the profile of an immigrant and request for their residency papers. A law that has caused so much uproar among both immigrants community and citizens alike all across the country since it was made public. It even led to the boycott of business dealings with Arizona by a handful of states and major cities across America......a move that clearly reflects the level of anger and rage everyone felt about the Arizona state administrators' outright xenophobic spirit towards foreigners. The law also makes it a felony punishable by jail time for those caught within the state by the state's law enforcement officers. Even the mayor of Phoenix, Arizona's largest city, was highly outraged by this law and plans to join a host of other entities across the country to file legal action with the court to challenge the legality of this Arizona state law against foreign nationals residing within the state.

In the suit filed by the Obama administration opposing such creation and enforcement of immigration laws by the state of Arizona after the controversial laws was made public.....the Nation's Justice Department on behalf of the Obama administration holds that such creation and enforcement of the nation's immigration laws by the state of Arizona will lead to racial profiling of citizens and non-citizens alike which will in turn lead to a gross violation of one or more of the nation's Bill of Rights as well as the violation of one or more of the nation's Constitutions. It also asserts that the creation of immigration laws and their enforcement thereof is solely the federal government's obligation and not that of any individual states within the country.

In July 2010, right around the time which Arizona state governor was about to sign these racially biased immigration provisions into laws, the judge presiding over the case at the Federal District court in Phoenix, Arizona, ruled by shutting down the most crucial parts of the Arizona version of the immigration laws that would have enable the state's law enforcement officers to stop anyone who basically look or sound like an immigrant......the laws which was intended specifically to target folks of Spanish descent in particular......and ask for their residency papers. If they are unable to produce them on the spot, part of these laws mandates the Arizona cops to arrest such aliens on the spot to face criminal charges and jail time as well as being deported after they finish serving their time just for being in the country illegally.

The state governor and her extreme-right Republican constituents did not like the federal district court judge's ruling, so herself and the rest of her rightist Republican teamsters in Arizona decided to appeal the court's ruling to the U.S. Court of Appeals for the Ninth Circuit in California. What a shame and a waste of taxpayers' money in a state that is so cash-strap to balance its fiscal budgets since 2007-08 that the Bush-Cheney's administration got the nation in a state of recession.

It was very sad but not a surprise that John Mc. Cain was a part of this Arizona anti-immigrants crusade just for his political survival. His flip-flop style on crucial national issues like this has robbed him twice of his shot at the presidency. It reflects that his intentions to the American public, like the rest in the Republican hard-line faction, are not sincere and relatively vague at best.

Whatever might have been the political reasons behind the Obama's administration reluctance in disclosing to the American public and to the rest of the world a full account of the cruelties done by the Bush-Cheney administration as well as holding the culprits accountable for their arbitrary acts and abuse of power, it should be equally mindful that there were numerous victims at issue across the globe whom irreparable damages of huge magnitude was inflicted upon without cause nor any redress yet. It should also not be forgotten that without accountability and full repentance, the process of forgiveness and of healing the wounds on either sides will remain incomplete till such threshold prerequisite is met in the face of God which America puts its trust.

All the vast-right conservatives in Washington has been busy trying their hardest to cover the Bush administration's dirt under the rug, but the dirty odor will not go away till the wound is properly treated and healed. For America to truly move forward from this dark past brought about by the Bush-Cheney administration, a full repentance and accountability of the administration's horrific past is a must and inevitable. The Bush-Cheney's team has been allowed to get away with the evil acts they ordered and executed on mankind in America and across the globe. The God that America trusted since it founding sent a Messiah, Barack Obama to come and safe the nation from Bush-Cheney's ruin. After all the hard work for 8 good years, the anti-immigrants faction who supports everything Trump says about Mexicans and other foreign nationals, went and voted him into office....essentially allowing Trump to wipe out all the progress made by the Messiah 'Obama,'...taking the nation back to the Wild-West colonial era once again.

Avoiding to get to the bottom of this often stalled atrocious events that marked the Bush-Cheney's eight years era by the succeeding administration, will only suggest to both the American public and the international community, that it also, to some degree, condones the culture of deception and the belief that a government officials' primary loyalty is not to the people, but to the power itself.

Mr. Obama had appointed one justice already in 2009 and had appointed another one in 2010 to the Supreme court that has been on the brink of being dominated by radical right-wing ideologues with so much conservative views of interpreting and applying the laws of the land. Imagine if Mr. Mc. Cain would have won the 2008 presidential election, he would have certainly picked rigid conservative ideologues who do not believe in level playing field when it comes to the rule of law and its application. Those who voted for Donald Trump and those who could have went to vote but didn't do so has now made it possible to turn the nation's judiciary settings upside down towards the extreme right for generations to come......especially at the nation's highest court.

## (c)   Harassment of Foreigners

**-- *HARASSMENT OF FOREIGNERS:*** Never has immigrants been highly humiliated and tormented in the history of America of recent generation as it has been during the Bush-Cheney/Trump administrations.

Armed Squads bursting into homes in the dead of nights with shotguns and automatic weapons, terrorizing families and taking away anyone who lacks identity papers, even if they have raided the wrong house. It may sound like Baghdad, but it is the suburbs of New York city during fall of 2007. Another case in point, among hundreds of communities where federal agents invaded homes and workplaces in search of immigrants to deport. Federal agents said the raids were a focused campaign to catch gang members and fugitives. That would be good if the Immigration and Customs Enforcement (ICE) agency were carefully extracting the dangerous criminal sliver from an estimated population of 12 million illegal immigrants. But as immigration raid have vastly increased these days in America, they have become something murky and ugly.

The U.S. Immigration agency, highly emboldened by the Bush administration.....and now that of Trump.....has been catching modest numbers of undesirables, but also a much larger by-catch of peaceable immigrants. The agency have been setting off waves of fear and outrage, not only among illegal immigrants, but among citizens whose privacy they have violated, through unchecked aggression, carelessness and incompetence.

In Sept. 2007, dozens of federal agents fanned out across Nassau County, Long Island, to execute warrants on accused gang members. County Executive, Thomas Souzzi and Police Commissioner, Lawrence Mulvey, were so dismayed that they refused to offer their cooperation on further raids until ICE agents gets its acts together.

They described a seriously botched "cowboy" operation by dozens of ICE agents.....some in cowboy hats, who had not trained together.....used inappropriate weapons and mistakenly drew them on Nassau officers. They said the agency misled them.....that what was supposed to be a targeted gang crackdown was something much more sloppy and indiscriminate. They said the agency ignored to check its list of targets against Nassau's up-to-date gang records, and ended up raiding many wrong homes. The raid were stunningly ineffective. Peggy De La Rosa- Delgado, an American citizen, said her Huntington Station home was raided by mistake during this crackdown at about 5:30 a.m. "It was the second predawn raid looking for the same man at the same wrong address. My husband and three teenage sons, legal residents, were terrified," she said.

ICE officials callously shrug off such mistakes as collateral damage, but advocate for immigrants filed yet another class-action lawsuit, asserting that the raids in the New York city area were unreasonable searches conducted by agents who did not show warrants and misidentified themselves as police officers. Mr. Suozzi wrote to the Homeland Security director at the time, Michael Chertoff, requesting him to investigate the Nassau debacle. Mr. Suozzi deserves praise for having the courage to oppose mindless immigration enforcement while affirming his county's commitment to sane policing and public safety. The Trump's immigration enforcement strategy currently in force is proven to be way worse than that of Bush. Trump is apprehending parent migrants along with their kids/babies…and then separating and forcefully taking their babies away from them to undisclosed locations. How cruel and heartless that can be done to human beings....babies for that matter.... in the nation of immigrants and the land of the free.

## (d)    Reckless Raids

--- **RECKLESS RAIDS:** The adverse economic impact of the mass-expulsion of foreigners by the Bush administration has started playing out in recent years. Some day the nation will recognize the true cost of its war on illegal immigration. Not in dollars, though those are being squandered in the billions. The true cost is to the national identity: the sense of what America stands for and what has truly retained those values. It will hit the nation when the enforcement fever breaks, when America looks back on what has been done and no longer recognize the country that did it.

A nation of immigrants is holding another nation of immigrants bondage, exploring its labor while ignoring its suffering, condemning its lawlessness while sealing off a path to living lawfully.

The evidence is all around that something pragmatic and welcoming at the American core has been eclipsed, or slipping away indeed.

An escalating campaign of raids in homes and workplaces has spread indiscriminate terror among millions of people who pose no threat. Following one of the largest raid ever in 2008,...at a meat packing plant in Iowa...hundreds were forcefully force-fed through the legal system and sent to prison. Civil rights lawyers complained, futilely, that workers has been steamrolled into giving up their rights, treated more as a presumptive criminal gang than as potentially exploited workers who deserve a fair hearing. The company that harnessed their desperation, like so many others, has faced no charges.

Immigrants in detention languish without lawyers and decent medical care even when they are mortally ill.The new Congressional majority are struggling to impose standards and oversight on a system deficient in both. Counties and towns with spare jail cells are lining up for federal contracts as prosecutions of illegal aliens fill the system to bursting. Unphased by the sight of children in prison scrubs, the Bush administration, before he left office, went on to build three new family detention centers. Police all over are now checking papers, empowered by the nation's right-wing politicians itching to enlist in the federal crusade.

Of course, it is not about forcing people to go home and come back the right way. Ellis Island is closed. The paths are clogged or do not exist. Some backlogs are so long that they are measured in decades or generations. A bill to fix the system died in July 2007. Of course the vast-right political faction in Washington would have never let it be in the first place. The current strategy, dreamed up by restrictionists and embraced by Republican extremists, is to force millions into fear and poverty.

There are few national figures standing firm against restrictionism. Late Edward Kennedy, Senate Democrat of Massachusetts, bravely done so for four decades before his death in Sept. 2009, but his Senate colleagues who were running for president seem by comparison to be hiding. Also, late John Mc. Cain seemed superficially supportive of sensible reform, but his full support for the Arizona anti-immigrant law clearly reflects his true position on the issue. He would rather flip-flop on his affirmative position on key national issues just to get reelected. Hillary Clinton has lost her voice on this issue more than once. President Barrack Obama, gliding above the ugliness might someday test his vision of new politics against restrictionists hatred, but he has not yet done so. The American public's moderation on immigration reform, confirmed in poll after poll begs the candidates to confront the issue with courage and plan, but they have been vague and discreet at best when they should be forceful and unflinching.

The restrictionists' message is brutally simple.... that illegal immigrants deserve no rights, mercy or hope. It refuses to recognize that illegality is not an identity, it is a status that can be mended by making reparations and resuming a lawful life. Unless the nation contains it enforcement compulsion, the so-called illegal immigrants will remain forever Them and never Us, subject to whatever abusive regime the powers of the moment may devise. Every time America has singled out a group of new arrival immigrants for unjust punishment, the shame has echoed through history. Think of the Chinese and the Irish Catholics and Americans of Japanese ancestry. Children someday will study the Great Immigration Panic of the early 2000s, which harmed countless lives, wasted billions of dollars and mocked the nation's deeply held values.

# 29
# GLOBAL IMMIGRATION ISSUES

EVEN THOUGH UNITED STATES, DURING THE Bush-Cheney era going forward, has helped established the nation's record in recent time as one of the worse, if not the worse, regarding the treatment of foreign nationals and their expulsion process, other Western nations and some Middle-Eastern Arab nations also adopts relatively hostile immigration policies against foreigners who emigrated to these places. Such hostilities ranges from harsh restrictions against them from becoming too integrated into their societies; to implementation and enforcement of laws intended to impede them from being permanently resettled, or even become naturalized citizens of such countries.

Immigration policies are so terrible in some of the Middle-Eastern Arab countries that the laws do not even permit the kids born in these countries by immigrant parents of the right to citizenship of the countries of their birth. Their laws makes such kids to automatically claim their parents countries, instead of their rightful countries of birth. Arab nations like Saudi Arabia, United Arab Emirates, Qatar, among others, continues to adopt such discriminative immigration policies...... even against their own Islamic kinds whom they share similar religious faith. Most foreigners in these regions are only allowed to remain there for a temporary basis.

However, upon notification to leave, their governments do not practice the cruel apprehension, detention and removal methods as the one started by the Bush-Cheney's administration in the U.S. before getting kicked out of the country.

In 2005, France experienced a mass youth reprisal that led to massive destruction of both private and public properties......in their attempt to finally get their long ignored point across to their government regarding the double standard treatment they have for so long been subjected to. These kids who took to the streets to vent their outrage against their government are born citizens of France by immigrant parents. They have for long been stereotypically profiled, marginalized and deprived of various socioeconomic benefits which other kids born there by French-born parents are fully afforded.

Following this reprisal, the French government, then under president Jacques Chirac, finally started taking these depraved kids' concerns very seriously...after decades of such racially motivated discrimination towards foreigners and their French-born kids.

Even if these kids parents are somewhat subjected to such socioeconomic impediment, such xenophobic cruelty by the nation's policymakers and leaders should, by right, never be extended to their offsprings born in the country. After all, these immigrants' children are born citizens of the country just like the so-called privileged leaders and the policymakers who enjoys every privilege and incentives the country has to offer its citizens.

The money spent by the French government to repair and restore private and public properties that was destroyed and damaged by these youths' violent demonstration could have for long been put to better use to create socioeconomic opportunities for these deprived kids long before they finally resorted to such violent cause of action that could have been avoided. Whatever the liabilities resulting from the incident, the French government and its leaders are to blame for its double standard style of discrimination on its citizens born there by immigrant parents, while their peers born by French-born parents continues to enjoy uninterrupted social privileges the nation got to offer its citizens.

It is a shame that sometimes it take a violent cause of action for the oppressed and the dispossessed to be heard. In certain circumstances, it is a practical fact that "if you make peaceful change impossible, you make violent change inevitable." The oppressors, in most cases, continues with their oppressive treatment of the oppressed until the oppressed gets pushed too close to the edge and resort into doing what they feels necessary to get their point across....either to compel the oppressors to completely stop the challenged behaviors, or to improve on the disputed condition at issue.

In the case of United States with a long history of foreign migrants of which its socioeconomic standing has always been attributed, it has every reason to always be more accommodative and tolerant to arriving foreign nationals than any other nation across the globe. Instead, the right-wing Republican faction in Washington and across the country rather chose the path of tormenting them, exploiting them and then devise wicked laws to have them kicked out of the country butt-naked based on often times frivolous grounds.

All American-born citizens of any race have ancestral roots that goes back to some immigrant parents who gave birth to the parents that gave birth to the ones of the current generation in America today...after they got to America from another parts of the world...except for the Native Indians who were the original occupants and native citizens and landowners of the Continental America.

The highly hostile immigration policies enacted by the Bush-Cheney administration....also emulated by some other like-minded anti-immigrants regimes....are intended to alienate foreigners, control the minority population, and shutting them out of every opportunities such countries got to offer, which in turn would have allowed such migrants the opportunity to gradually integrate into such societies. Like Mr. Bush administration, the so-called ultraright conservative hard-liners' mission in Washington has been to do any and everything within their means to shut every doors that may have enabled the new wave of migrants to America from ever attaining a meaningful level of accomplishment which was afforded them through their ancestral migrant parents...a privilege that subsequently helped them to reach their current state of socioeconomic an geopolitical status.

There are in fact some very sickening immigration policies practiced in some of the Islamic countries as well. Some of the Arab nations even discriminate among their own kinds.

As a Muslim Arab migrant in another Muslim nation, one would think or at least expect that such Muslim migrants would be very welcomed by their more affluent sister Arab nations to stay as long as they wish, or even naturalize if they wish to do so.....at least for the sake of religious oneness. It is surprisingly not so in some of the Arab nations.

In nation's like Saudi Arabia, United Arab Emirates (U.A.E.), and Qatar, among others, these nations do not condone long term stay by immigrants, be they Christians, Muslims, Hindus, Buddha, or even Pagans, or whichever might be their religious orientations. Almost every immigrants in these countries are only allowed to remain there for relatively short period of time. After such short period of permitted stay, they are promptly notified by their Immigration Authorities to start packing up and be ready to leave their country.

No matter how long immigrants manage to remain in these countries, their laws do not permit immigrants to ever become naturalized citizens, nor do the immigrants' kids born there are entitled to citizenship. The kids are rather considered citizens of their parents' countries.

At the current rate of which war is being waged against foreigners in America today, it won't come as a surprise to see the rightist hard-line policymakers in Washington attempting to push for yet another immigration bill that will completely pull the plug on immigrants of ever becoming naturalized, or even create tough immigration laws that will bar kids born in the country by migrant parents, legal or non-legal, from citizenship entitlement like the case in the Middle-Eastern Arab countries. Some sick public officials in the state of California and in Washington are already beating their drums of hatred towards such unconscionable proposal....they even got the balls of publicly debating their support to such move on a federal level.

Nicolas Sarkozy, former president of France was playing the drumbeat along with his right-wing constituents to wage antiimmigrant war on immigrants living in the country. Even if France has a somewhat hostile policies on immigrants, the immigration situation in United States is a totally different scenario because America is and always has been an immigrant nation and should not tolerate the current right-wings' anti-immigrants uprising across the country that is getting worse whenever a Republican gets elected as U.S. president.

What's happening, presumably, is that modern movement conservatism attracts a certain personality types. If you identify with the downtrodden even a little, you don't belong. If you think ridicule is the appropriate response to other people's woes, you fit right in. Some Republicans disillusionment with Mr. Bush's ideologies did not appear to signal any change in that regard.

So, once again, if you are poor, or appear to be at the oppressors' mercy, or you're sick or don't have health insurance, remember this: these people think your problem are funny.

# PART-II

# *WAR ON IMMIGRANTS*

# 30 THE STRONG-ARM GAME

REALISTICALLY SPEAKING, AMERICA IN RECENT GENERATION is increasingly still a country that dreams are too often deferred.

As the saying goes: "No man is an Island." As individuals, we all need one another at some point in time. Similar principle applies to various nations across the globe. Mutual co-existence is vital to the growth of individuals and nations as we continue to live under this planet. Anyone with sound state of mind will agree with this line of reasoning......so also will any democratic society. However, it is human nature to sometimes disagree on things with others due to our differences in ideological point of views. Nonetheless, if such ideological differences persist and becomes a thorny issue capable of undermining mutual co-existence among such parties, muscling up or strong-arming the weaker team to conformity is not always the smartest or the boldest move to make.

In most cases, engaging in bi-lateral dialogue with the adversary to bring forth meaningful compromise is a much smarter and effective move to make rather than taking the other route. At least the attempt to resolve things amicably is always better than the ruthless offensive style often preferred by some folks. The offensive style always brings about chaos, mayhem and all the like. It often create an even more heightened hostility and a delicate balance than when the problem initially started.

This brings to question on how to best address the socioeconomic and geopolitical differences that often come up among individuals as well as nations around the globe. If parties are cognizant of the fact that their interdependency for survival and growth is inevitable, then there should be profound necessity for their peaceful co-existence. The rogue strategy of strong-arming the presumably weaker party, as some of the Western nations still practice today after centuries of such bygone imperial style of engagement, is becoming more or less outdated and counter-productive in effect in this day and age. It is a strategy identified with the bygone colonial era which by then, was a relatively effective style of imperial dominance.... but not very effective today.

This type of selfish colonial era strategy is sadly Donald Trump's favorite style. He thinks, America having stronger bargaining leverage will sway or force the presumably less stronger nations to cave in to his selfish demands. So far, on trade, sanctions, tariffs, and other international issues, this outdated strategy of his has yielded zero result for the nation he currently leads.

Such imperial approach is not only illegal in today's globalized world of interdependent economies, but also is counter-productive and brings about regional unrest that often times escalates to deadly confrontations that usually spreads beyond the confines of the conflicting factions. Such sentiments which could be racial, political, or religious in scope sometimes can even have a global impact, just like the battle against Islamic Radicalism had gotten when the Bush administration chose a wrong approach in dealing with the issue.

The Bush administration, just like the other American presidents, was fully cognizance that America and its economy needs the vital oil resources of some of the oil-rich nations it was waging endless war against to power its economy. Whichever way it had chose to spin the argument to justify its failed unilateral act of aggression against the targeted oil-rich Middle-Eastern nations, accused of using some of their oil wealth to fund acts of terror against its interests, Mr. Bush's unilateral military incursion to topple the governments of these regimes has proven to be non-effective and irrational at best.

Typically, from the colonial playbook, the presumably superior power prefers to use extreme hostile measure to silence the presumably weaker party into submission. A typical strong-arm tactics often used in forcefully taking what do not rightfully belong to such person without the willful consent of the rightful owner to give it up. In today's day and age, such provocative style definitely means paving way for immediate or future chaos to erupt. If a revolt does not follow right away, it is usually a matter of time before it eventually happen. The strategy is like "a thief in the middle of the night" scenario......coming to take someone's possessions at force, without the owner's consent. But the Bush-Cheney's administration was worse than the "thief in the night" scenario. The administration's leadership style can best be described as that of "the thieves in the broad day light" coming to steal from you with deadly force right in your face. This has been one of the strategic rogue foreign policies which the Bush-Cheney administration had adopted that had proven not only counter-productive, but also has left America and the rest of the world relatively unstable and in a state of chaos and mayhem that was non-existence before his presidency that lasted for eight horrific years.

Mr. Bush's leadership style prefers the confrontational approach with his so-called adversaries over engaging in constructive dialogue to resolve the root cause of their differences...a typical rightists' style of engagement. And his vice, Dick Cheney, was the brain behind all the wicked and provocative policies executed during the 8 years tenure of the administration. The administration was undoubtedly an arrogant and oppressive regime...perhaps the most outlawed, arrogant, oppressive and repressive administration in the United States history. An administration that felt too pompous to engage in any form of constructive dialogue with its so-called "axis of evil" states to amicably resolve their grievances. Instead, he deployed the "thief in broad daylight" strategy to destabilize those regimes and still ended up not accomplishing the Republican's vast-right ambiguous motives with the so-called enemies.

However, despite Trump's greedy colonial era ways of dealing, he nonetheless at some point sees the urgent need to dialogue with his adversaries for mutual resolution of contentious issues when he finally acknowledge that his one-way-street mentality approach is not working and won't work......like the meeting he held with North Korea leader after he became president and his change of gears with the NAFTA trade deal with Mexico and Canada that he was bluffing to re-write his way or pull the U.S. completely out of it.

The sad part is that the execution of these failed arrogant and oppressive foreign policies came with enormous price tag at the expense of the hard-working American taxpayers' money, and all the innocent human lives lost so far in the process as these unforeseen consequences of the unilateral invasion of Afghanistan and then Iraq continues into an unforeseeable future. The Bush- Cheney's administration strategy of combating Islamic radicalism accomplished nothing other than further sowing more hatred between the West and the Middle-Eastern Arab and the Muslim religious factions across the globe.

The Unilateral invasion tactics of the Bush-Cheney administration and its other foreign policies can also be analyzed in view of a man who admires a woman sexually, but chose to ignore the normal process of first establishing friendship and courtship. Instead, he orchestrated a short-cut strategy to satisfy his sexual desire with the woman, like a thief striking at the middle of the night...confronting the woman at a discreet location and forced her against her will into sex by way of rape...without her willful consent. Such move portrays a coward, arrogant, tyrant, and self-centered mindset. A friendly and peaceable dialogue is the proper approach, then the sexual intimacy will follow with much ease.

Such dialogue which will establish some level of acquaintance might even open the door for an improbable romantic connection between them. This strategy of engaging in dialogue with an adversary has been proven universally to be very effective way of amicably resolving minor or critical conflicts or differences among parties who don't see eye-to-eye. Those who normally ignore the amicable route are either doing so with the intention of starting some trouble and could care less of the consequence of their action, or just simply seeking the destruction of the rivaling party. When such act of aggression is made against another nation, such move can only be perceived no other way than an act that provokes trouble. It is usually an act in pursuit of territorial dominance of another man's sovereignty.

Dialogue between grieving parties helps to heal old wounds and open the door capable of killing two birds with one stone. With constructive dialogue, old animosities are resolved and new mutual relationships can be forged with even stronger mutual trust among both parties than before. The Bush-Cheney's administration did not like such peaceful diplomatic way of representing the interest of American public abroad. He prefers the strategy of crushing his adversaries and bringing them to submission and take control of their resources by act of force and intimidation. The so-called world gorillas always underestimate the underdogs' defensive capabilities. The so-called underdogs got to do what they got to do as well to protect their own interest.

Donald Trump operates along that path too, if not worse, but with all the changes that was brought about resulting from the Bush-Cheney's failures, he too has cautioned himself in a lot of ways to not make similar or worse moves.

If you choose the aggressive cause of action to crush, eliminate, or bring your adversary to submission, and your adversary proves not to be an easy meat to swallow as you had first anticipated, that automatically screws up your 'superman' morale that you had relied so heavily upon. On top of the shattered morale, the so- called gorilla have to deal with the aftermath of the mess that had spilled all over the place, while intended result had backfired. The folks whose well-thought opinions you had earlier flunked are the same ones you now ran back for help in cleaning up the mess you created. Such has been the case with the Bush administration and his misdiagnosed handling of the war on Islamic extremism.

Only a dictator administration prefers a unilateral act of war when the rest of the world strongly suggests a peaceful and diplomatic alternative to an offensive cause of action. The American public are still puzzled if the Bush-Cheney's administration was in fact an indirect dictatorship government right from the outset, or a democratically elected leader who turned a dictator after getting in office.

Shockingly surprising to all....including himself, Donald Trump won the 2016 U.S. presidential election and got elected as the next U.S. president after Obama. He has such an untamed Wild-West colonial era mentality. He goes against everyone but his own selfish gut. Even himself, most times don't know the outcome of his wild cause of action. When he was doing his thing in the private sector, the adverse consequence of his wild moves was only his problem to bear. But now that he is actually elected to serve in a public office......the U.S. president for that matter, the adverse consequence to any of his wild cause of actions while in office will be felt and affected by the entire nation and beyond. We all have to stay-tuned...also fasten our seatbelts just in case!

# 31 REPUBLICANS V. DEMOCRATS

ELECTED LEADERS CAUGHT LYING TO THEIR country citizens, not once nor twice, do not have the best interest of their people at heart.....and are not fit to be allowed to continue leading. Leaders like that should be summoned by their country people who elected them into office to resign from such public office for the interest of the public they serve. In most cases, once a person lies more than once, it has been proven that there is very strong likelihood that such individual will continue to be a liar.

During the last years of former president Bill Clinton in office, a sex scandal erupted at the White House that was blown out of proportion by the then Republican majority in Congress. A trumped up incident that ended up tainting Mr. Clinton of making inappropriate sexual advances on the then White House intern, Monica Lewinsky. A mild scenario that was relatively so minor and should have been irrelevant and treated to that effect. It shouldn't have called for such highly trumpeted outcry by the vast-right Republicans in Washington.....those whose primary motive was an aggressive and a relentless pursuit for a window of opportunity to seek Clinton's demise.

The incident, as usual, was spotlighted by the media all across America. The issue was made out of nothing just to help Republicans build their frivolous accusation against Mr. Clinton's Democratic leadership lapses while in the nation's highest public office. It was also an hindsight attempt to garner enough public consensus so that the Republicans could seize on the opportunity to push for his impeachment.

Shortly after the incident that showed Mr. Clinton giving an innocent peg on the White House intern's cheek in a public forum, the Republicans build up their allegation with the help of the overreaching media publicity of the video clip. The American main-stream media networks which are sadly becoming more of instigators of events than facilitators. The primary role of journalism of news information to the public should always be an unbiased and independent presentation of the news information shared with the public.

At the end of the day, the Republicans' conspiracy attempt to impeach Mr. Clinton using this mild incident failed. Mr. Clinton survived the blow and prevailed through the end of his second term in office. Majority of the American public who had voted him in office on both terms did not support the Republicans' call for his resignation because his good deeds outweighed his relatively minor missteps that Republicans intended to capitalize heavily upon.

Comparing Mr. Clinton's job performance during his presidency on America's overall national security, the nation's socioeconomic and geopolitical stability to that of Mr. Bush's presidency, who succeeded him, would be like comparing day light to a total darkness. The level of governance was the exact opposite among these two individuals. A very sharp contrast can be drawn to reflect the fact that during Clinton's era, though not perfect, was a prosperous and peaceful regime that strongly believes in dialogue to strike a mutual balance with his adversaries both at home and internationally. Strikingly, Mr. Clinton served as a leader whose priority was to advocate and advance peaceful co-existence among the American public and the international community as a whole.

Global tranquility reigned during Mr. Clinton's era as opposed to that of Mr. Bush.

Mr. Clinton was a great negotiator on behalf of the American government. He sat, walked, and talked with his adversaries and made good of their existing differences and won them over. Clinton, like Mr. Obama, can be described as a true leader for the masses with relatively genuine political skills. He was quite proficient in executing and regulating his vested executive authorities and not abusing them like Mr. Bush.

He understood and knew when to apply justified aggression in solving problems and when to adopt diplomacy in balancing things out amicably. His governing style, in most cases, always had resulted to a win-win situation for him as well as the opposition team. This is the leadership skill needed by any American president that Mr. Bush had lacked.

Mr. Bush's leadership, in contrast, conveys his message with provocative aggression and high level of arrogance. He always try to portray in a wrong and arrogant way the level of power, military and otherwise, which America possess to the international community, and that it can apply such power to overreach in the world stage at any given moment without having any second thought of the unforeseen consequence of such reckless style of leadership. Such authoritative and dictatorship style of aggression inspires similar radical reciprocal behavior from the opposing party, or the adversary. His provocative foreign policies towards his so-called 'enemy of states' triggered similar reprisal. Instead of quenching the fire, his leadership strategies helped to further inflame the preexisting tension.

With Mr. Bush's proven counter-terror strategies adopted both at home and abroad against foreign states and foreign nationals, particularly the mess he created in Iraq, it became overwhelmingly evident that his leadership skills in international playing field was all the way crude and counter-productive to accomplish the desired results deemed appropriate and acceptable by the America public and the international community.

Mr. Bush and his like-minded vast-right Republican teamsters never brought forth nor promoted peaceful co-existence for all. In other words, Bush's leadership style did not unite. It scatters and break bonds. His leadership intervention in any affairs, private or governmental, serves rather as a catalyst that fuels and escalates preexisting crisis among conflicting parties. His intervention into existing conflicts is not intended to mend, but to further poison the minds of the grieving parties who he ostensibly had lend a helping hand in reconciling their differences. Similar character traits applies to his like-minded right-wing conservatives in Washington and across the country. Simply put, Mr. Bush and his like-minded teamsters are all trouble makers. The world do not need any more leaders like Bush whose leadership doctrine will not bring peace but add more to the already existing troubles and chaos around the world.

Sadly for the nation, those who loves and believes in the 'one-way street/arm-twisting' style of Donald Trump went out and gave him enough vote to win the 2016 presidential election. As he has promised his base, he's been stirring up the waters again that was made calm for 8 years by Obama.

## (a)   The Failed Foreign Policy Approach

**--- *THE FAILED FOREIGN POLICY APPROACH:*** Just as the United Nations and the NATO member states had foresaw the likely consequence of Mr. Bush's short-sighted act of aggression to combat terrorism, the world today, after eight years of his unilateral occupation and warring against the so-called suspected terrorist regimes, continues to suffer the consequences of his reckless cause of action. Rabid fundamentalism have sprung up, particularly around the Middle-Eastern regions, at an exponential rate, further leading to global insecurities, heightened chaos and bloodshed of innocent souls.

International communities as well as the American public had widely condemned Mr. Bush's strategy and approach as being counter-productive to fight terrorism. Counter-productive measure that has done nothing but inspires and breeds more Islamic radicals. Even though Mr. Bush and his vice, Cheney, had left office, the effect of their misguided and dysfunctional policies continue to linger and affects the masses thereon after. Plus, his ultra-right Republican Congressional policymakers still in Washington today are yet to turn a new live from that distorted mind-frame of leadership.

International figures across the globe even weighed in over the years of Bush's futile occupation......sharing their points of view regarding their observation of the actions and reactions from both sides of the warring parties and the hunted insurgents. They all came up with similar inferences that "focusing on the killing of rabid Islamic fundamentalists will and have not stopped extremism, but have only increased it. That reasoning hold true relative to the increasing evolution of extremist activities all over the globe. Mr. Bush rejected the non-offensive dialogue approach strongly recommended by the international community to address the root cause of the Islamic radicalism against America and its interests at home and abroad.

The international community believes that if Mr. Bush had heeded to their suggested soft power approach of constructive communication with these so-called enemy states, tremendous milestones would have definitely been reached since all these years of hostility and warring. Radical minds would have been converted and extremism would have been greatly reduced against America or anyone else across the globe.

The Bush administration was rather busy implementing offensive strategies to capture the so-called bad apples of the Taliban's Al Qaeda group dead or alive. While doing so, his approach to extinct or silence these radical groups has, in retrospect been helping to fuel and breed new radicals at an exponential rate. It was also discovered over the years of Bush's warring that the new breeds of Islamic radicals are now taking the Al Qaeda cause but not necessarily affiliated with the group.

The strategy Bush-Cheney and the rest of his right-wing Republican faction was adopting to eliminate the problem is in turn brewing increasing level of resentment among the targeted group, which in turn has been giving rise to an exponential new breeds of radicals who are not even directly affiliated with the so- called targeted radical groups, but are adopting their cause. In other words, the so-called Islamic radicals are increasingly growing and expanding into so many fronts far beyond the widely publicized Al Qaeda group. To succeed in defeating these growing number of fundamentalists using the Bush strategy, will simply means that majority of the world's Islamic population will either have to be captured and held behind bars, or be extinct. That may be a far- fetch goal which may never be accomplished by the Bush's style of combating global terrorism....particularly identified with Islamic radicals.

With Mr. Bush's unilateral arrogance of flexing his executive muscles by imposing imperial-style foreign policies, most international observers truly believes that the administration's goal was not to truly combat the real threat of global terrorism, but rather to seize the window of opportunity provided by the 9/11 incident to impose its implicitly concealed Western imperialism on these targeted nations. The ugly events and saga following the invasion of Iraq indicated misleading signals contrary to Mr. Bush's publicly declared reasons to bolster his unilateral cause for the invasion. The post-invasion occupation by the U.S. and the reckless loss of huge civilian lives even added more doubt to the legitimacy of Mr. Bush's declared mission to invade Iraq.

If in fact Mr. Bush's unilateral act of war was that legitimate as his right-wing Republican faction in Congress had gave him the green light to proceed, then he should have been readily willing to change gears when his master plans brought forth more of the problem than he was trying to solve in the first place.

People in position of high authority, in most cases, loves to camouflage with their executive leverage to orchestrate false political pretense to fool the general public about their true mission and position in serving the public. With time such deceptive style of leadership eventually runs afoul when the result fails to match up with the executed policies....and in particular, when such cause of action runs counter to the interest of the society. After such misleading priorities starts to manifest adversely on those it was intended to protect while the actor still insist to stay on cause anyway with the same flawed policy, that is when you know that such policy was ill-intended and was all based on deceptive motives from the get go.

# 32

## THE MEDIA POLITICS IN AMERICA

IT IS A NO BRAINER THAT every nation loves to use their media to paint rosy pictures of themselves to the outside world, even though the picture might not be that rosy as they are being portrayed. But it is no longer cool when you only portray yours as the 'beautiful and the flawless' while portraying those of others as the 'bad and the ugly,' If there is nothing good you can say about others, it's better to say nothing at all. Such one-way street media politics reflects a mindset that do not wish others well.

The Western developed countries, especially the U.S., have been engaging in the business of media politics since the advent of the industrial revolution up till present time. As one of the nations that sets the pace of technological civility, United States, without a doubt, has been using the leverage to its full advantage, which is quite normal of any civilized society. But at the same time, it has been using the same media power to portray often inflammatory and distorted profile of the rest developing nations around the world......creating a wide-spread, and in most cases, false or distorted public impression of these nations.

In recent time, those strategies are becoming less effective as they once were during the Western economic hey days. The reason? Most of the developing nations are now catching on as well to the media myth of the West to which they have been victims for so long. These other countries are now more than ever telling their own stories to the world....adopting similar influence of the media to counter the West's often inflammatory portrayal of their socioeconomic and political standing in the world.

A relative case in point has been the Arab media network, Aljazeera, a United Arab Emirates' (U.A.E.) news network, that, since the war, had been filling in on war updates in Afghanistan and Iraq and other Middle-Eastern Islamic nations…giving a more accurate account of the war news compared with the often distorted and censored version of the American news of the same events. The Bush-Cheney administration blockaded the free flow of the nation's Constitutional right guaranteeing 'Freedom of Speech and that of the Press,' The American version of international news, especially the ones focused on foreign policies, and the war in Iraq, or terrorism-related issues shared with the general public, often got so watered down during Mr. Bush's administration to the extent that such sensitive news highly anticipated by the general public got regularly altered to fit the context of what the administration wanted the public to hear, or the intended impression it wish to create in the minds of the public. Since the Bush-led war in Afghanistan and Iraq, his administration tried so hard to manipulate the American media to champion his failed unilateral mission to invade Iraq. Most of the conservative-owned networks happily obliged.

The Bush administration labeled Aljazeera as a mouth piece for the Islamic extremists and their supporters. In his attempt to counter the Aljazeera news about the war, which are widely viewed by those from the Islamic descent, the administration funded the establishment of an Arab television station in South Carolina to broadcast the American version of the Arab news of the war. The Bush administration also wanted to use this American version of Arab Television to divert the viewership of the Aljazeera's audience. Of course the strategy did not work because the public quickly catch-on to the administration's motive of trying to rival the Arab news network.

As a result of the often distorted account of things presented to the public by the Western medias about events or the state of things in other countries…..developing countries in particular…..China recently launched its own international version of 'News and Information' network to set the record straight. It is focused on telling its own story first hand to the international community as opposed to the Western media giving an often distorted account of what goes on in China to the international community. In 2010 China opened a branch of this newly launched International News Network bureau in New York city as well in other major cities across the globe.

In the fall of 2006, about 10 journalists from the Miami Herald news paper was implicated in a scandal of accepting tens of thousands of dollars from the Bush administration to participate in a news coverage of the United States Radio and Television Broadcasting Agency. It was lured into the government influenced culture of bias journalism to publish and air what appears to be a blackmail version of news report targeted at Spanish audiences of Cuban descent concentrated in the Miami region of Florida. The administration's effort was focused on spreading a more or less fabricated account of some of the flaws associated with the Cuban government to win the support of the exiled Cuban-Americans living in Miami. As the scandal unfolded, three journalists from this Miami-based newspaper got fired as the probe ensued.

It is not a surprise to find out that most of these mainstream media markets in America are owned and operated by individuals, in most cases, with well-connected politically conservative roots. In a situation where the nation's Commander-In-Chief happens to be an outlaw conservative like the case of Mr. Bush, and the mainstream medias across the country are owned and operated by like-minded Republicans alike, that explains the degree of polarization and double standards that had reigned very heavily during the Bush administration.

The Miami Herald incident, among many others that never made it to the public further affirms the public's wide-spread perception that American media has long been accused of being at the back pocket of American government, as opposed to the "Freedom of Press" guaranteed by the nation's First Amendment Constitutional doctrine.

Harsh as it may sound, it is the absolute fact which most of the American public are already aware of that, for America to be able to return to its hey days which has been on a gradually decline, it has to confront the hard absolute reality that it must discard of the ill-intended vast-right policymakers in Washington during election period. These bad apples wants to re-write the nation's constitution and the existing statutory laws to fit their twisted imperial ideologies. The implementation of their ideologies have been causing major shift and division in the socioeconomic and political values that once made the nation stood out among the rest nations. Socioeconomic values that has for long been the hallmark of America's growth and strength. These bad apples are using their elected position in public office to push for selfish and arbitrary policies......toxic policies which effects has, over the years, been slowly eroding the core values of the American society.

Nonetheless, quite a few of the American media networks, like the old-fashioned Public Radio networks, Public Radio International, and even the New York Times, among few others, still stands out and remain independent of the government of the moment in delivering their journalistic duties to the public. These media and news information organizations have tried to stay course on the authenticity of their news report without much spin. American public must not allow these bad apples to continue watering-down the well-founded values and image of the nation. To be more precise, Mr. Bush and his vice, Dick Cheney and a handful of his administration's like-minded vast-right conservative policymakers have been among the very bad apples in the history of United States' government of this generation. Their vision and leadership style has been playing out, even after they left office, as more of a residual liability to the U.S. government than any good anyone can think of. The policies they implement and champions are always highly contagious like H.I.V. virus when contracted, and thereon after slowly weakens both the subjects' and the innocents' immune systems alike. Public consensus within America and across the world showed that the Bush-Cheney's administration has been America's worst nightmare of the current generation.

Even though they are no longer in office today, but the havoc the administration had done will continue to affects millions of people in America for decades ahead.....and also millions more in other parts of the world where the administration had went to wage its terror war.

## (a)    Call for Media Reform

**--CALL FOR MEDIA REFORM:** Governmental interference on news information, or media service as a whole, undermines the credibility of such nation's democracy. The issue of media politics is, to some extent, more or less an ubiquitous phenomenon which varies in levels of governmental regulation and interference on a nation-by-nation basis. Some governments completely blockade the airing or publishing of some sensitive but critically important news information by their private or national medias. This is somewhat less damaging from insiders' or outsiders' point of view, because accounts of event, either censored or uncensored, was never even shared with the pubic in the first place. The most damaging is the one when certain governments deliberately affect the alteration of news information gathered by journalists, or news agencies itself.... in effect, creating a misleading perception of the event in the minds of the citizens and the general public.

Majority of the America public as well as the international community believes that most of the news which American news networks covers on national and global terrorism and Islamic radical actors during the Bush administration has been recklessly and overly portrayed and misrepresented as opposed to the underlying facts of the matter itself. Western media, the American ones in particular, has for decades been on the forefront of global journalism with great degree of reliability on certain news and information contents they shared with the public, but in recent time, major shift away from that status has been raising a widespread concern among the American and the international community, strongly recommending a total overhaul and reform of the American journalism due to its huge influence on domestic and international audiences.

The call for reform is to be focused on news media presentation of facts without spin and independent of governmental censorship on sensitive issues that are closely followed by the general public.

The public feels that there is utmost need to fix the American conservatives' owned main-stream media into a more transparent and unbiased journalism about global events in particular, like the coverage of the war in Iraq and the terrorism-related news which has been, in most part, stereotypically publicized with bias by the conservative-owned news and information networks. They always pluralize the acts perpetrated by few Islamic radicals within the religion as acts practiced by all Muslims and their affiliates.

Akbar Ahmed, professor at the American University for Islamic Studies, was a guest on a Philadelphia public radio show, hosted by Terry Gross during the fall of 2006. He emphasized on the troubling developments of the reckless representation of news of events presented to the public by

American and other Western media networks regarding Islamic radicals in connection with the religion and Muslims as a whole and its doctrine.

Professor Ahmed, among other academic figures across the globe, condemned the American medias' role in assisting the Bush administration in fueling the terrorism propaganda out of proportion on the minds of the American public. He blamed some of the mainstream American media entities for dancing to the tunes of the Bush administration.... advancing Mr. Bush's personal perception, which in most part were vague and outright speculations of the existential degree to which this extremist acts actually exist within America as well as its suspicion to infringe on its interest across the globe. In effect, the public's perception has been overly heightened by the medias' drumbeat, causing the general public to have mixed signals as to the exact nature and the very magnitude to which the rabid Islamic fundamentalism is present in America and elsewhere.

Professor Ahmed was concerned as well as other world renowned intellectuals, that the Western media, led by the American journalism has failed to play a constructive and instrumental role as provided within their professional capacity and protocols, in abridging the news of war and extremist activities they have been feeding the public since the aftermath of 9/11 and the war in Iraq. He feared that the exact nature of things continues to be misrepresented by the American and other Western conservative mainstream medias.

The 2006 Miami Herald media scandal that implicated some of its journalists that later led to the dismissal of three of its top journalists and others within the company, led to a brief boycott of the newspaper readership which are predominantly Hispanics and Cuban-Americans. To stave off the boycott and appease the readers, the management resolved the tension by making one of the Spanish officials resign his post....ostensibly taking the blame for what had happened while the three journalists who were initially dismissed were re-hired and the rest other staffs that was implicated were all exonerated. A managerial strategy adopted by the newspaper's administrative circle to cure and quell the public's outrage over its gross ethical and professional missteps.

The resignation of one of the top Spanish administrative directors made it rather appear as if the only bad apple in the midst has fess up and accepted responsibility for his action and has been rooted out. Whereas, the whole conspiracy goes further than that.

This, among several others, has been how the Bush administration helped to tarnish the professional integrity of the American news media and the news and information they share with the public.

The role of any news and information media is to give an accurate account of events without spin. When this utmost responsibility is being compromised and stifled by whatever reason, then the very role which the media and the journalists suppose to serve becomes dangerously compromised while the entire public are being deliberately led astray on the actual stand of things.

It is very shameful that United States of all countries continue to play implicit role in hindering the accuracy of news contents which private media entities shares with the public......essentially abusing the governmental authority by influencing the nation's media and news information networks to assist it cover up its dirt while exposing that of others.

Despite all that has been put at stake and sacrificed by Mr. Bush in his unilateral act of war and style of governance, no significant milestone was so far attained all through his eight years reign with his multifaceted strategies of combating global extremism. The only thing that has significantly changed for all that has been sacrificed has been increased bloodshed, violence and radicalism among the Islamic communities. A cause of action intended to quell an uprising extremism is itself fueling and breeding more of it. That tells the public that the cause of action or the manner of its execution is faulty and counter-productive and needs a new approach. A much better approach was implemented by the Obama administration.

If the Bush's tough military stance and bullying strategy has failed to quell and accomplish the desired goal, be it legit or ambiguous, as it has been playing out over one years of warring, then the new approach has to be the reversal......the soft power, which the international community had recommended and expect to yield much better result.

# PART-III

# AMERICA......THE SOCIO-ECONOMIC POLITICS WITHIN

# 33   *THE LAND OF OPPORTUNITY*

WITHOUT A DOUBT, UNITED STATES HAS CHANGED so drastically in recent time from all its appeals of few decades ago. Every aspect of its glorious hey days seems to be fading out as each year unfolds.....particularly from when Mr. Bush took charge of the country back in 2001 to 2008. Obama came and revived the nation for 8 good years.

In the U.S. thousands, if not millions apply for enrollment to colleges each year. The top 1 percent will go to elite universities. Some of the others will go to second-tier schools, at best. These unfortunates will find that, while their career prospects aren't permanently foreclosed, the odds of great success are diminished. Suicide rates, and the accompanying Attention Deficit Hyperactive Disorder (ADHD), at these schools are high, as students come to feel they have failed their parent....likewise their anticipated future career projections.

When questioned about the enormous income inequality in United States, the cheerleaders of the America's unfettered market countered that everybody has a shot at becoming rich here. The distribution of income might be skewed, but America's economic mobility is second to none. With emerging economies like China, India, Brazil, Russia, among other nations becoming increasingly active and relevant on the world stage, that once robust U.S. economic status appears to be on a shaky footing and have been gradually diminishing for quite some time now relative to that of some of theses emerging economies.

To reverse this shaky state of income mobility in America, a drastic reform of the nation's commerce law must be effected to mandate a change of morale in both public and the private sectors. The Obama administration has put in place bills that will put various American business sectors on check, particularly the financial sector....creating a more effective laws and oversight that will end the conservative corporate America's style of unbridled business practice and insatiable personal greed.

As they usually do, the beneficiaries to this type of wild capitalism in America has been lobbying hard, conveying their opposition to such reform through their vast-right conservative peers in Congress, to obstruct the commerce reform laws from passing. Nonetheless, the Obama administration made very impressive headway in passing the necessary reforms.

Sadly, Donald Trump conned his way with the American voters to win the 2016 presidential election. In effect, he has been reversing all the gains made by Obama. Trump is giving business organizations within the country leeway once again to conduct their businesses as they wish with the general public with little or no governmental oversight at all. The general public are in for a wild ride again.

That image championed by the free-market conservatives is wrong, and these days, it abets far too many unfair policies, including cuts in essential programs like 'head start' or Medicaid. The poor, we are told, can use their own bootstraps. The Bush administration got away with huge tax cuts for the rich, in part, because non-rich Americans who make up most of the population, believes everybody has a chance of making it in the club. Unfortunately, the American dream is not that broadly accessible. Simply put, American dream is under assault.

A research surveyed by the Organization for Economic Cooperation and Development, a governmental think-tank for the rich nations, found that mobility in the United States is lower than in other industrialized countries. One study found that mobility between generations.....people doing better or worse than their parents......is weaker in America than in Denmark, Austria, Norway, Finland, Canada, Sweden, Germany and France. In America, there is more than forty percent chance that if a father is in the bottom fifth of the earnings distribution, his son will end up there, too. In Denmark, the equivalent odds are under 25 percent, and there are less than 30 percent in Britain.

America's sluggish mobility is ultimately unsurprising. Wealthy parents not only pass on that wealth in inheritances, they can pay for better education, nutrition and healthcare for their children. The poor cannot afford this investment on their children's development.... and the government doesn't provide nearly enough help.

In one of his speech back in 2007, the Bush administration Federal Reserve Chairman, Ben Bernanke, who succeeded Allen Greenspan, argued that while the inequality of rewards fuels the economy by making people exert themselves, opportunity should be "as widely distributed and as equal as possible." The question is that the have-nots don't have many opportunities either.

There is an immense problem of inequality in America. It is getting worse, not better. It cannot be solved entirely by tax policy. And it certainly cannot be solved by monetary policy....but we can take a stab at it. Even if it's a small stab, by sharing the skills and connections that some of us have....and were born with.... those young people who have what it takes in their cerebral cortex but needs an outside connection. Effort in this direction will not change everything for everyone, but it will change life for some, and that would be a good day's work.

## (a)   *The National Minimum Wage Politics*

***THE NATIONAL MINIMUM WAGE POLITICS:*** It is quite ludicrous to learn that the very nation that loves to take all the credit of being the most industrialized, the wealthiest and the largest economy in the world, puts its workforces, who brings forth all the growth, at the bottom of the list, while the select corporate executives ends up with remarkably huge executive pay packages.....regardless of companies' profitability or loss.

No matter how ingenious these corporate leaders are in their managerial skills or risk-taking, every organization, either for profit or otherwise, needs strong and effective workforces to have them operate effectively as well. With their managerial ingenuity, these corporate heads nonetheless, can not do all the work. In fact, none of the so-called celebrity-status corporate chiefs' ingenious managerial expertise can be carried out without the input and the human resources of these undervalued workforces. The success and growth of any given private or public establishment is just as good as the managerial skills of the corporate or organizational leader, and such managerial competency is just as good and important as that of the human resource workforces who actually gets the physical jobs done. Workforces should be equally as valued in essence to their financial compensations just like that of the corporate executives.....or at least close to it.

All the organizational credits and the financial perks should not always be attributed to only the organizational leaders alone as if they were the only ones who did all the work.

For over two decades, the national minimum wage in United States has remained at a steady $5.25 per hour for average unskilled workforce which makes up about sixty percent of the nation's total workforce in the private sector, while the corporate executives of most of the corporate chains are paid annual pay package in the millions......plus millions more on company stock options and other incentives like the unlimited use of corporate jets, and other extra perks that even extends to their wives and kids.

To even make matters worse, some of these corporate executives, after a period of lousy job performance, are handsomely compensated with sign-off packages in the range of eight to nine digit payoff figures. What a reward for a terrible job performance by an executive, while the average productive work forces, doing all the hard work, continue to remain at the lowest income bracket. An income barely enough for these hard working people to utilize in sustaining their daily living till the next paycheck. Not to even mention other surcharges and mandatory governmental deductibles that still gets taken out of these meager wages. In the case of the corporate executives, its an all year-round Déjà vu experience for them.

In Japan, another highly industrialized developed nation ranking so far as the third largest economy in the world after United States and China.....the corporate culture and the value placed on the industrial workforces is totally the opposite to that in the United States, or that of typical Western industrialized nations.

Not only do the Japanese corporate culture places very high value on their workforces, but they also make sure their earnings are proportionate to their average expected standard of living and relatively sustainable to their livelihoods.

Japan corporate culture caters to its workforce by guaranteeing them a lifetime employment regardless of market fluctuations or business short or long term performance. Though that hospitality has slightly dropped in recent time due to drastic change in global economic structure. Even so, the slight drop in employer-employee job security in Japan is still nowhere near the ruthless employer-employee job insecurity corporate culture in America. Japan's spirit of corporate loyalty to their employees still remain intact despite the drastic changes that is taking place in the global economic environment of the recent decade.

In Japan, a person's place of employment was a part of his identity and unflinching company loyalty was the highest of virtues. When the country had Asia's hottest economy, fast-growing companies could afford to buy employee loyalty with guarantees of lifetime jobs and a sense of belonging at a company that treated workers like extended family. But that social contract started disintegrating in the economic stagnation of the 1990s.

In all, the Japanese corporate culture accommodates its workforce in both ups and down times. They believe that their workforce were part of the organization's good days, so they should be accommodated also during the organization's down times till better times comes back around. Unless in an unavoidable situation where an organization is shutting its doors and going out of business, then letting go the employees at that point is inevitable and understandable by everyone affected.

Anyone with a two-way street mindset should see Japan's corporate culture as a pretty rational and reasonable managerial ethics that would not only translate to more future growth, but also boosts organizational efficiency and employees' morale. It is the direct opposite in the American corporate culture.

In the American setting, whenever an organization happens to be performing poorly in terms of earnings, for whatever internal or external reasons, that automatically translates to mass-layoff of most low-end workforces.....practically treating them like production machines that can easily be put away when not in use and could be reengaged only when they are needed to get some serious jobs done.

In contrast, the American corporate theory implies that workforces must be discarded at down time to minimize operational cost, regardless of how invaluable their job performance were in good seasons. A typical American business organization don't think such workforces deserve some reservation to be retained at organizational low points. They basically care less about how these laid-off workforces will at least sustain themselves till they may be called back to resume work, or till they are able to secure another job. So long as such layoffs helps the organization cut cost and eventually brings the organization back to profitability.

The sad part is that the lower-end workforces are always the first ones to be discarded. And they are the most vulnerable income bracket workforces in America who are ineligible to receive unemployment checks from the government. That simply means they are on their own whenever they get laid off.

There is nothing wrong in working towards organizational recovery, but the method the American corporate entities takes in accomplishing that goal reflects a selfish corporate culture that only cares about the company's bottom line......and not that of the hardworking workforce whom the company depend on in getting the various jobs done. Instead, the accumulated windfalls made by the company when business was good are rather reserved to be split among the administrative level executives as additional incentives on top of having already been well paid for their executive job performance. None of such prior earnings are ever used to retain these low-end workforces in American corporate culture when business is slow.

Absent the culture of corporate greed, it is very good managerial policy for organizations to spend some of the windfall profits they made during good business times to provide some form of minimal income for the laid off workforces whose low income bracket makes them ineligible to receive unemployment benefits from the government. That will at least sustain them till things improve, rather than just laying them off at down times like unproductive machines. They should not be treated by these organizations like machines that has no life in them...that can just be put off till their services are needed again.

In the government's part, it should have a more comprehensive Unemployment Benefit policy than what it currently has now. It should have an Unemployment Benefit program that will cover all American workforces, not just for the median to the high- end workforces alone. The low-end workforces have similar daily human needs to meet just as the rest groups of workforces whom the government caters for when they happen to get laid off.

Most corporate executives are retained in American business organizations during down times. So also should the low-end workforces be retained as well, while working towards Organizational restructuring. Even during the colonial era, the slaves masters were still responsible to feed their slaves regardless of any fluctuation in the demand of their farm products, or other climatic factors. The slaves were fed even though they had suffered other forms of cruel and inhumane treatments from the hands of their masters.

Corporate greed has become so terribly entrenched in the hearts and souls of American corporate leaders.....with almost no reservation at all for any form of socioeconomic or humanitarian flexibility for the average employees who works so hard to make the company a success that the so-called owners enjoys and takes all the credits for.

The American corporate sector has a well funded team of lobbyists that helps get their concerns across to their vast-right conservative peers in Congress in Washington.....who in turn helps them to stifle the progress made by the American Labor Union to hike the national minimum wage for decades.

A case in point, among many others, was that of the former Washington lobbyist, Jack Abramoff, who got caught in 2006 in the act of fraud and conspiracy of lavishing gift on Washington lawmakers in return for a wide range of relaxed trade laws that is intended to help boost the bottom line of the concerned corporate players. Abramoff was subsequently indicted and convicted in 2006 for his role in corrupting government officials in an influence peddling case. He was sentenced to serve prison term for this crime. Mr. Bush, whose administration was an accessory to this type of unbridled playing field, even attempted to grant him presidential pardon to avoid him serving his jail term, but there were just too much high-level political watchdogs monitoring the matter. The Bush administration was always partner to the culture of corporate and political deception.

Even though Abramoff got caught, there are still a lot more of such folks out there pushing envelopes for the behind-the- scene bad apples in the public sector. The right-wing Republican leaderships in America always allow them to have things their way at the expense of the general public. Mr. Trump operates this way in his private businesses. Now that he is president, he has been paving way for large business organizations to operate their way....with little or no governmental oversight.

The dangerous culture of enabling influence peddlers to impair the judgment of public officials is still widely tolerated by the rightwing faction in United States and is causing major havoc to the nation's economy as a whole...and the general public.

About two months before the November 2006 U.S. Congressional election, the American Labor Union again lobbied to have the national minimum wage increased from $5.25 to $7.25 per hour. Both Houses of Congress, which then was still majority Republicans, voted on the bill. Sadly, the bill was shut down by the majority right-wing Republicans who were against such increase. The Republicans did not allow the bill to pass.

Two months later, after the Congressional election, Democrats swept both Houses of U.S. Congress and changed the nation's legislative power structure that was under the Republican control since 1994. With new leadership and majority in both Houses of Congress, the national minimum wage bill was once again revisited. In fact, this was one of the top agendas on the Democrats list of priorities to be addressed within their first 100 hours of inauguration on January 2, 2007 as the new Congressional majority leaders.

Votes were casted once again, but this time Democrats were the majority in both Houses. The bill that has been stalled by Republicans for decades was finally passed in favor of the Labor Union to increase the national minimum wage to $7.25 per hour. Thanks to the America public who overwhelmingly voted Republicans out of the majority sits in the Congress then.

Most American public and the outside world are now clearer than ever that typical American right-wing Republican leaderships can not be trusted with their words......and in most cases, their leadership priorities are always misguided, skewed, self-centered and not necessarily to benefit everyone but those within their immediate circle. That's not the leadership America needs ever again until the nation's vast-right Republicans are fully repentant of their misguided and distorted culture of leadership.

During the last few months to the end of Mr. Bush's presidency, the result of his dysfunctional economic policies almost brought the nation's financial and economic standings to its knees. The economic downturn continued to unravel as the administration got ready to leave office...with major financial institutions along with products and services institutions going under within a very short period of time.

The worst political and economic debacle in recent generation was caused by the Bush-Cheney's Republican administration in America, and not long after that it quickly spread to other parts of the globe due to the policies championed by the Bush team along with his like-minded vast-right conservative faction in the U.S. and some other Western nations.

## (b)   Moral and Financial Threat

***MORAL AND FINANCIAL THREAT:*** The people who created America built a moral structure around money. The Puritan legacy inhibited luxury and self indulgence. Benjamin Franklin spread a practical gospel that emphasized hard work, temperance and frugality. Millions of parents, preachers, newspaper editors and teachers exploited the message, the result was quite remarkable.

The United States in most part has been an affluent nation since its founding. But the country was, by and large, not corrupted by wealth and personal greed like it is in recent generation. For centuries, it remained industrious, ambitious and frugal. Over the last 30 years much of that has been shredded. The social norms and institutions that encouraged 'frugality and spending what you earn' has been undermined. The institution that encourage debt and living for the moment have been strengthened. The country's moral guardians are forever looking for decadence out of Hollywood and reality TV. But the most rampant decadence today in America is financial, and in large part, moral decadence, the trampling of decent norms about how to use and harness money.

The deterioration of financial mores has meant two things. First, it meant explosion of debt that inhibits social mobility and ruins lives. In a 2008 report conducted by the Institute for American Values and other Think-Tanks called "For a New Thrift: Confronting the debt culture," between 1989 and 2001, credit card debt nearly tripled, soaring from $238 billion to $692 billion. By 2007, it was up to $937 billion.

Second, the transformation has led to a stark financial polarization. On one hand, there is what the report calls the investor class. It has tax-differed savings plans, as well as an army of financial advisers. On the other hand, there is the lottery class, people with little access to 401 (K)'s or financial planning but plenty access to payday lenders, credit cards and lottery agents.

The loosening of financial inhibition has meant more options for the well educated but more temptation and chaos for the most vulnerable. Social norms, the invisible thread that guide behavior, have deteriorated in America......thanks in part to the neo-cons and the vast-right free-market masters of the universe who have been the purveyors of this terrible culture. Over the next past years, Americans have been more socially conscious about protecting the environment and inhaling tobacco. They have become less socially conscious about money and debt and morality in general.

The agents of destruction are many. State governments have played a role. They aggressively hawk their lottery products, which some people call a tax on stupidity. Twenty percent of Americans are frequent players spending about $60 billion a year. Aside from the financial toll, the moral toll is comprehensive. Here is the government, the guardian of order, telling people that they don't have to work to build for future. They can strike it rich for nothing. Yet, most of those habitual lottery players work pretty hard to earn the money they use in state sponsored gambling.

Payday lenders have played a role. They seductively offer fast cash at absurd interest rates......to 15 million people every month. Sadly, those credit streams have ran very low since the economic crunch and financial meltdown that started to unravel during Mr. Bush's last years of presidency. The Obama administration had sound restrictions in place to keep their predatory lending practice in check, but Mr. Trump came and lift the restrictions...sadly allowing these lenders to continue raping the general public. Trump operates this way so he is very pleased to approve other businesses to do likewise at the expense of the general public.

Credit card companies have played a role. Instead of targeting the financially astute, who pay off their debts, they have found out that they can make money off the young and vulnerable. 56 percent of students in their final year of college carry four or more credit cards before the 2007-08 economic meltdown.

Congress and the White House have played a role. The nation's leaders have always have an incentive to shove costs for current promises into the backs of future generations. It's only now becomes respectable to do so. The huge debt incurred by the Bush's act of war in Iraq and elsewhere is already becoming an inevitable financial liability for the current and future generations in America.

Wall street has played a role. Bill Gates built a socially useful product to make his future. But what message do the compensation packages the hedge fund managers get send across the country?

The list goes on. However, good criticisms should be accompanied with viable recommendations to at least help fix the problems as well. First, raise public consciousness about debt like the anti-smoking activists did with their campaign. Second, create institutions that encourage thrift.....a practice that is becoming fastly widespread as the state of American economy continued to tank during the last years of Mr. Bush's eight years of chaotic presidency. Foundation and churches could issue short-term loans to cut into the payday lenders' predatory business. Private and public programs could give the poor and middle class access to financial planners. Usually laws could be enforced and strengthened. College could reduce credit card advertising on campus. Kids-save accounts will encourage savings from a young age. The tax code should tax consumption, not income, and in the meantime, it should do more to encourage savings up and down the income ladder.

There are dozens of things that could be done. But the most important is to shift value. These are not recommendations that can only be adopted in American society. Other governments can adopt them as well. Impressively, the Obama administration made some inroad implementation towards such direction during his 8 years' tenure. None of such values are encouraged by Mr. Trump who took over from Obama.

# 34 GUN-RELATED CRIMES AND THE ISSUE OF GUN CONTROL IN AMERICA

WHY ARN'T THE CONGRESS GOING AFTER THE ROGUE dealers, or even control the entire arms business directly from the manufacturers? Because a substantial amount of tax revenue is generated by the government from the firearm industry. The industry is also backed by powerful lobbying team. Also, the Wild-West mentality still lingers heavily in most parts of America today.

In a typical U.S. Republican leadership, a familiar slogan is: "Business as usual," so long as the government is getting a piece of the action...... even though allowing such business operation to thrive may be extremely detrimental to public's safety.

Since 2001, the National Rifle Association (NRA) has been calling the shots on gun control policy all through Mr. Bush's Republican administration. After Mr. Bush took office, his administration rewarded the gun lobby with series of laws and regulations that prohibits the Alcohol, Tobacco and Firearms (ATF) from releasing gun-related info to the public.

In September 2006, the House of Representative attempted to further castrate the agency by passing the A.T.F. Modernization and Reform Act, which makes it harder for the Feds to prosecute gun dealers who break the law. Another law up for debate would prevent the A.T.F. from disclosing gun-trace information to local authorities for use in lawsuits and make it a felony for law enforcement in one state to share gun-trace data with colleagues in another.

As long as the federal government don't control the gun laws and allow it to vary from state to state and Congress continues to bow to gun lovers, dealers will continue to sell to traffickers without penalty and traffickers will continue supplying states where demand is highest and the saga along with the nightmare will continue. Meaning you might want to invest in gun yourself for protection.

As some American public might argue that the provision of the nation's 2nd Constitutional Amendment permits them of the right to bear arms. Fine, but the purchase of such arms should be directly through the government itself, instead of permitting such sales of weapons or business entities whose primary goal is to amass as much profit from their business operation as they possibly can. These private gun dealers could care less of verifying how many guns are owned or purchased by the customers, and the intent to which such purchases are focused. The more guns the dealers can sell the better for them regardless of who the buyers are or how many guns they already own, or their purpose for purchasing the guns. More gun sales translates to more profit to be made for the private dealers. There is just no incentive on the dealers part for such aggressive and extensive details with their potential customers like the government would have done before the guns are sold to the public.

As most right-wing Americans and even the conservative justices at the nation's Supreme court had chosen to interpret and kept claiming that the nation's 2nd Amendment Constitutional provision permits them the right to own a firearm, the government in this case should be the right medium through which anyone in America who really feels the need to own a firearm for whatever their reasons are, to get their guns from. This way, the government will make sure it verifies the legality of every firearm sold to the public, and also cap its sales to one gun per person for those citizens eligible to purchase or own one. Guns should not be allowed to be owned as souvenirs because they can be used by anyone as lethal weapons, which they actually are.

Second, the 2nd Amendment right to own or carry arms needs to be revisited in earnest by Congress for amendment and clarity of the provision in a way that will best serve and protect the safety and interest of the American public at large. Such amendment should assert the absolute authority to sell any form of firearm to the public only by the government itself, and no longer to be sold directly or indirectly by any private individuals or business entities. Such provision will not only put the private individual gun dealers out of business of dealing guns for profit guns that are predominantly sold to folks with devious motives, that ends up being used to harm and destroy mostly innocent lives.....but will also greatly reduce the number of guns that used to be easily purchased through private dealers by ill-intended individuals.

## (a)  Gun Vilence within America

***GUN VIOLENCE WITHIN AMERICA:*** Ever before the war on terror became the talk of the nation after 9/11, there have always been a disturbing level of violent crimes committed in various cities across America. An increasingly troubling trend that continues to threaten the safety and security of innocent law abiding citizens. Among the various acts of criminal violence, those committed with the use of gun are considered the most lethal.

For so many decades, legal access to guns by citizens have remained one of the highest, if not the lead cause of human premature deaths across America. Even the effect of any form of controlled-substance, that somewhat impairs human judgment as well as their physical health when consumed, can not, in most cases, subject the users immediately dead like what a gun shot would do to a victim. Though, the impairment effect caused by drug usage can cause such users to wrongfully use a deadly weapon within his or her reach to settle scores against the next person.

Even illnesses which are bound to plague mankind from time to time, still won't take a man's breath away instantly as the wrongful use of gun will do.

Yet, for all the past decades of turmoil and the lost of human lives due to the availability of guns for sale to the public as a form of profit-driven enterprise in America, the lawmakers in Washington have at best only enacted laws to take the so-called illegal guns off the streets of America and impose tough penalty for their illicit usage by criminals, but has taken the back seat on legislation that will essentially ban the sale of this lethal weapon itself to the public by private individuals or business entities.

So much American public taxpayers' money has been spent by the federal and state governments in hunting down and prosecute the unlawful users, but no effort from the federal government has yet been made to put the gun retailers out of business.

This makes an average citizen wonder why the government of United Sates has for so long been reluctant to legislate and enforce a law that will strictly ban gun sales by private sectors, except for government use only, which can be obtained by the government directly through the manufacturers. Or, if the government wants a piece of the revenue made from gun sales that bad, it should then take absolute control of the sales operation to the public like it does with the liquor market. That way, whatever the citizens end up doing with the guns, the government could share part of the blame as well.

Allowing civilians to own firearms, other than the kind used for hunting, do not serve the public's interest in any shape or form.....nor does it serve any constructive purpose for public's safety other than the motive of the holders of the weapons. Why would the government of any sovereign country legalize the sale of firearms to its civilian population, knowing that it is a lethal weapon that can be deployed to cause severe bodily harm or death if they happen to fall in wrong hands, or in the hands of folks under influence of drugs or alcohol? If everyone in America were to be carrying guns for their own protection as the 2$^{nd}$ Amendment is construed by the American conservative ideologues, then it should make sense to argue that there is little or no need at all for having the armed cops out there securing the streets of America. If the 2nd Amendment allows everyone in America the right to own and carry firearms for their protection, then there is no need for the government providing the cops to protect the streets, property and the public, because the so-called misconstrued Constitution already allowed anyone to own and carry a weapon to protect themselves.

The burden of police to control firearms crimes is shifted by the federal government to individual state law enforcement agencies across America, while the authority to own and operate a firearm business by private citizens is permitted by the federal government itself. Something don't look right with that equation. Basically, those far-right policymakers in Washington have all along been implicitly telling the American people that the revenue the government generates from the firearm dealers is more important than legislating the law to ban the business for public's safety. Or maybe the nation's rightist hard-liners' vague self-protection doctrine trumps public's safety particularly that of the innocent ones, who ends up, in most cases, being the victims of gun-related crimes.

Similar policies has been applied by the U.S. government in restricting cigarette smoking in government buildings, along with a bunch of other ads and marketing restrictions through the public media. Even some states across America have legislated their own laws that ban cigarette smoking in bars......of all places, restaurants, or even in the car while any minor is within the vehicle. These lines of restrictions are quite reasonable for health reasons to non-smokers within such vicinity. But if the government is so concerned and mindful of the adverse health effect of smoking by its citizens, why not just make the law that will ban its retail sales completely.

The cigarette makers, just like the gun makers, are paying the government huge fees on operational taxes, while the same government turns around waging all kinds of war against the consumers of these products that it permits the manufacturers to produce and market their products to.

Any government with a democratic setting like the United States, should not abet or be a partner, directly or indirectly, in crime or anything that, when made available to the general public can pave way to being utilized as a form of lethal device or health hazard to either the user or another fellow individual....or cause physical or mental deficiencies to the end consumers or innocent others.

In New York city, a law was put in place in early 2007, banning the smoke of cigarette in any vehicle while a kid or minor may be inside. Violators are issued citation of x-amount of dollars by the city police to be paid by such violators to the government coffers. And in Philadelphia, the city administrators also made an ordinance in 2007, banning cigarette smoke inside all bars and in public parks. Any bar owner who allows their customers to smoke within the bar and gets caught, will be issued a citation by the city's cops. Such citation carries specific fines expected to be paid by such violators to the city's treasury. Similar citation and fine applies as well to those caught smoking in the public parks. Other cities across the nation have also followed suit to implement their own ordinances as well. The municipal authorities saw it as a window of opportunity to generate extra revenue from the public.

In all, the government keeps avoiding to address and tackle the root cause of problems. Instead, it prefers to adopt policies that will somehow shift the burden and penalty of inaction to the innocent end-users of these products, while their makers are allowed by the same government entities to continue making and supplying these products for public's consumption.

Taking a close look at both ends of the equation, it appears like the government is getting paid from either ends. One, through taxation of such products like cigarette, sold to the public by the manufacturers, and also getting paid as well by the end-consumers by way of implementing bogus restrictions on consumers that will enable the law enforcers to issue citations for violators of such unjustified ordinances.

Yet, the root cause of the underlying problem itself remains unattended, while their adverse effects continues to plague and affect people's lives in the society.

In the case of the cigarette war, the end consumers seem to be getting the raw end of the deal by being made to foot the entire bill of keeping the product makers in business, as well as being forced to pay the government unjustified fine just for consuming a legally purchased products. Instead of the federal government putting a complete stop to the sales, or even the making of such health hazard products, it rather chooses, in most cases, to circumvent its own authority by adopting other vague policies to further exploit the end-users of these products. Is this justice for public's interest, or the use of public office to enact policies that exploits the public that supposed to be protected by such public officials? That is a question for the administrators in such public offices to answer.

Back in the days, gambling was a lucrative hustle operated by the Italians in New York city. The government subsequently discovered that a lot of money was being generated through this process without the government getting any piece of the action. A law was later enacted rendering gambling by private entities illegal. Shortly after that, the government assumed full control of the gambling business and made it officially legal by turning it into a statewide lottery enterprise.

Having declared similar form of gambling as illegal by the government because it was seen, in most part, as illegitimate profiteering enterprise that rips the public off their money with very slim chance of them getting anything back for the money spent, the government itself should not, for any reason, embark on such deceptive form of enterprise. Most notably, the gambling activities do not serve any public's interest but that of the insiders in charge of the operation who ends up richer with the money of the often losing players. It is, in most cases, a fast cash lucrative operation devised only to enrich the team owners, while the victims, in most cases, are left feeling like they are chasing a mirage.

Yet, knowing the socioeconomic imbalance caused by this form of 'robbing Peter to enrich Paul' lucrative "theft by deception" enterprise, the government rendered the operation illegal from being operated by private citizens in New York city at the time. But thereon after, the same government sets up its own shop doing the very same thing it had stopped the private citizens from doing.... with the same insatiable motive of amassing profit at the public's expense.

There are just some businesses, no matter how lucrative they might be, that are just unfit for any democratic government to involve in, or permit to flourish, because they do not serve the citizen's interest. It is just like someone using an illegitimate means to meet legitimate needs.

Instead, this type of enterprise paves way to increased criminal activities and disorients people's lives within societies. And it is sad that the government itself is an accessory to it.

Government entities should be the only sector in control as well as the utilization of any form of firearms and should never permit civilians or any private sector to become firearm dealers to the public. Until American policymakers enact stringent laws to address the issue, the judiciary's effort to curb gun violence and murder across the country will continue to seem more like someone beating on a dead horse.

Governmental interest of generating huge revenue from its operation or sales of deadly or health hazard products or services should not trump the value it places on human lives. Compromising illicit revenue over public euphoria and physical safety is bad governance. Government officials championing such style of governance should be sanctioned to relinquish such public office and be replaced by well-intended bilateral- minded representatives with incorruptible track record of prior leadership competency.

Key issues of this nature can properly and effectively be addressed if the American public starts to pay very close attention in electing their leaders in both the executive and the legislative branches of the government.... and also at the judicial branch as well. It is extremely crucial for the citizens of any democratic society to elect leaders and policymakers with no ambiguous motives when it comes to making specific reforms as expected by the public who voted them into office. Either we choose to be proactive or just want to stay at the sideline like some of us are not affected by some of the terrible policies championed by such unbridled public officials, or just want to remain in denial of how devastating some of these laws really are, such policies, good or bad, impacts everyone's lives one way or another in America or elsewhere.

The public must also be extremely cautious not to fall for spin masters who would say all the good stuffs that voters loves to hear just to get them voted into office...and then do the direct opposite of what they vowed to do after getting elected. A case in point has been Mr. Bush's administration of eight long years of tumultuous leadership in America.

In a case seeking judicial clarity over the U.S. 2nd Constitutional Amendment clause regarding citizens' right to own or carry firearms, the U.S. Supreme court, in June 2008, ruled in a 5 to 4 majority for the gun makers and the dealers that citizens are permitted to own or carry guns as guaranteed by the 2nd Amendment.

This particular 2nd Amendment clause has been misconstrued in so many instances to appease the firearms industry who are backed by powerful 'special interests' at the expense of the American public who are the victims of these lethal weapons allowed to be sold and owned by the public.

Following the 2008 (D.C. v. Heller) Supreme court ruling that the 2nd Amendment protects an individual's right to possess gun.....sits decision went under assault......from the right. Two prominent federal Appeals court judges, Judge J. Harvie Wilkinson III of the Fourth Circuit court of Appeals in Richmond, Va. and judge Richard A. Posner of the 7th Circuit, said that Justice Antonin Scalia's majority opinion in the case, D.C. v. Heller, was illegitimate, activist, poorly reasoned and fueled by politics rather than principle.

Judge Posner, viewed as the nation's most influential judge not in the Supreme court, referenced on his (2008) book "How Judges Think,"… which argued that Constitutional adjudication by the Supreme court is largely and necessarily political. After Heller was preceded, the Heller decision, he wrote in the New Republic in 2008, "is evidence that the Supreme court, in deciding Constitutional cases, exercises a free-wheeling discretion strongly flavored with ideology."

Warren E. Burger, after retiring as Chief Justice in 1986, called the individual rights view "one of the greatest pieces of fraud... I repeat the word 'fraud,'...on the American public by special interest groups that I have ever seen."

Despite the substantial strides made by the Obama administration to get America pass the old brain-dead politics by ensuring the American public and the world...that America is a nation ruled by laws and Constitutions, not the whims of the unbridled rightist ideologues, while trying to eliminate the red states and blue states politics, the temperamental conservative groups who readily yokes with the culture of deception and who believes that a government officials' primary loyalty is not to the people, but to the power itself, were not quite pleased with such pragmatic change of direction towards the right path.

Such anxiety became quite evidence in mid 2009 when the conservative faction, still backed by the pharmaceutical and Healthcare industry's special interest group, mounted heavy opposition against the Obama administration's Healthcare Reform Bill......even though it was so obvious that the proposed reform is intended to serve the interest of the entire American public. The rightist conservative faction in America hates any governmental policy that will bring forth a pluralistic benefit for everyone. If it's not a policy that will only benefit their faction or the select few, they most likely will oppose it by any means they possibly can.

After quite a contentious battle by the Democrats over Trump's second pick for the Supreme Court Justice, his nominee, Judge Brett Kavanaugh from the Circuit Court in Washington D.C., ended up with enough vote to be confirmed for the job. He is now Justice Brett Kavanaugh sitting as the ninth Justice at the nation's highest court.

It is very clear to all what are at stake to have an individual strictly from the right side of political reasoning to enter opinions at the nation's highest court on crucial cases of national priority. This was the main reason for the high level of resistance put up by Democrats not to support this second pick by Trump.

The nominee, now Justice Brett Kavanaugh, is from the right for sure and fully aware of the national politics at stake across the country to be sitting as one of the ninth deciding justices in the nation's Supreme Court.

Without a doubt, he will surely deliver for his right-wing constituents when crucial cases lands at the court for argument. His position on matters brought before the court will definitely not be based on legal reasoning but rather based on whose side he's with on national politics......including the likelihood of ruling over matters involving Donald Trump himself who picked him.

It is a scary shift of judicial power towards the right on important national issues that will be brought before this court with expectation of fair and balanced rule of law...some cases that will impact millions of American public for generations to come. Stay tuned in.

# 35

# RACISM ISSUE IN AMERICA

AFTER EIGHT YEARS OF CHAOTIC LEADERSHIP of the Bush-Cheney administration, history at long last was made in November 4, 2008, when the American public overwhelmingly voted a black candidate for the first time as the United States president. In preparation for the November 2008 election, the political mantra was "CHANGE,"

Barack Obama, a Democratic U.S. Senator from Chicago, Illinois, identified by the mainstream American public as a black African-American, emerged as the victor of the 2008 presidential election.....making him the first black and the 44th president of United States. Even though he is referred to as black, he is actually half black and half white or half Caucasian. Born by a black father from Kenya and a white American mother. So, that actually makes him a half black and half white person, and not the so-called African-American he is commonly referred to by the Caucasian Americans.

Anyway, he transcended the issue of race in the run-up to the election even though the Republican counterparts tried their hardest to make race an issue during the election. Without a doubt, racism is still deeply rooted in most rural states and counties across America.

A case in point is South Carolina where confederate flag still flies on the grounds of the state capitol. A disturbing example of how difficult it is for people of good will to dispose of the exotic layers of bigotry that have accumulated of several long centuries.

A bygone era like Benjamin Tillman is still being honored in this state, which is very much like honoring a malignant tumor. A statue of Tillman, who was known as "Pitchfork Ben" is on prominent display outside the state house. Tillman served as governor and U.S. Senator in the late 19th and the early 20th centuries. A mortal enemy of black people. He bragged that he and his disenfranchised "as many as we could" and he publicly defended the murder of blacks.

In a speech on Senate floor, he declared: "we of the South have never recognized the negro to govern white men, and we never will. We have never believed him to be equal of the white man, and we will not submit to his gratifying lust of our wives and daughters without lynching him." Wonder how he would have felt after the November 2008 presidential election if he was still alive today to witness a black man in America at the helm of the highest public office and calling the shots as well for the entire nation.

Real change is more than problematic in a state so warped by its past that it can continue to officially admire a figure like Tillman.

Bud Ferillo, a white public relations executive who produced and directed a documentary called "Corridor of Shame" in it, called attention to the neglect of rural schools in South Carolina. If you were to walk into some of those schools......which are spread along a crescent-shaped corridor on either side of interstate 95 from the southern edge of North Carolina to the northern edge of Georgia...you might forget that you are in United States.

This, we may say, was probably inevitable. In South Carolina, the Confederate flag is flying right out there in the open and Pitchfork Ben is on display for all to see. In most other places across America, hostilities towards blacks and other races still goes on quite discreetly.

No one wants to deal with it. The eight chaotic years of the Bush administration was a reminder of the American Wild-West era. The level of hostility and assault on the rule of law and human liberty by the administration was excruciating, particularly against foreign nationals residing in America.....and beyond.

## (a)  *Forced Migration (Uprooted People)*

***FORCED MIGRATION (The Uprooted People):*** In a nostalgic celebration that marked the Cherokee Indians' heritage, a crowd of

Cherokee Indians who had journeyed on April 16, 2009 to Red Clay State History Park in Cleveland, Tennessee from Oklahoma, North Carolina and elsewhere, gathered for a reunion that lasted for three days.

Head of the Cherokee Nation, Principal Chief Smith, presided over the event which was the first in 25 years of the two groups gathering for celebration of a history and culture unknown to many outsiders. They stood transfixed, as though transported to another time when their ancestors' lands covered much of Southeast America.

Red Clay, just across the border from Georgia, holds deep historical significance for the Cherokee. This was briefly the capital- in-exile for the Cherokee Nation in the 1830s after an increasing hostile Georgia government forced them out of the state. It was here that legendary John Ross learned that appeals for help from Washington had failed and his people learned that they were to be pushed off their land, forced-marched to Oklahoma on what became known as the "Trail of Tears."

In 1838, federal troops rounded up 18,000 for the long torturous trek to Oklahoma, during which more than 4,000 died. A thousand more went into hiding, many fleeing into the mountains of North Carolina. The descendants of those removed to Oklahoma became the Cherokee Nation; the descendants of those who stayed behind are the Eastern Band of the Cherokee Indians.

"Red Clay reminds....us all about the harshness of government policies, federal and state, that led to the Trail of Tears," says Principal Chief Chad Smith at the event. Principal Chief Michel Hicks of the East Band of Cherokee Indians also noted that the reunion was vital for Cherokee children... "The true history is what our children needs to learn," he says. "We don't need to let them forget where we came from."

The reunion comes amid fresh public attention on the experiences of Native Americans. 'We Shall Remain,' a five part PBS series on that history broadcasted on April and May of 2009, featured an episode on the 'Trail of T ears' on April 27.

The Cherokee Nation numbers around 280,000. About half live in Oklahoma.

In the 2000 census, 729,533 people said they were Cherokee alone or in combination with one or more other races or American Indian tribal groupings......the U.S.A's largest tribal identification by far.

By the 1820s, the Cherokees lived on 36,000 square miles of North Georgia and Alabama. In 1825, as Georgia's rapidly expanding white population pushed into what had been Native American territory, the Cherokees formally established a national capital called 'New Echota' in northwest Georgia. It was one of the first efforts of self-government by an Indian tribe; the tribal council built a Council House and created a Supreme Court.

"The establishment of a written Cherokee Constitution in 1827 prompted the Georgia Legislature to enact anti-Cherokee laws," Smith says. These laws set up a process to seize their land, divide it and offer parcels to white Georgians in a lottery.

When Andrew Jackson was elected president in 1828, he made removal of eastern tribes a national priority...quite similar to how the Bush's 2001-09 eight years administration made the expulsion of foreign nationals, both documented and undocumented, from United States, a national priority.....and now Donald Trump as U.S. president, along with his hateful and angry crowd, may succeed in taking the nation back to that era once again.

In 1930, Congress passed the Indian Removal Act. The Cherokees sought help from the U.S. Supreme court. In 1832, the court ruled that Georgia had violated the Cherokee Nation's Sovereign status. Jackson refused to enforce the ruling. Under increasing pressure, the Cherokees began holding their Council meetings in exile at Red Clay in 1832. In 1838, they left on the Trail of Tears.

The gathering in 2009 was a powerful experience for many, like stepping on hallowed ground. Wilma Mankiller, who was the first female Principal Chief, also noted that the meeting was incredibly moving and incredibly emotional. "When I step to this area where the Cherokee people had actually met a couple years before removal, where they had to decide whether to stay and fight to the death for their land or go peacefully, I feel connected to the people and the families who attended those meetings." Ms. Mankiller passed away at the age of 64 from pancreatic cancer the following year (April 2010) after this historic gathering.

## (b)  Perils of Racism and Hatred

**PERILS OF RACISM AND HATRED:** On September 2009, right after the passing away of the U.S. Congressional old guard, Ted Kennedy,

Democrat U.S. Senator from Massachusetts, president Obama addressed the nation in Capitol Hill to give the American public, as well as the Republican opponents to his proposed Healthcare Reform, more clarity to the proposed reform.

As soon as the president said his proposed Healthcare Insurance Reform for the Americans will not cover undocumented immigrants living in the country, a Republican Congressman, Joe Wilson of South Carolina rudely and resentfully interrupted the president by saying: "you're lying".....ausing a brief moment of silent. A statement signaling an extremely disrespectful act and unprecedented line of ethical misconduct by a U.S. Congressman to a sitting U.S. president for that matter.

The level of disrespect caused by his action towards the president left him with no other choice but to apologize to Mr. Obama as soon as practicable. The president accepted his apology......even though it was not the Congressman's free-will intention to do so. Because the foul statement he had uttered that had caused the uproar during the president's speech to the nation was not a mere slip-of-tongue, but rather a verbal expression of how he actually felt as a typical vast-right conservative Republican with the usual bias towards Democrat leaderships who tries to put an end to the American rightists' culture of unleveled playing field that sadly has failed to serve the nation's best interest for so many decades.

The Congressman's action won't be much of a surprise if one remember the history of what part of the nation and state he is from and representing. Joe Wilson is just like one of the many (Pitchfork Ben) Benjamin Tillman types of the late 19th to the early 20th centuries era in South Carolina that are still sadly among today's generation of policymakers in America...who is still stubbornly stuck on those obsolete bygone era imperial ideologies.

The Pitchfork Ben type of ideologies, who, during his time then as a governor and later a U.S Senator representing South Carolina, declared on the Senate floor that: "we of the South have never recognized the right of negro to govern white man, and we will not submit to his gratifying lust of our wives and daughters without lynching him." Congressman Joe Wilson, among many other likeminded ultra-right-wing Republicans, both private and public citizens across United States, are among many of their kind who are still yet unsettled with the notion and the changes unfolding right before their eyes that an individual partly from a black race finally happens to be the one calling the shots at the nation's highest office to those like him, among many others who thought it will never happen in America.

With such recent time intrusive and racially biased comment uttered by Republican Congressman Joe Wilson of the same South Carolina during president Obama's healthcare reform speech in Capitol Hill, it is undoubtedly evident that he, as well as many other like-minded rightist Republican U.S. policymakers like Republican Senator Linsey Graham of the same South Carolina, retired Senator John Beohner still share similar mindset as that of Tilman of almost a century ago.

The most interesting part to all these is that the young generations in America today are becoming more engaged than ever before on how the biased policies and ideologies of these type of rightist characters has, for so many decades, robbed them the wrong way, and in effect, now more than ever, are engaged in electoral process to vote out such biased-minded right-wing ideologues from office.....replacing them with level-playing field citizens with no present nor future bias sentiment and nothing but a genuine best interest of everyone at heart when and after getting elected into public offices.

Despite big and important advances over the past several decades, including Mr. Obama's crossover campaign, racism remains alive and well in much of America. And yet no one.....not even Bill Clinton, the man touted (absurdly as the nation's first black president, or even his wife, Hilary Clinton, who lost the Democratic presidential nominee ticket to Obama and later joined the Obama's cabinet as the U.S. Secretary of States, or Barack Obama himself, the first half-white half-black elected U.S. president to occupy the White House.....is willing to talk honestly and openly about it.

# EPILOGUE

THIS BOOK IS NOT ABOUT SETTLING scores, but rather to share with the public at large of the suffering and torments inflicted on foreign nationals within America and abroad by the Bush-Cheney administration and its continuing trend by Donald Trump who won the 2016 U.S. presidential election......all under the premise of protecting the homeland. It is intended to serve as a way to create awareness as well as preventing such ruthless regime and their dark imperial ideologies repeating itself in America or elsewhere across the globe. Sadly, those who went and casted their vote for Trump has allowed this very recent dark past to repeat itself. It is also a way to restore some level of dignity to those who were robbed or denied it by the Bush-Cheney era....and now by Trump.

What the book does so well is to remind people, as if it needs reminding, that the leaderships of Bush-Cheney/Trump administrations and that of the rest extreme-right Republicans across America had essentially toiled with the nation's most unique reputations, increasingly turning it into a nation operated with deep hatred towards foreign nationals, and doing so with little or no regard for the nation's rule of law by the government officials themselves.

Those who may repudiate the content of this book, which are based on true events that in most part unfolded in the U.S., are those who readily accepts the culture of deception and who believes that a government officials' primary loyalty is not to the people, but to the power itself. The

Bush-Cheney team applied such delicate ideology all through their eight years of leadership......highly distorted ideologies that had sadly soiled the once good image of America across the globe. He had also applied similar skewed ideologies in implementing the nation's economic policies that led America into a state of recession during the last years of his presidency.

The succeeding administration of Mr. Obama, who won the 2008 U.S. presidential election by the popular vote of the American public and that of the world community, worked sincerely hard to return America back to the fundamentals of the founding fathers and reversed the nation's right-wings' politics of division in America and the rest of the world. On the other end, the Republican policymakers in Washington continues to thwart those efforts by doing the direct opposite to the nation. With Trump leading the nation now, common decency in all levels of his administration is like 'a pie in the sky,'

# *INDEX*

## Symbols



## A

American Native Indians  63

American public  xii, xiii, 5, 16, 22, 50, 57, 59, 62, 65, 69, 74, 82, 90, 101, 102, 105,
        107, 115, 119, 128, 134, 144, 150, 157, 159, 163, 164, 197, 204, 207, 208,
        211, 224, 225, 228, 230, 235, 236, 238, 250, 256, 257, 261, 262, 263, 264,
        265, 269, 272, 279

American taxpayers  17, 55, 82, 83, 224

Andre  21, 22

Andrew Jackson was elected president  268

Annabel Park  86

anti-Cherokee laws  268

anti-immigrants  33, 69, 128, 150, 163, 164, 198, 207, 208, 215, 216

Anti-immigrant sentiment  57, 140, 163

Arab nations like Saudi Arabia, United Arab Emirates, Qatar, among othe  213

Arab television station in South Carolina  234

Arnold Schwarzenegger  141

Article 3 of the Geneva Convention  126

Attention Deficit Hyperactive Disorder (ADHD)  243

axis of evil  223

Axis of Evil  57


# B

Bagram  xi, 127

Barnard Maydoff  9

Benjamin Franklin  251

Benjamin Tillman  266, 269

Bi-lateral dialogue  221

Bill Clinton  4, 13, 192, 227, 270

Bill Clinton was the president  192

Bill Gates  65, 253

Bill of Rights  204, 206

Board of Immigration Appeals (BIA)  69

Brazilians  190

Brett Kavanaugh  106, 263, 264

British Columbia  13

British King  105

Browning of America  139

Bud Ferillo  266

Bush-Cheney  xi, xiii, 13, 56, 60, 72, 73, 74, 90, 91, 94, 104, 105, 106, 107, 110,
        125, 127, 128, 129, 130, 132, 134, 146, 147, 150, 151, 153, 154, 159, 160,
        161, 163, 164, 169, 174, 181, 190, 191, 192, 193, 194, 197, 199, 200, 201,
        202, 203, 204, 205, 207, 208, 214, 223, 224, 225, 231, 234, 236, 251, 265,
        271, 272, 279

Bush-Cheney/Trump administrations  104, 129, 132, 154, 169, 190, 192, 201, 208,
        271

# C



# D



# E

Western imperialism  231
Western medias  234
Western Phoenix  141
Wild capitalism  56, 244
Wild-West  42, 72, 83, 125, 133, 160, 208, 225, 255, 266
Windfall profiteering  49, 52
WPP  108

## X

Xenophobia  15, 197

## Y

York, Pennsylvania  35, 40, 42, 45, 46, 50, 53, 54, 56, 117, 145, 146, 151, 182, 189, 192
Yugoslavia  17, 170

# ABOUT THE AUTHOR

'Thompson' K. George, author of **Once Upon a Time in America** shares with the world an intriguing and yet very heart-wrenching eye-witness account of events that was and still being inflicted on mankind in the 21st century in America some of which remains best kept secrets to most American public and the rest of the world at large.... chronicling the destructive policies that trails the dark past of the Bush-Cheney's era...and now Trump. An uncut revelation of the true state of things in America today with immigrants and citizens alike and the lowdown dirty inner-workings of the conservative right-wing ideologues in Washington.

'Once Upon a Time in America' tells it all. It portrays everyone's story and a message for all. A pure and timeless masterpiece of history of the 21st century. The author lives in New York and currently working on an upcoming documentary based on this masterpiece.

9 781958 690444